HELLBENDERS

HELLBENDERS BOOK ONE

RICHARD PROSCH

WOLFPACK
PUBLISHING
—— EST 2012 ——

Hellbenders
Paperback Edition
© Copyright 2021 Richard Prosch

Wolfpack Publishing
5130 S. Fort Apache Rd. 215-380
Las Vegas, NV 89148

wolfpackpublishing.com

Paperback ISBN 978-1-64734-758-1
eBook ISBN 978-1-64734-757-4

For Wyatt in his 18th year

HELLBENDERS

CHAPTER 1

OCTOBER 1859

LIN JARRET RODE ONE-HUNDRED FIFTY MILES ON RAIN-soaked horses southwest from San Antonio and ferried his bedroll and Maynard carbine across the Arroyo Colorado on his Uncle Oscar's bidding. The bay came from a trusted hostler on the low side of the river, and by rights would be his final mount on the journey to Rancho de Jada and the Rio Grande troubles. The carbine he carried came from an Arkansas gun drummer and was less than a year old.

A Tejano named Cardoza was stirring up trouble on the American side of the border and Tom Sinclair needed an extra hand. Maybe an extra gun.

Lin Jarret had the guns. Lin Jarret was a Texas Ranger.

When he broke camp under a persimmon grove on the last morning of his trek, a Wednesday, he was saddle-sore and on edge, ready to rein in and tuck away something other than campfire chow. He looked forward to making the ranch, shaking Sinclair's hand, and getting his first good night's sleep in a week.

With a goose-down pillow—if the stories he'd heard about the extravagant ranch were true.

On the Palo Alto range, dawn's hard-pounding rain gave way to a fine mist.

Lin rode at moderate pace. Uncle Oscar had been shy on details, but Lin got the impression the sooner he arrived, the better.

Still and all, he was careful. The place was new to him, and he had no intention of blunder bussing into the situation.

Above him, tattered clouds spread themselves thin over a milky yellow sun.

Autumn was a fickle gal this season. Riding south, he expected to catch up with summer's heat. Instead he found a cold drizzle.

Damn it all. Lin slapped his gloves on his thighs and pulled his wideawake cap down closer to his scalp.

He continued to push to the southwest, toward the fork of the upper and lower Carlito Rivers in the direction of the big Rio Grande.

The sun climbed steady in the sky. The higher it was, the warmer it got.

Tendrils of fog rose from the yellow green scrub ahead of Lin. Gnats raced around in clouds at eye level, and a cotton-tailed rabbit ran ahead of him for a while, ducking through clumps of shrubs and patches of columbine grass.

He was close to the rancho now, he thought. Might even be riding on Sinclair land, though he'd passed nothing looking like a property line marker.

When Lin heard a girl cry out, he spurred his bay gelding into a fast gallop across the mud slick llano.

More shouting, and the din of several men steered him toward a bosquecillo of gnarled mesquite, cedar elm, and persimmon running to the south and east.

The bawling of a calf and a fresh shout from the girl gave Lin a second wind.

"¡*Cuidado, cuidado*!" she cried, and there were male voices too.

At the prickly tree line, he urged the bay forward with a firm, commanding voice.

Solid in the saddle, Lin clamped a glove down on his hat with one hand while warding off a spider's web of mesquite branches and thorny twigs reaching for his rough-whiskered face with the other.

He held fast to the primed Maynard rifle riding along-side in its short boot, and the bay kept to its path, nimbly finding its way over uneven ground.

Ahead were the sounds of a scuffle. A crash. The wet pop of splitting wood.

A score of chattering birds burst into the air, heralding Lin's arrival as he plunged into a patchy wet clearing of windmill grass and creeping chisme a hundred yards wide. More than a dozen cattle grazed here, and an equal number were trapped inside a wide rough-hewn corral. To the west, four vaqueros dressed in light cotton shirts with wool coats harried a fenced cow chute. Two of them wore straw hats, one had a kerchief knotted around his head. The fourth was bare-headed and older, with a shoulder-length mane of gray.

The fifth vaquero, shapely and tall with a single black braid, was a woman.

"Ay, ay!" she yelled.

The locus of the skirmish was an oversize longhorn calf, its wild neck and shoulders straining against a wooden yoke. It was caught between a long hinged squeeze gate, partially broken and weighed down by the vaqueros, and the far side of the chute. One of the straw-hat cowboys swung a glowing iron back toward a caliche block firepit piled high with ash and glowing embers, and the animal's hip smoked with a fresh brand. Lin smelled the singed fur and burnt flesh even as he noticed the former bull's male parts, freshly removed, slick and glistening atop a pile on a canvas tarp. Naturally, they'd be saved for frying.

The calf bellowed again.

Not his lucky day.

He bucked hard against the chute's broken fence. One cowboy stumbled, landed on his backside.

The beef gave as good as he got.

Most of the Rio Grande valley was traditionally sheep country, but to Lin's relief, the Sinclairs raised beef. Before getting on with the Rangers, Lin had worked cattle in north Texas, hiring out as a trailhand to the big boss men of the day. He didn't know sheep from shingles.

Lin well remembered mornings like this one. Castrating bulls and branding. Dipping an ornery herd with kerosene bug juice. Come dinner time, there'd be a celebration for a job well done with fried prairie oysters and homemade beer, sweet corn and sorghum bread.

In this case, they'd waited too long before tending this particular calf. Half again the size of the other beeves, he was too big for the crush and was busting up the chute. And he was shitting all over the place.

The two vaqueros with hats lunged against the failing gate. Joined by the girl, they barely kept the poor devil contained.

Lin rode closer and saw the steer was blind in one eye —red-rimmed and pus-green in the center. Maybe it was the reason they had delayed today's procedure. Standing back and away from the others, the old gray-hair edged close with a white pasty clump dripping from both hands. A poultice for the sick eye.

The beast was struggling, desperate to escape, falling sideways against the plank-built wood crush. Bawling, he kicked his back hooves with a violent spasm, smacking the tallest vaquero on the shin, sending him back with a jerk.

Lin never hankered to be a cow man, but he had an instinctual knack for handling the beeves, for keeping them calm. A spooked yearling like this one shouldn't present this much of a challenge, though the four clumsy hands made things worse with their squalling. With animals you couldn't take anything for granted.

Same with people.

He dropped from the saddle. "Hello, the ranch," he yelled.

The big steer swung its head around, catching stub-like horns on a rope hackamore held by the bare headed cowboy. Torn from his grasp, the hemp line whipsawed through the air to slap his female companion. The shapely vaquero made a dive for the rope, missed, and took a face full of mud for her trouble.

Another few seconds and the heavy beef would be free.

"Hup, hup, hup," said Lin, clearing a path to the side of the broken squeeze gate.

He slid to the wood planks and added his strength to the tallest vaquero who had rejoined the fray. Together, they pushed the dun colored animal upright, keeping him on all four hooves, firmly braced against the solid opposite wall of the crush. The bare-headed cowboy regained his lariat, gathering the length in one hand while holding fast to the loop around the steer's nose and letting his weight pull the head around.

The girl was back on her feet beside the gray haired man.

"Barb, *aplica la cataplasma*," she said.

The oldster now hurried forward, his hands filled with a poultice smelling of liniment and woodrot and at least a half-dozen other pungent odors catching in Lin's throat. With Lin's added weight bolstering the gate, the steer had ceased its ferocious fight, occasionally trying to lift a hoof in half-hearted resistance.

"He knows when he's licked, eh boys?" said Lin.

Barb cupped his wrinkled fingers over the calf's weeping, sickly eye, applying the medicinal paste with a quick, practiced motion. In an instant, the job was done, and he nodded at Lin and the other wranglers. As one they stepped back to relieve the pressure on the steer while, at the same time, the bare-headed gent slipped away the hackamore.

Within seconds, the animal was free, careening across the meadow, bellowing its indignations even as it kicked its rear heels skyward and divots of sod flew into the sky.

Lin tipped back his cap and ran the sleeve of his flannel shirt across his brow, grinning at the men in their straw hats. They were natives, rough skinned and tall. Kickapoo maybe, thought Lin. Maybe Apache.

The thought made him shudder.

The men smiled back without words, but their expression quickly soured as the female member of the team brushed past Barb to confront Lin.

Tan skinned, her ebony braid pulled away from her smooth forehead in a severe knot, she wore loose-fitting clothes like the others, but her coat was new with hand carved wood clasps and lined with sheepskin. Lin tipped his hat, but green eyes like the grassy flint hills of his childhood warned of hidden sharp edges. Her full lips pursed in disapproval.

"Careful, Miss Reece," said one of the Indians.

Lin took off his sloppy wet gloves and tossed them to the ground.

He recognized the name.

So this was Reece Sinclair.

"I'm mighty pleased to meet you, ma'am."

She lifted her sharp chin and looked down a pert, straight nose.

He wondered how he looked to the heiress of Rancho de Jada.

Compared to these rugged men who worked the cows with their wind scarred cheeks and dust reddened eyes, he figured he came off pretty good. He kept his sandy brown hair cropped close to the scalp, and the day's harvest of whiskers shading his chin accentuated a square jaw.

A filly in Dodge City once told him his eyes were as straight-shootin' as his teeth, and Lin took it as a compliment. He ran his tongue over his back molars and swished around a quick spit bath hoping to impress Miss Reece with his clean white ivories.

How could she help but fall in love with him?

Reece planted a fist on both hips. "Who the hell are you supposed to be?"

That's one way to say hello. How to answer?

"Name's Lin Jarret," he began.

But before he could continue, one of the vaqueros spoke in a native language he didn't understand.

And all hell broke loose with the crack of a gun.

CHAPTER 2

EVEN AS THE MID-MORNING SUN CLEARED THE LAST OF its ropy thin clouds, a line of seven men on horseback crashed through the trees and into the clearing with volleys of thunder, catcalls, and smoke. Seven intruders on heavy thoroughbred stallions hoisted their six-shooters and carbines toward the sky, tossing fire around like confetti, spooking man and beast alike. The free cattle charged away in mad flight, the penned animals jostled into bunches and crashed into the fence, eager to make an escape.

Lin clutched Reece's hand. To his relief, she didn't resist.

The outlaw outfit pounded in at lightning speed with high-money tack and expensive outdoor clothes. Leather dusters slapped in the wind, catching the dust of more than two-dozen churning hooves. Polished boots flew free of their stirrups, and leather *reatas* sailed in wide arcs through the sky.

Lin pulled Reece back toward the relative safety of his bay horse. He got a boot in the stirrup and swept Reece up and into the saddle in front of him. He pulled the short-barrel Maynard from its boot and tried to point the gelding away from the tumult.

A red-haired hard case with a thick, greasy beard dripping from his chin reared in close, but his attention wasn't on the couple. Instead, he swung a wide lasso and tossed the loop at the corral. Watching over Reece's shoulder, seeing the rider's plan, Lin backpedaled.

Red hair's rope caught a corner post, held fast, and immediately he was joined by two more of his riders with lariats.

The men were experts in the saddle, gigging their horses into a cooperative tug, straining against the corral post.

The other bandits kept up the dizzy percussion, triggering their pistols as they rode in circles around the perimeter of the corral, driving the cattle into a wild frenzy.

One rider kicked apart the branding pit, sparking a flurry of scattered coals, and his horse hammered the noon banquet of prairie oysters into the fresh plowed mud. Each fresh round of destruction was followed by lusty shouts and peals of laughter.

Reece's native vaqueros were doing their best to flank the bastards on foot, the tallest one clenching the castrating knife in his teeth.

The three ropers continued to tug at the corner post. One of the men whipped his horse with a braided leather quirt. Another shouted gleeful encouragement. Lin understood their intent, to stampede the pent-up cattle. He tried to steer his reluctant bay into the fray, but to no avail.

The corner post came out of the ground with a violent eruption of earth.

As the fence failed, Lin felt the ground rumble even

as his ears registered the concussions from dozens of hooves driving tons of muscle and bone straight at them.

"Get around," he said, slapping the horse's rump even as the first longhorns tore past. Up until now, snug against Lin in the saddle, Reece had been complacent. Now she moved before he could react, grabbing the reins from his hands to spin the bay around. She meant to thread back through the charge of cows, her defiance focused on the bearded man.

Half way towards him, the horse reared up and dumped Lin flat on his butt in the middle of the stampede, still gripping his rifle.

The cows came at him in random clumps of two or three, and he took a blow to the shoulder. Then his knee. The red hot shards of agony made him want to roll into a ball, tuck his head down, and pray for salvation. The voice of experience told him it was a sure way to have his skull cracked open like an over-ripe melon. He struggled to his feet as a snorting brown bull rushed past, with five or six more stragglers streaming in from behind.

Heads pumping vigorously, hooves churning up the soil, Lin was glad the longhorns weren't yet full grown. Which wouldn't matter much if he went down again. One false move, one stumble, and the beeves would trample his guts into paste flour and there'd be nothing left of his to scrape up and identify.

A fast heifer blindsided him then, clipping his left hip, spinning him into the path of a couple young bulls, their horns sharp and widespread. He launched a reckless dive to the side, landed flat on his belly, losing wind.

Losing the rifle as it flew out of his grip.

Instinctively, Lin rolled onto his back, and there, above him, was one of the cowboy intruders, wheeling around on his midnight black mount, his face branded with a pair of puffy long scars. Grinning at Lin, he showed only a handful of teeth.

Lin sat up, unarmed, and Scarface levered his pistol down, aiming with a careful wink. Whether the rider meant to kill him for fun or for business, Lin never knew. Before Scarface could pull the trigger, a bone-chilling scream cut through the stampede. The tallest native vaquero leapt out of the confusion onto Scarface's arm, cranking him out of the saddle.

Lin shuffled away and sprang to his feet as the two men slammed into the earth. The tussle was furious, like the jacked-up play of two Tom cats, the Indian on top, Scarface fumbling is desperation for his gun.

The vengeful vaquero still clutched the castrating knife, but now he held it in his right hand.

Scarface did his best to push away, to increase the distance between him and his opponent, but in the end, he lost his balance. He tumbled back to earth with the vaquero on top. Scarface went rigid as the razor thin blade, already gleaming crimson red in the high morning sun, slashed down across his neck in a single swift motion.

Three more calves kicked past, and Lin retrieved his carbine from the chopped up field of grass, checking the percussion cap, making sure the weapon was primed to fire its thumb-sized hunk of .52 caliber lead.

Reece was visible now, turning in circles on the bay horse as cowboys circled her with jeering taunts, striking out at her with braided leather quirts. The other three gathered nearby at the remnants of the corral.

Marching toward the invaders, Lin couldn't get a clear shot, and his boots complained in the chewed-up sod.

One of the men was bigger than the others and sat atop a finely tooled and ornate saddle. He wore with a high crowned hat and silver string tie—this man was the leader. His blowing gruff horse took a few ominous steps toward Lin, then stopped.

The hair stood up on the back of Lin's neck, and he felt the boss man watching him, waiting to see what he'd do.

Lin skirted a length of broken fence and stepped over a section of splintered rail. Then he stopped to turn his attention to Reece and her trio of tormentors. Thirty feet from the action, he bucked the short barreled Maynard to his shoulder.

The three men Reece had in orbit could have been brothers, triplets in their uncanny resemblance. Each of the dark horses they rode wore a distinct blaze on its nose. Each of the men had a swarthy complexion marked by long oiled sideburns. One grew a heavy waxed mustache under a bulbous pink nose, but all three were dressed in loose sweaters and baggy dungarees, sombreros and heavy boots.

The mustachio wore a .30 caliber cartridge belt slung over his shoulder, and he carried a rifle in the bota. They pranced around the girl with lewd suggestions and obscene gestures, swinging the quirts, laughing.

"Hey, señorita, you maybe let us take you home. Take on all three of us at once?"

"I know these Sinclair women, Carlos," said another. "They like the whip. They beg for the *wheeeeep*."

Reece Sinclair answered with haughty mockery of her own. "It's you who beg for the whip, *chico*. You and your *el niños*."

The one called Carlos flipped the leather braid sideways and down, drawing a thin line of blood across the girl's forearm.

More the fool him.

Before he knew it, Reece had snatched up the frayed strap in both hands and jerked backwards with all her might. Already leaning out over his center of gravity, Carlos lost his balance and tumbled from the saddle, landing with a bone crunching thud, screaming as his startled horse mashed his fingers under a back hoof.

Damn, but this girl had spirit. Lin lowered his carbine.

Reece took advantage of the break and spurred away from the men, circling her horse around to reunite with Lin. His wordless query was answered with a curt nod. She was unhurt, but her face was an animated flood of rage and frustration.

Lin took command of the bay's bridal, and the big man approached them on his giant steed.

The monstrous stallion sauntered slow and easy, matching the rider's own aloof demeaner. Lin tried to remember the last time he'd seen such an impressive horse. As tall as a draft horse at 15 to 16 hands high, it was sleek limbed and couldn't be more than a few years old.

The horse was muscular, the man in the fine saddle, mostly fat. Fleshy jowls forested with a curly black beard and heavy liver spots differentiated him from his men. Indigo blue veins showed at his temples like a child's tracing of a puzzle, and he carried a silver flask in his coat's outer breast pocket. His nose was red and puffy, like an eggplant, and his lips were chapped. When he reached for his flask, his pudgy fingers shook with a nervous palsy. He drank from the flask, his watery eyes were like red fungus set deep in soft rotting wood.

His gaze was fixed on Reece Sinclair.

To her credit, she didn't flinch, but instead met his gaze head on until the fat man turned and took a drink.

He swallowed. Replaced the clasp of his flask, then returned the container to his pocket.

Behind him, Carlos lay curled on his side, cradling his ruined hand, moaning with agony.

Behind Reece and Lin, Scarface bled out into the mud.

The vaqueros were nowhere to be seen.

The corral fences were a total ruin, and the crazed herd of cattle had scattered to a shallow valley east of the corral grounds where they continued their mad clamoring.

Lin figured it would take all day to gather them back. Maybe longer.

Carlos bemoaned his broken hand, and his boss man bared yellow teeth to croak out an order. "Shut him up."

The red-haired hard case with the greasy beard jumped down and kicked Carlos in the ribs.

Lin's jaw clenched at the impact.

What kind of leader held such contempt for his men?

"Dub Hornsby," said Reece, "You rotten son of a bitch. Explain this outrage."

Hornsby's remaining riders lined up next to him, keeping their pistols ready to fire. Greasy beard climbed back into his saddle.

Again Hornsby showed his vile brace of teeth, and a thin line of brown saliva spilled over his white lower lip. "It's you who brought me here, Missy Reece. It's you not doin' right."

Lin kept watch on the *pistoleros*. With all the shooting they'd done to scare the cattle, Lin figured they couldn't have many shots left over. Like he'd been able to keep count during the furious fandango.

Reece, on the other hand, had done just that.

"You have two bullets left, *jefe*," said Reece. She

nodded at one of her three Mexican tormentors, then at red-head with the beard. "Your Segundo better be sure of his aim."

Lin wondered at her certainty. He'd known card sharps and gamblers his entire life and recognized a bluff when he heard it. As a Ranger, he knew plenty of tall tales, and he could almost always detect an outright lie. When Reece said their opponents had two bullets left, she wasn't bluffing.

She was more than confident.

She *knew*.

He tucked away the odd bit of information for later.

Feigning amusement, the corners of Hornsby's mouth twitched. His voice was a hard whispering thing, a wind soughing through barren trees. Lin imagined the man's heart buried under the mountain of flesh, laboring away like a steam engine.

"Marko generally hits what he aims for."

"I very much doubt it," said Reece.

Hornsby stated his case. "Three weeks ago, I told your old dad to pack up his things and clear out. You've got no rights here, Miss Sinclair."

"Rancho de Jada belongs to us," said Reece. "No matter what Cardoza tells his lapdogs."

This time the insult was like a slap in the face and got the same reaction. Hornsby's eyes blazed with indignation.

"I'll show you who's the lapdog, you little—"

Without hesitation, Reece reached down and plucked Lin's rifle from his hands, leveling it squarely on Dub Hornsby's chest.

"One more word," she warned, "and I'll blow you to hell. I promise you."

Lin walked between the horses. "Let's hold up here a

minute," he said. "I need everybody to put away their guns and take a breath."

"You need?" said Hornsby. "And just who are you?" He looked at Reece with honest curiosity. "Who is this man?"

Lin stepped forward, brushing aside his slicker to reveal the heavy leather rig slung around his waist with its secured Colt Walker Model 1847 six-shot revolver. He pulled the .44 caliber iron from its rose-tooled cradle, lifting it until the engraved cylinder reflected a flame of sunlight.

"I'm Lin Jarett," he said. "I'm a Texas Ranger." He couldn't help but flash a smile back at Reece before delivering the news to Hornsby. "And you, sir, are under arrest."

CHAPTER 3

"UNDER ARREST? YOU THINK I'M YOUR PRISONER?" Dub Hornsby's laugh was an ugly guttural croaking. But it was genuine.

"I'll be go to the devil," he rasped. "Did you hear, boys?"

Hornsby's four gunmen chuckled in unison.

"You hear what he said, Marko?"

The redhead scoffed. "Every swinging dude west of the Mississippi comes to Texas and right away starts calling himself a Ranger."

"It's true, Mr. Jarret," said Hornsby. "You've got even less authority here than she does."

Lin pointed his Colt at the man's chest. "This gun is all the authority I need. Climb down off there."

Hornsby called his bluff, launching a long stream of tobacco spit to the ground in front of Lin's boot. "You're a funny kind of man, Mr. Jarret. Ranger or otherwise."

Marko snickered again.

Lin felt his temper boiling up from deep inside. He didn't like being laughed at.

If he shot Hornsby from his saddle, he'd likely save the world a heap of trouble.

He chewed on the dilemma. Was this the trouble his uncle had brought him down here to fix? Lin figured as much. He'd never heard of Dub Hornsby, but Reece just now mentioned Cardoza. And Cardoza was the man Uncle Oscar had told him about.

Hornsby's quartet each had a gun trained on his forehead.

Considering the cacophony of explosions they'd just been through, was he ready to trust Reece Sinclair's bullet tally with his life? Two bullets she said.

Two bullets was all it would take. One for him. One for her.

With her clenched jaw and white knuckled grip on the carbine, it could well be Reece Sinclair was just as crazy as Hornsby.

Maybe even more so.

Now Carlos, the soldier with the crushed hand, had found his horse and rejoined his comrades. He too now held a gun, albeit in his left hand, his right being little more than a scarlet pulp.

Lin lowered his Colt, and Hornsby tipped his chin.

"My respect for you Rangers don't amount to a thimble's full of piss," said Hornsby. "But you're likely a smarter man than most of your colleagues."

"Go to hell."

"You're meddling in other people's affairs, Ranger. This ain't your business." Hornsby's eyebrows rolled up his forehead as he turned back to Reece. "Or maybe I'm wrong. Is it his business, Miss Sinclair? Maybe Ranger Jarret here is your new beau?"

Lin cleared his throat. "Let's assume for the moment

what happens here is my business." Lin circled the muzzle of his revolver. "In a roundabout way."

Hornsby shrugged, answering Lin's pronouncement. "It doesn't matter to me one way or the other." He told Reece, "I'll give you another week. You tell your dad." He signaled his men to move out and pulled up the reins on his stallion. "One more week."

Lin motioned toward the gruesome corpse sprawled out near the corral. "Aren't you forgetting something? Aren't you gonna bring home your man?"

Hornsby's expression reflected the disgust in his voice. "You bury him," he said. "It's not like you have anything else to do. No cows to work, eh *amigo*?" Again the guttural laugh.

With surprising familiarity, Reece jerked the rifle up to her shoulder and aimed down the iron sites. It wasn't the first time she'd hoisted a long gun.

"No," said Lin, his grip moving up to hold her arm. "Let it go for now."

Hornsby followed his five men back to the tree line and disappeared into the bosequillo, leaving Lin and Reece with only the echo of laughter and the whinny of horses.

"The pig. What were you thinking? I should have butchered him here, now, and been done with it." Reece swung the rifle back into Lin's grip like a rail hammer.

He almost didn't catch it.

"For what it's worth, I was thinking the same thing," said Lin. "But shooting a man in cold blood isn't the answer. Then I'd be arresting you."

"We'll rue the day we missed our opportunity. I pray I am there with you to remind of you how foolish you were."

She jumped from the saddle and faced him like no

woman he'd ever seen. She was trembling, not out of fear or delayed anxiety—but out of anger.

"Now it's your turn to explain yourself. You told Hornsby you have business here?"

"I have business with your father," said Lin.

"My father doesn't do business with Rangers." Like she wanted to spit on him.

"You're welcome, missy."

She turned her back and started to walk away, but Lin continued. "You know, if it wasn't for me pulling you out of the stampede, you'd be so much ground up sausage right now. I'd say you got off lucky."

Reece pivoted on her right heel. "And my men? Were they lucky? Where are they?"

Lin had wondered the same thing. As soon as Hornsby started talking, the vaqueros, including the old man Reece called Barb, had vanished.

"They're Apache, aren't they?" said Lin.

"Lipan herders. *Amigos nativos*. Unless you rile 'em up. Best damn cow men you've ever seen."

Lin nodded to himself. He knew just enough about the Apache to wet the back of a postage stamp. But he knew the Comanche. Knew the native fighting spirit.

"You're right about them being riled," he said. "I can't imagine the four of them letting today go without payback in the future."

"Only three of them are Apache," said Reece. "Ramon, Simon, and Juan. Old Barb Sanchez is a Tejano—a Mexican living in Texas. He grew up on Rancho de Jada."

Lin saw the concern on her face, the worry in her eyes. "He's family to you?"

Reece said he was. "He is my cousin. As much heir to the Spanish porciónes as I am."

She wiped her hands on the thin cloth of her trousers. The sun was past the morning midway point.

"We should go find the cows," said Reece, still filled with the excitement of the past hour's cyclone.

"I need talk to your father first," said Lin. He nodded at Hornsby's dead soldier. "Need to look after the corpse. We can review our options afterwards."

"Let the coyotes and buzzards fight over him. They'll take care of him soon enough."

He appealed to reason and hoped she would listen. "My guess is Ramon and Barb are off rounding up those cows. If you and me ride out there, we'll just get in the way. And two of us on one tired horse? We might just cripple this poor bay." Lin rubbed the horse's gentle nose. "The most important thing now is to let your dad know what happened here. There's plenty of hours of daylight remaining."

Reece kept quiet while he talked, and Lin knew she weighed her words against an almost overwhelming urge for action, for vengeance. She wanted to make things right again—now, immediately.

In Lin's experience, impulsiveness got you killed faster than anything.

He dared put a hand on her shoulder, and if she noticed, she didn't react.

Finally, she agreed with him. "He needs to know about the cows."

"You mentioned Cardoza. What's Hornsby's relationship with him?"

"Hornsby is Cardoza's foreman. He's the ramrod at Cardoza's sheep ranch in the Diablo Flats on the other side of the Rio Grande."

Lin could tell there was more to it, but Reece wasn't

talking. She had a healthy suspicion of wandering strangers who just happen to show up out of nowhere.

"But enough questions. You haven't yet explained what you're doing here," said Reece. "Let's start there."

Lin led the bay around, then stepped into the saddle. After he helped Reece onto the horse with him, he said, "Truth to tell, I'm not sure myself."

CHAPTER 4

TOGETHER ON THE BAY, THEY RODE DUE SOUTH, AWAY from the wreckage of the corral until they came to the fork of the upper and lower Rio Carlito with its flat rocky outcroppings and dense brush full of cattails and cypress trees. The llano to the west was rough grazing ground near an old way station called Defilement.

Reece told Lin her father had pasture ground there. "It's probably where Barb and the Indians will take the cattle once they round up the herd."

Most of the south central flatland water drained here at the fork into the heavy upper branch of the river and was carried away toward Jade City and the Rio Grande, but a lesser flow, called the Little Carlito, paralleled the trail they were on.

"Does the little river run through your property?" said Lin.

"It skirts the east side and is reunited with the wider river at Jade City."

"It's the source of your water?"

"Part of it. There are springs near the fork feeding the lower branch."

The day had finally warmed up to Lin's liking, though he couldn't discount the heat of Reece Sinclair pressing against him.

They followed the Little Carlito across the floodplain until Reece pointed out a second trail. The way veered sharply west away from the water's course for more than a mile. Eventually they met up with the water again, and Lin got the impression what had been a steady stream now seemed to be a pitiful dribbling.

Across the stream, they face a stand of mixed hardwood fronting a line of old, dilapidated jacals. Lin judged the thatch-roofed mud huts to be older than he was. Slave quarters, he supposed, and was interested to see they were not lived in.

Reece kept her hands on the bay's withers but nodded her head. "There's the home place ahead."

The clay-paved ranch yard was cracked and indifferent to their approach, and three swaybacked frame structures standing there were evenly spaced apart. Lin supposed the footprint of the homestead buildings had once appeared square, but now the outbuildings wandered to the north and east. The main house and its brick retaining wall tilted south toward the distant Rio Grande. Planted in the center of the widespread triangle was a round hand-dug well with block walls.

"Most of our water comes from there."

Reece steered the bay toward a tin-roofed livery barn with its open center runway and horse stalls on either side. To the west, a handful of wood-fenced pens wrestled with a forest of weeds and lay half buried under a dusty stack of hay.

The livery's white-washed siding had weathered with age and now appeared gray and dingy between patches of yellowing ivory flakes. Unkempt yellow grass lined the chipped rock foundation, and tall milkweeds, their shriveled pods burst open and spent, were a snarl in front of a half-open side utility door.

Upon seeing them, a surprised tiger-striped gray barn cat darted inside.

Once they dismounted, Lin slung his leather bag over his right shoulder and carried his bed roll on the left. He gripped the Maynard in his right hand. Reece turned the bay over to a young African dressed in a mismatched Sunday suit wearing a bowler cap. "Please make sure it's brushed, fed, and watered?" said Reece. The hostler nodded without a word and took the gelding inside toward the back of the barn. Lin listened to the echo of hooves recede in the distance.

"Sounds kinda lonesome in there. My uncle suggested you had a well-stocked *remuda* of horses," said Lin.

"Summer's gone," said Reece. "The winter season is slow. The Jensen brothers are here, but we've had to lay some men off. Had to sell some stock, too. I'm afraid they see us at the Rio Grande City stockyards more than I like. We don't ever get a decent price."

Her tone dared him to challenge it.

"I understand," he said. Cattle were big business in the north. Here they had yet to catch on. He offered a word of consolation, "Another few years, this whole region'll be thick with beef."

"*¿Quien sabe?*" she said.

Who can tell?

"Shall we go see my father?"

The brush grew tall along the path beside the long bunkhouse and another trio of sorry jacals squatted under a line of gnarled mesquite trees on the opposite side. Like the livery, the siding here had turned gray with the seasons. In its day, the shingle-roofed dormitory might've housed a score of beds secure from the elements. Now its glass windows were cracked and open to the wind. "I suppose I could drop my gear off here?" he said with some reluctance.

"Bring it to the house, and we'll see what my father has planned before you get settled in," she suggested.

They pushed on, up a small incline, past the well. When he'd received the message from his uncle, Lin had expected more from Rancho de Jada. It was hardly the jewel of the Palo Alto he had been expecting to see.

Perhaps most disappointing of all was the single-story ranch house, forty feet long on a grassy rise running east to west, the immediate property in the rear dappled with a few hunched over trees. The weary roofline was broken and missing shingles like a toothless old coot, and the three foot high retaining wall encompassing the front yard had lost a score of bricks. The façade and its three windows faced north with a red front door, sun-faded to pink, on the end.

A square shack with an open porch hunkered into the sod nearby, and a flock of scrawny chickens clucked and pecked around the grounds. Lin was judicious where he stepped as he approached the door.

"Just let me do all the talking," said Reece.

Lin followed her inside a musty parlor and straight back to Tom Sinclair's office.

———

"A BODYGUARD?"

Reece stomped her foot in the open space between her father's unorganized acreage of a desk and the *caliche* fireplace keeping his office at bake oven temperature.

"You hired a Texas Ranger to be my bodyguard? To watch over me like a baby?"

Lin clutched the black felt brim of his felt hat tight with calloused hands and waited for Tom Sinclair's response.

The rancho sat behind a soggy half-burnt cigar smoldering on his lower lip. When he spoke, a flaking caterpillar of ash tumbled onto a paper brush pile.

"To give an old man peace of mind," he said.

At the foot of the desk, his gear piled at his feet, Lin shook his head. "To be a pain in my ass is more like it. My Uncle Oscar's idea of a joke."

"I'll not have foul language used in front of my daughter."

The cigar bobbed up and down while he talked, and puffs of gray sent a smoke signal warning.

Lin dismissed the rebuke.

"In case you haven't noticed, sir, your daughter's plenty grown up. I expect she's heard worse from the drovers around here."

"Not in my presence, she hasn't."

There was no point in arguing. Lin chewed on the proposition like a rancid plug of tobacco. Now knowing the details of the job, he was inclined not to take it.

When his uncle asked him to visit Tom Sinclair and his daughter, Lin assumed a few locals under this Cardoza fellow were stirring up trouble. He'd been more than willing to lend his gun hand to the men of Rancho de Jada.

He hadn't cottoned on being assigned guard duty over a spoiled heiress.

"You've got the wrong man, Sinclair." Lin slapped his hat back on his head. He turned to leave.

"Folks in Jade don't think much of the Rangers," said

Sinclair. "I don't either, but I fought with Oscar Bruhn in Mexico City. I need a job done, Oscar says you're the hombre to do it."

It wasn't Sinclair's words stopping him, as much as the weary resignation they conveyed.

"He's a good man, sir." Lin tugged at the blood red kerchief on his neck. "A lot of Rangers are good men."

"A *lot* of them aren't. There've been a passel of indiscriminate shootings. We've had local Tejanos mysteriously killed. We can argue your definition of *a lot*." Sinclair mopped a loose strand of slick gray hair away from his thick Anglo features. "But we'll do it later on."

The man reminded Lin of a rough-hewn hickory carving of George Washington he'd seen when he was a kid, but with extra slabs of timber at the jowls and a dozen more termite grooves. His voice rumbled up from a mud-packed well and his eyes were chips of hard turquoise.

"For now, you prove to be a quarter the man Oscar is, we'll get along," he said. "You keep my daughter from getting caught up in this Cardoza mess, you'll earn your pay."

"She's already been caught up in it," said Lin. He turned back to Reece. "Do you want to tell him about this morning, or should I?"

Reece came forward and related the sequence of events starting with the one-eyed calf and the interruption by Dub Hornsby and his raiders. Reece left out the parts about pulling Carlos off his horse and threatening Hornsby with the Maynard.

Lin didn't see any reason to add to the story.

Reece was adamant. "He says the ranch is his, dad. His and Cardoza's. He says we have one week to vacate."

When Reece finished, Sinclair dismissed her like a school girl.

"If you'll excuse us, daughter, Mr. Jarret and I have much to discuss."

"Yes, you do," said Reece. "Like how soon he'll be leaving. I don't want—"

"Daughter."

The one soft-spoken word did more to end the conversation than any round of exclamatory declarations. Sinclair had had enough of his daughter's petulance, and his voice carried notice.

Beyond this point there be dragons, thought Lin.

"Maybe I ought to just go," he said.

"You do that," said Reece. She stood at the foot of her father's desk and faced him square. "I always thought Rancho de Jada was a symbol of freedom," said Reece. "It's what you told me. Everything else can succumb to the darkness, but we stand for *freedom*?"

It was an odd thing to say.

"We do stand for freedom," agreed Sinclair.

"For everyone except your daughter? I am finished with this conversation."

Lin watched the beautiful young woman turn and stride from the room with a flourish. Tom Sinclair may have asked her to leave, but Reece made it clear she was the one who decided to go.

Opposite the exit, behind Sinclair's desk, tall plate glass windows presented an expansive scenery of the Rio Grande valley with the flat winding river like a swirl of quicksilver on the horizon. In another part of the house, he heard Reece Sinclair cross a room and slam a door hard enough to shake the big window.

He wondered what she'd meant about the ranch standing for freedom.

"My daughter will be twenty-one years old next month, Jarret. I don't like being overly harsh with her, but I'm not a kind man. Not in reality."

For the first time since they arrived, Sinclair plucked the cigar from his mouth.

"Oh, you'll hear otherwise. You'll hear about generous old Sinclair. Wonderful, charitable Sinclair. But it's a myth."

"The West is built on myths, Sinclair. As I'm sure you're aware."

"Myths don't fight the weather, endure the droughts, or whip the Comanche. My family fought—and died—for everything we have here. We fight the Tejanos, who we shouldn't be fighting at all." Holding the cigar stub between his right thumb and forefinger, Sinclair rolled his hands over to display the rough, worn palms. "The fighting life sort of squeezes out the usual pleasantries."

There didn't seem to be anything to say, so Lin waited for him to go on.

Finally, Sinclair clenched the cigar back between his teeth and said, "I'm glad you were on hand this morning."

"I am too, sir."

Lin understood this was as close to an expression of gratitude as he was likely to hear.

Sitting back in his chair, the pronouncement was followed by a wet-sounding wheeze.

Sinclair was about as sturdy as the rest of the ranch. Which was to say not sturdy at all.

A strong wind might carry the old man away.

The room reflected its occupant. Chipped plaster walls, termite chewed beams, crumbling rock founda-tions...they all gave the illusion of strength, but it wasn't the truth. The lintel beams at the doorways and windows bowed with strain. Books and file folders were piled everywhere, with spilled shelves bearing witness to past book slides.

Lin had hoped for goose-down pillows. Looking around the room, now he figured he'd be lucky to get straw.

In a warped frame on one wall was a single spark of vitality—a stunning portrait of a beautiful woman with a single waist-length braid like the one Reece wore. So vivid was the palette, so sensuous the rendering of flesh and silken hair, Lin almost expected the woman to step from the painting and speak.

Sinclair caught his gaze. "My wife," he said. "Jada Sanchez. We lost her three years ago."

"Rancho de Jada," said Lin.

"Her family received the porciónes, the land grant, two centuries back. The old man you saw today, Barb Sanchez, is Jada's cousin. His parents, now long gone, founded Jade City. Barb lets Reece run the mercantile because it means he can spend more time here at the ranch."

Lin scratched the back of his neck. "I'm not sure I understand. The Sanchez ranch is yours, even if your wife is gone. It belongs to your family. If you have the porciónes, you needn't worry about Cardoza."

"I worry about everybody. The reason you're here is because I worry." Sinclair jabbed a tired finger toward a chair stacked high with old books. "Just toss them on the floor and sit yourself."

Lin remained standing.

Sinclair glared at him under hooded eyes, a man accustomed to being obeyed without question.

An ailment leaving him vulnerable, thought Lin. Especially where his spitfire of a daughter was concerned.

Sinclair likely believed it was just the opposite.

"I want to be sure we're clear, Jarret. I'm not paying you to act as another vaquero. Between the Indians and the Jensen boys, I've got all of them I need. I'm not looking for a gunman to scare off Hornsby or Cardoza either. You leave it to me. All I want is for my daughter to be safe in the crossfire. She's all I have."

"You have the ranch, the cattle."

"Spoken like a man with no children. The ranch means nothing if I lose her."

Sinclair was making it awfully hard to say no.

"Tell me about Dub Hornsby and Cardoza," said Lin.

"A Tejano boss named Juan Cortina has been making war on the city of Brownsville. He's been leading incursions, causing trouble for the authorities. You've no doubt heard about this from your uncle."

"More or less," said Lin.

"The man's a butcher."

"From what I hear, the Anglos ain't much better. Sounds like there's plenty of blame to pass around."

Sinclair fumed. "Cardoza is one of Cortina's lieutenants. He runs sheep at Diablo Flats on the other side of the Rio Bravo. Dub Hornsby is Cardoza's foreman."

"What's his claim to your rancho?"

"Cortina's war on this side of the river has emboldened Cardoza. He's determined to drive out all the smaller rancheros on this side of the river. He means to use Rancho de Jada as his new base of operations and make war from here. Worse—he believes he's justified in doing it."

"Yes, but again—by who's authority?"

"The same Spanish land grant we live under. See, son, before the Treaty of Guadalupe-Hidalgo, this was all one big Sanchez spread on both sides of the river." He spread his arms out to each side, symbolically holding thousands of acres.

"When the treaty went into effect, it established a new national boundary. The Rio Grande cut the Sanchez land in half."

Lin understood. "It's a boundary Cardoza doesn't recognize?"

"Cardoza was married to Jada's sister," said Sinclair. "She is also now sadly passed on."

"Which means Cardoza is your brother-in-law." Lin's spirits sunk. Getting in the middle of family squabbles was always a bad idea. "I think Hornsby was right. This isn't any of my business."

"I never knew a young man who wasn't in the business of making money." Sinclair bent forward and reached into the bottom drawer of his desk. He removed two sacks filled with gold liberty-head double eagles. He tossed one through the air and Lin caught it. "One sack now, one sack when the job is done."

Lin had to admit to himself he liked the sound of the coins rubbing together, admired the heft of the sack.

"All I'm asking you to do is keep an eye on my daughter for the duration."

"How long is the duration?" he asked.

Sinclair's answer was direct. "Until I am able to kill Cardoza with my own two hands."

Like all too much in Sinclair's life, the threat rang hollow.

CHAPTER 5

BEFORE THE LUNCH HE'D BEEN PROMISED, LIN WASHED up and combed his hair in the guest room at Rancho de Jada.

His back ached, his joints were stiff, and there were plenty of angry snarls coming from his stomach he wondered if somebody had smuggled a wildcat into the room.

He'd been sleeping outside for so long, his bedroll had his backbone in knots.

And too, he'd had better mornings. Mornings didn't include being knocked around by longhorn cattle. Or having loaded guns pointed in his direction.

He stretched in the floating dust motes and sunshine, then pulled a clean shirt from his duffle.

Catching sight of himself in the old bureau mirror, the angry red scars on his ribs and abdomen reminded him he'd had worse mornings too.

Like the day he went toe to toe with a Comanche warrior.

The poor devil would never see another sunrise.

How easily it might have been the other way around

—Lin underground, feeding the wild flowers and the young brave on his way to becoming a tribal chieftain.

Fate was what it was, he thought, pulling on his blue linsey-woolsey shirt.

He'd decided to stay on at the Sinclair place.

The sack of gold stashed in his satchel had almost entirely convinced him to take up the old man's offer. The daughter's green eyes and womanly figure had carried him the remaining distance.

To be sure, he resented the affair almost as much as Reece did. He didn't like being bossed around, by his Uncle Oscar, Tom Sinclair, or anybody else.

And he didn't like playing nursemaid. But gold coins and female assets have a way of turning a man's head.

Not always for the better.

He took a minute to check on his payment. He knew the gold was there, in his leather saddle bag. He could see it from across the room where it sat on a chair beside the door. Crammed in alongside his powder flask, percussion caps, toothbrush, and other necessities, the gold sack made a tell-tale bulge on one side. Taking a look inside the sack was a small thing, but it put his mind at ease.

Now he strapped on his leather gun belt, spun the revolver's wheel and dropped it into place.

Then the smell of fresh coffee and fried beef drove everything else from his mind. He pulled open the door and traipsed down the hall, following the aroma.

The ranch house floorplan was like an upper-case letter H seen from above: two wings joined by a hallway. The west wing, where the front entrance was, led into the foyer and Tom's office in the back. The east end of the house contained the kitchen and Tom Sinclair's bedroom.

In between was the hallway with a room on each side.

His guest bedroom was the front side of the hall, Reece Sinclair's room directly across the way at the back of the house.

The privy was just outside Tom's room in back.

Hungry, Lin was lured into the kitchen by fine aromas, but was disappointed to find thin rations at the table.

Tom Sinclair's idea of lunch was a sliver of anemic beef, two runny eggs, some leftover beans, and day-old biscuits—served for two. Barb Sanchez—yet to return from the range—usually prepared meals for the rancho. Lin got the idea Tom Sinclair was slightly embarrassed at the mean grub.

Besides Sinclair, two other men sat at the table. Both were short and pear-shaped with loose suspenders over red flannel shirts. Their pants were worn and baggy. Neither man carried a gun nor a full set of teeth.

"Clyde and Cecil Jensen," said Sinclair by way of introduction. "Two good ol' hands."

Clyde had a head of curly hair the color of sour milk and a beet-red complexion. His brother was equally flushed but bald with a shock of dark sideburns.

"Pleased to meet you, boys." Lin poured some coffee from a tin pot waiting on a quilted hot pad, then set to loading his plate with eggs and beans.

Other than a lingering scent of familiar lye soap, there was no sign of Reece.

Her father read his mind.

"She's hitching up her wagon for town," he said as he washed down his lunch with a quick swallow of coffee. "Wanted me to tell you to go back to where you came from."

The Jensens laughed.

Lin grinned and slathered the surface of his halved biscuit with sour butter. "Is it what you want, Sinclair?"

"We already settled our business. How do you find the accommodations?"

Lin had to admit the bedroom wasn't half-bad. Sinclair nodded. "I'd rather have you here than down at the bunkhouse. Likewise, you'll take all your meals with me and Reece," said Sinclair. "Ride back and forth to town with her."

"She goes to town often?"

"Like I told you, she runs the mercantile for Barb. Keeps things stocked. Jade City's just over the property line. There ain't a lot of customers except a few rannies from the neighboring spreads, but there's the store, a cantina."

"Who runs the cantina?"

"You keep your nose out of there."

Clyde Jensen agreed. "And be not drunk with wine, wherein is excess; but be filled with the Spirit—Ephesians, Chapter five, verse 18."

Lin chewed his biscuit, kept the conversation casual. "I'm not much of a drinkin' man."

"The cantina's called the Muleskinner," said Jensen.

"Hollister Morse owns it," said Sinclair.

"Morse a friend of yours?"

"He's not friends with anybody but himself, if you take my meaning."

Lin drank his coffee. "I hear you."

"Morse is an attorney and acting constable of Jade City," said Jensen.

The grub wasn't the best he'd ever had, but he soon realized it wasn't the worst. Surprised at his hunger, he slicked his plate clean and went for seconds. "Takes care of lunch," he said. "Or do you call it *dinner*? Up where I'm from, we call dinner the night time meal."

"Supper's at night," said Jensen, reaching for his hat. "If we want any, we best get to work."

Lin hadn't noticed before, but the brothers had perched both of their toppers crown-side down on the floor behind their chairs.

As one, they rose and plopped the hats onto their heads and looked at Lin.

"Thought we'd see about the corral you all busted up this morning," said Clyde. It seemed like he did all the talking for the brothers.

Sinclair told them to forget the corral and ride out to the east pasture near an old sheep station called Defilement. "Barb was talking about taking the cows out there after we worked 'em. See if they've got 'em pulled together yet."

Both of the Jensens nodded their good-byes. After they left the house, Sinclair turned his attention back to Lin.

"Those two are as Christian as they come. Loyal as the Carlito."

Lin's look in response must've puzzled Sinclair, and he added. "Wet weather or dry as a bone, the river runs true. Just like those old bachelors. Glad to have 'em around."

After a pause, Sinclair said, "I love my daughter, but a man could wish for a son to take care of things."

Lin finished his coffee, poured another cup. "If you don't mind me saying so, your daughter's an extraordinary woman."

Sinclair agreed. "She is, indeed. Reece spends most of her time organizing the store for Barb, keeping things up. She's got a strange way with numbers. Does math in her head, and always calculates it right. She's a fair hand at gunsmithing too, if you can believe it."

"I believe it."

"There's something else to keep your nose away from," said Sinclair, putting as much menace into his voice as he could muster. "Despite what I said about a son, I ain't looking to marry Reece off, especially to a Ranger."

"I'll remember it," said Lin. Then with a wink, "Make sure Reece knows."

"Are we gonna have trouble, Jarret?"

Lin talked around a mouthful of beef tips. "With chow like this, you're damned right."

Sinclair held his gaze for a full ten seconds, then broke into a look of amusement. "Alright you son-of-a-bitch, you win. You win." His chuckle turned into a series of spasms, and he coughed phlegm inside his wrinkled flannel napkin.

Lin sat in a chair with his back to the cook stove and finished the meager fare. Each rancid bite got him to thinking. Each swig of bitter coffee worked on his curiosity. After cleaning his plate, he said, "I don't mean to pry, but just how well are you fixed for things around here, Tom?"

Across from Lin, Tom Sinclair mopped his egg yolks up with a bread crust and shoved it into his mouth. "Been better. Seen worse. We've got some salt pork hanging in the summer kitchen—the little shed out here in the front yard. A few beans. You've seen the chickens. Reece says we got some freight in yesterday. I guess she's going in after it." After he finished his coffee, he said, "Your uncle's supposed to be coming in today or tomorrow. He usually packs something along too. A few hams or bacon. Something."

The wheeze again.

Lin carried the coffee to his lips one last time, then stood up and retrieved his hat. "I'll go find Reece," he said.

"S-she's up at the barn," said Sinclair, still trying to tame the coughing jag. He pointed toward the parlor and the hacienda's front door. "She's got the high-wheel rig."

Lin said he'd find her.

But when he got to the livery barn, there wasn't a wagon to be found. The African he'd seen in the morning was likewise gone. Lin poked around the place twice, calling for Reece, without getting an answer.

He plucked a piece of dry grass and stuck it between his teeth.

Then he walked inside.

A half-dozen animals occupied the left-hand stalls, and the equestrian smell of horses and tack was a welcome, familiar thing. To his relief, the animals appeared to be well cared for with shiny coats and clean pens. A good supply of leather occupied a *bodega* on the east end of the place, and a couple spare saddles were available on a pair of heavy sawhorses.

The gray tiger cat he'd seen earlier in the day ducked around a side pen, hiding.

A few pens occupied the opposite side of the alley, but most of it was reserved for a walled-in grain closet reaching all the way to the rafters. A beat-up door hung on three rickety hinges, and Lin unhooked the iron clasp and looked inside. The dusty, dim room smelled of oats, but was otherwise empty, and its crusty walls were lined with dobber nests.

The barn's open center alley showed wheel marks in the dust and a few boot prints.

Lin walked to the end of the alley, assessing the

square pens until he found his bay, brushed with clean bedding, hay, and a trough with fresh water from the well. To find his horse well cared for spoke well of the Sinclairs and their hired help. In the long run, how a person treated a horse was more important than just about anything else.

Lin strolled back outside to lean against a hitching post and looked around, studying the ranch.

The old Spanish land grants were narrow strips of land running north and south from the Rio Grande, and Lin figured the original Sanchez spread must've included thousands of acres of prime grazing land along with the stickery meadows and sparse hard wood forests he'd already encountered. His uncle assured him Rancho de Jada on the north side of the river had an abundance of land and enough livestock to assure a high crown in future economic and political royalty—but considering what he'd seen thus far, Lin wasn't too sure.

The cattle pens from this morning were a shoddy, rickety mess, and across the open yard from the stable, the one-story frame hacienda was a sprawling skeleton of a once-vital home. The bunkhouse wasn't in any better repair, and aside from the old stack of hay he'd seen the night before, the inventory of surplus feedstuff in the barn was non-existent. The outside of the building was likewise covered in run-down siding. Lin wondered if it was too late to consider raising sheep.

On the bright side, at least the air was a lot less humid than it had been earlier in the day, and the sun was bright.

More important, it had finally warmed up.

Alone, Lin leaned against his post and removed a compact sack of tobacco and the makings of a smoke from his shirt pocket. He took his time, sprinkling a heap of leaves onto the rolling paper, cinching the sack shut with his teeth, rolling the cigarette between his lips. He scratched a lucifer on the heel of his boot and touched it to the paper. Breathing in the smoke, he considered the footprints.

Before setting off for town without him, it looked like Reece had hitched up her wagon by herself.

Which was something else bothering Lin about the ranch.

He'd lived and worked on cattle and calf operations. There were certain expectations to be met. Early mornings at the bunkhouse, big tables full of food at noontime, and a hustle and bustle around the corrals. A ranch this size, Lin expected at least five or six hands, even during the off-season.

Other than Barb Sanchez and the two old Jensen brothers, Lin hadn't seen a soul.

Surely the modest grouping of cows he'd seen didn't constitute Sinclair's entire herd?

He squinted through his smoke, taking in the adjacent bunkhouse, its front door open, creaking on old hinges back and forth in the breeze.

Back and forth.

Back and forth.

A buzzard swooped low, then circled up in ever wide loops, riding the warm air currents. If Lin were the superstitious type, he wouldn't like the omen of carrion birds circling the homestead.

What was it, Reece had said? *Rancho de Jada symbolized freedom.*

At the moment, it sure was free of people.

The cat soft-padded up to the door behind him and offered a curious meow.

Taking one last draw off his cigarette, Lin dropped it

to the ground and twisted it out under the toe of his boot.

Nothing to be done but saddle up a horse and ride to Jade City.

He righted his cap, hitched up his belt, and made his way back inside the barn and the horses there.

Sinclair had given him pick of the available animals, and since the bay he'd ridden in on deserved a rest, he figured to choose a new ride. He retrieved his blanket and saddle from the bodega and walked down the open galley post to the pen where his bay was stabled. The horse's eyelids were heavy and he was still enjoying a fine rest in a stall by himself, but a blue roan mare next door seemed eager to go. She nickered at his approach.

"Howdy, gal," he cooed in response.

"Howdy yourself, pard," said a voice coming in the opposite way.

Lin hid his surprise at this first sign of human contact and walked back the way he'd come to meet the tall, lanky gent who approached from outside.

"I'm Jim Carvell, but folks call me Stick." He was several inches taller than Lin's 6 feet and had longish blonde hair hanging from a dark felt hat. "*Stick* 'cause you give me a job I stick with it. Same with friends, family, or a ranch—I stick. Some people they don't. Some people talk a big game but when the chips are down, they can't hold to a commitment. Stick Carvell, though, he's something else. Yes, sir. Put me on it, and I'm gonna—"

"You're gonna stick," said Lin. "I got it."

"You Lin Jarret?"

Lin said he was.

"Miss Reece gave me a message for you. Pretty as she is, she's sorta stand-offish and hard to live with you understand. So when she says something, it don't necessarily mean what you think. With her, you gots to read between the lines. I'm just telling all of this to you so's you don't get mad, plus she's a little odd in the head, I mean compared to women you might've known before. She works as a gunsmith, and—"

"Just give me the message, Stick."

Interrupting Stick Carvell could get to be a habit.

"She says go back where you came from."

Read between the lines is right, he thought. Never once had he mentioned his boyhood home to the girl. And Sinclair hadn't mentioned it while in her company.

She'd been asking about him.

Lin almost blushed as his stomach fluttered like a boy in short pants.

"What else did she have to say?"

"Huh? Oh, sorry. I was just noticing your gun."

"I said, did Miss Reece have anything more to tell me?"

"Just to say if'n I saw you to give you the message."

"Her dad said she's gone to town."

"Yes, sir." Stick didn't bother to be discreet as he bent his knees to examine Lin's Colt. "There's a mighty nice hogleg. You're a pretty fair shot, I'd reckon."

"Pretty fair."

"Truth? I told you Miss Reece works on guns, didn't I? She had one of these a few months ago. I could've bought it from her, but I didn't. You say you're a good shot, huh? You wanna show me?"

"Not particularly."

"I'm a pretty fair shot. Want me to show you?"

"Not particularly."

"Miss Reece said you've got a Maynard rifle up there. Fifty-two cal? With the paper percussion cap roll?"

"Yup."

"You ain't carrying it with you?"

"Does it look like I'm carrying it?"

Stick made a show of giving Lin the once-over. "Nope." Then he said, "I sure would like to shoot your rifle sometime."

"We'll work something out," said Lin. "Sounds like Miss Reece told you a lot about me."

"Want me to fix up your saddle on the roan?"

"I can manage."

Stick walked across the way to a pretty palomino. "I was planning ride to town myself. Durned shoe leather is falling apart on me." Bouncing up and down, Stick held up his right foot to show Lin where the heel of his boot had broken away from the sole. "Normally I'd fix it myself but I'm plumb outta tacks and..."

Lin allowed Stick to chatter on while he worked to outfit the roan for his ride into town.

Lin cinched up the saddle and pretended to listen.

He couldn't get Reece Sinclair out of his mind.

Her defiant schoolgirl posture might be a façade to hide her true feelings.

She hardly seemed agreeable. But what if it was a mask?

She'd noticed his Maynard and told Stick about it. Could be she was mooning over him?

When the roan whinnied, Lin realized Stick had stopped talking several minutes before, and he'd long finished saddling up the horse.

Get a grip on yourself, hombre.

"Ready to go, Mister Jarret?"

"Call me Lin."

Stick flashed him an army salute. "It's a fine thing to make your acquaintance, Lin."

The roan was good-natured and carried Lin genially

out and around the barn where he waited for Stick and the palomino to join him.

The afternoon was quiet and peaceful, and he almost couldn't imagine violence like he'd seen earlier in the day. He knew Dub Hornsby and his men were still out there. He knew Cardoza wielded an even more malevolent hand over the region.

But here, with a hardpan of blue sky above him and the spicey smell of silverleaf tickling his nose, his thoughts wouldn't go there.

He'd seen Reece Sinclair in action too, and Stick said she worked on guns.

As he sat astride the affable horse, enjoying the pleasant pace, Lin pictured Dub Hornsby on one side and Reece Sinclair on the other.

He wondered who posed the greater threat to his future?

CHAPTER 6

THEY FOLLOWED THE WOODED BANKS OF THE LOWER Carlito into town.

Lin Jarret and Stick Carvell had covered the distance from domicile to main street in easy fashion with the taller man telling most of the tales, one right after the other, barely pausing to take a breath.

"To understand the valley, understand the Tejano," said Stick. "To understand the Tejano, understand the Spanish, and the Indians too. This land belonged to them long before the sweet wonder of Texas came to be."

Lin couldn't disagree with him. "Are you from Texas, Stick?"

"Born and raised. Seen it all and lived to tell." Which was funny in itself, thought Lin. Stick couldn't be more than twenty-one or twenty-two. At least five years younger than Lin.

Stick steered his pal around a chug hole in the trail. "What about you?"

Lin shared some of his background. "I've been here in Texas the past ten years or so. Been up and down the trails. Worked in the country. Worked in town. Reckon this landscape grows on a man."

"You wait another few years, you'll never call anyplace else home. There's no place in the whole world like Texas."

Lin took Stick's paternal advice for what it was worth.

They came to Jade City by way of an open spot in the road where the trees gave way to a panoramic desert-like range. A misshapen adobe building snoozed through the afternoon, orange against the clear blue sky, and a sign above the door identified it as The Muleskinner—the cantina.

A stock tank and a fenced corral with a few more adobe buildings across the dirt street was the business district of the town. Far away at the end of the road, Lin saw a wagon parked with two horses in front of a board-walk. He assumed it was Reece.

Riding along under the trees in dappled shadow, Lin decided to use Stick's candor to his advantage. "How is it Tom Sinclair runs such a wide spread with no more than a few hands? Other than you, the Jensens, and the Indians I saw, seems like nobody's around. You got some vaqueros out on the line?"

For once, Stick didn't answer right away, and when he did he was more guarded than ever before. "Could be we're a little short at present."

"Before lunch, I met an African who watered my horse. What's his name?"

"I don't know who you mean," said Stick.

At the end of the woods where the Carlito made an abrupt turn to snake around Jade City to the east, they followed the road into town.

"How many men total does Sinclair have on the payroll?" said Lin.

Stick worried the question like a mental algebra problem.

He almost seemed ready to answer when they rode up a short incline to the boardwalk in front of the cantina.

Two men were stretched out on the planks, their bodies mutilated and buzzing with flies.

Stripped to the waist, they might've been enjoying a full-bellied siesta, except the skin of their necks and torsos was cut and peeled away like fruit rind. Blood had massed and coagulated in the lacerations, and their skin was mottled and gray. Whoever had killed them had left the faces intact, and one of the men had a familiar crushed right hand.

Lin stilled the urge to retch at the grisly sight and said, "I know this man. He's called Carlos, and he was with Dub Hornsby when they were at the cow corral this morning."

Stick's reaction was more stoic and detached. He dismounted and squatted down on his heels like a detective to examine each of the victims and their wounds. Cupping his chin, he said, "Yeah, it's Carlos all right. The other one's name is Rollie Martinez. Can't say as I'll shed a tear for either one of them skunks."

A series of vicious Spanish interjections came from inside the cantina.

"Didn't sound too friendly-like, did it?" said Stick, dropping his voice to a whisper.

"Friends of the deceased?" said Lin.

"Having an informal wake."

"And the killers? Who could've done this?" But after watching the ease with which the vaquero used the castrating knife on Hornsby's man, Lin had a pretty fair idea.

Stick figured the same. "Miss Reece filled me in on

your morning adventures. It's likely these fellows learned it just ain't wise to cross some men."

Lin knew Stick was talking about the Lipan Apaches. "This is awfully strong retribution for cutting loose a herd of cows," he said.

"I wouldn't call it retribution as much as I'd call it sending a message," said Stick.

Again, a string of profanities and vile declarations came from inside. This time, Lin was able to pick out some words less slurred, along with the name *Ramon*.

It sounded like Hornsby's riders had come to the same conclusion about the Apache herders and the killings.

Tom Sinclair's vaqueros were escalating the skirmish with Cardoza whether their boss asked for it or not.

"Let's go find Reece," said Lin.

Stick agreed. "She's up there at the Sanchez store, or at least I seen her wagon when we rode in. It's the adobe with the T-shaped hitching post out front and the green window shutters."

Stick took another look at the carved up cadavers and breathed in deep. "Hell of a way to die," he said. "But maybe it'll learn 'em to stay away from the ranch."

Somebody inside the cantina called for another round of drinks.

"Somehow, I don't think we're gonna be hit it lucky," said Lin. He motioned for Stick to follow him up the road.

The problem with vengeance, Lin thought, was it tended to get traded back and forth.

Forever.

And messages weren't always received the way they were intended. Communication was tricky.

Lin figured the Sinclair spread was due more trouble than ever.

When they were far enough away from the cantina to talk out loud, Lin said, "How many men do you think were in the cantina?"

"Three or four. No more."

Lin walked in silence past the stock tank and a big, round *noria* equipped with winch, rope, and bucket for fresh water. Sprawled in the shadow of the well, a lazy yellow dog flicked its ears at a pass fly.

Lin hoped they could pick up Reece and get out of town without trouble.

But Stick wouldn't let it be.

It was just possible he envied the morning's misadventure.

"You figure we might need to take them bastards on, Jarret? By God, we could do it too. Drunk as they're sounding, you and me could whup 'em good. Shucks, we wouldn't even need the hand cannon on your hip. Bet we could take 'em with bare knuckles."

"If it's all the same to you, I'm planning to collect Miss Reece and get the hell gone."

"Get the hell—?" Stick was dumbfounded. "You don't mean run? From Hornsby's men?"

Lin didn't answer. He understood Stick's confusion. The idea gnawed at him too. Lin wasn't one to run from a fight. "I've got a job to do," he told Stick. "My job is to keep Miss Reece safe. It's what I'm being paid to do, which means she's my priority."

"Wager you five dollars, she ain't willing to go home until she's good and ready. Most times it means sundown. She has lots of customers come in at twilight after evening chores. She won't appreciate you telling her what to do. After all, she's a scrappy little thing. Why, the other day I walked up to her and said—"

"Let's just make sure she's okay," said Lin.

They picked up their pace until he reached the intersection of dusty streets where the Sanchez mercantile waited. The high-wheeled wagon was parked there with a pair of brown mares hitched up to the tongue. The brake was set, the spring seat covered with a blue patchwork quilt, and the box contained two short round wood barrels full of cornmeal.

Across the street, a line of one-room shanties stretched four deep toward the line of the border river beyond, and Lin saw what looked like a sawmill and lumber yard.

A fresh-pegged sidewalk similar to the one in front of the Muleskinner fronted the Sanchez mercantile. Lin tied his blue roan to the post and stepped up onto the boards.

He wondered aloud if Reece had any more barrels to load.

"You might go ahead and ask me," said Reece, appearing in the doorway.

Lin's heart couldn't help but skip a beat, and once more his stomach fluttered against his rib cage. Since the last time he'd seen her—storming out of her dad's office —she'd pinned her hair up into a bun at the nape of her neck. Two long, loose ebony locks floated up on the west wind, and a smattering of sand rattled against Lin's boots and bounced off the wagon wheels.

"Howdy, Miss Reece," said Stick, lifting his hat. "Want me to haul some freight?

"If you would, Stick, with my thanks." The blonde man clomped over the boardwalk and into the store.

"You're a peach," said Reece.

Her hair wasn't the only thing different since the last time Lin had seen her. She was dressed different too, with a man's red and white checkered gingham shirt and canvas trousers accentuating her figure. The uniform suited her. She seemed capable of doing anything a man could do.

All of which didn't excuse him from being a gentlemen.

"I'll help too," he said.

Stick returned to the boards with a short round barrel on his shoulder. "These unmarked ones were here by the door. Are you planning to take 'em out to home?"

Reece nodded and Stick passed the barrel over to Lin.

It was heavier than anticipated, and he almost toppled over climbing off the boardwalk.

Quickly righting himself, he said, "What's inside these things?"

"Essential goods," said Reece.

Lin dropped the barrel into the back of the wagon, then followed the others inside.

The Sanchez store had a spacious interior, more than the outside let on. Glass windows added to the effect, casting a favorable light on three stacks of canvas bags in the middle of the room. Filled with coffee, flour, and salt, they nailed down an inventory replete with everything a river ranch might need.

Lin couldn't help but think the full mercantile was the complete opposite of Sinclair's spartan ranch. Iron tools hung from pegs on the far wall: a hammer, a pick-axe, a levered jack. A fine stock of brooms and mops dangled from the rafters behind the counter. A variety of speckled pots and pans were for sale.

Immediately inside the door, two glass-fronted display counters lined the left-hand wall, culminating in a third set at a perpendicular angle. Here a brass cash register perched over an assortment of colorful hard candy, gee-gaws, small toys, and frilly ephemera.

Lin picked up another barrel.

"Anything else you need loaded?" he asked.

"Coffee beans," she told him. "Some flour. I'll get it later on this evening after I finish sweeping up."

"There isn't going to be any later on," said Lin. "I want you to come home with us now, as soon as we get these barrels in."

Reece opened her mouth to reply, and her brows rose with the startled query, "Now?"

She followed Lin out to the wagon. "The mercantile is open Monday, Wednesday, Friday, and Saturdays until six-thirty. I'm expecting more than one customer today, regulars who will be in for supplies. Buck Louis alone will buy most of the cornmeal for his family of ten. I'll be here at least until sundown"

"Buck Louis can make do," said Lin, traipsing back inside the store. He wanted to be on the road for home before the men in the cantina finished their current round of drinks.

"Excuse me" the girl threaded her way between Lin and Stick, walking backwards through the store in front of him. "I don't know how they do things where you come from, but down here we help one another. I've got a new wagon load of freight in the back room, and I've got needy folks who want it."

Reece planted herself behind the counter with her hands on her hips. "I will not ask my customers to make do."

Lin slung a third barrel onto his shoulder and carried it out the door. "You better. If you know what's good for you."

"What's this about?" said Reece. "Stick? What's this about?"

At the side of the wagon, Lin didn't hear the ranch hand's response. He was too busy listening to the increased volume of noise from the cantina.

A figure stood in the doorway of the Muleskinner looking in the direction of the Sanchez store. The wind picked up again and a dust devil scurried along the street, sweeping up bits of chaff and cypress leaves.

The cantina man wore black and had a red and yellow poncho over his shoulders. His tall dark hat was pushed far back on his head, and he swayed as if affected by the breeze. While Lin watched him, the inebriated reached out a hand to steady himself on the doorjamb.

The distance wasn't very far, and Lin easily recognized Dub Hornsby's segundo, the red-head with the well-oiled beard. "Marko," he whispered under his breath, and the stocky man perked up his head almost like he heard his name.

Like a dog whistle, thought Lin.

Marko saw Lin—recognized him too.

Judging from the quick way he moved back inside, the dogs would be coming.

"Here we go," said Lin, as Marko disappeared inside the cantina.

Lin ducked in, picked up the last barrel, and called for Stick and Reece. "Get in the wagon," he said. "Right now. We're gonna have company calling, and I'd just as soon not be here when it does."

He hurried forward, sloppy, trying to take two steps at a time. When his toe hit the wooden edge of the threshold, he tripped and the barrel rolled out of his hands, backwards. It crashed down with a magnificent crack, three of the staves giving way even as the top popped loose.

A loud scattering of forged lead fanned out across the floor.

Some of the bullets disappeared into the hard wood cracks, others rolled under the display cases and sacks of coffee and cornmeal.

Bullets?

Lin was struck dumb.

Behind the counter to the left of the door, a line of shelves offered a variety of pellets, caps, and powder. They came from factories and hand mills both local and distant. All of them were packaged in paper or inexpensive wood.

Reece sold plenty of bullets over the counter.

To have six extra barrels...

Lin caught Reece's eye. "You fixin' to outfit an army?"

"What if I am?" She pulled a broom from a sample lineup at the counter and started to sweep. "Don't just stand there. Help clean these things up."

Lin hunkered down and did his best to salvage the broken barrel while retaining the remnant of lead inside. "Looks like .36 caliber?" he said.

"In one barrel, yes," said Reece. "There's different stock in different barrels."

Stick moved to the doorway, poked his head outside. "They're coming, Lin. Just like you said. They're staggering drunk, but they're coming."

"How many?" He had the broken barrel upright and shoved it up behind the counter with the cash register.

"Three. Bearded gent in the lead is called Marko."

"I know him from this morning," said Lin.

"They've been to the store before," said Reece. "They

won't do anything. Maybe knock over a display. Try to scare me by stealing some candy."

"And your dad lets it continue? Allows these fellas to hurrah you without doing anything?"

"He *did* do something. He had you uncle call *you*."

Lin pulled his Colt Walker from its holster.

"Good point," he said.

"I can handle them just fine," said Reece. "I've done it before."

"They're splittin' up," said Stick. "One of 'em's going around the back."

"Where's the rear entrance?" said Lin.

Reece nodded toward a narrow door opening into a back room. "Through the pantry, the back door leads to a latrine."

Lin stationed himself in front of the cracked pantry door.

"What's this all about?" said Reece. "Marko on his way, and you two all hellbent to get out of here?"

Stick told her the truth. "Ramon sliced up two of Dub Hornsby's men and left them down at the cantina as a message," said Stick.

Lin squeezed the butt of his Colt.

"It was more like a declaration of war," he said.

CHAPTER 7

THEY WAITED INSIDE SANCHEZ'S STORE, REECE BEHIND the counter with a British-made muzzle loader 12-guage, Lin beside her at the pantry with his Colt watching the rear entrance and Stick Carvell inside the front door with an old model No. 5 revolver. The store's back pantry was an arsenal, and they had ammunition to spare. If no real time to reload, should they need to do so.

Except, now the men outside had vanished, with the threat left hanging in the air like the smell of horse apples in the warm autumn afternoon.

After a tense five minutes, one of the wagon mares whinnied and took a step forward, rocking the box.

Nervous.

It caught Lin's attention and caused him to forget about the pantry and fixate on the wagon out front. The horse whinnied again and moved enough to clank the wagon hitch.

Something more than wind and dust was bothering the old gal.

She stomped her back hoof, and the wagon shuddered. She flicked her tail back and forth in a way that showed her discontent.

Lin told Stick, "Cover the back for me."

Lin stood at the front threshold, closer to the outside, and Stick zig-zagged around the counters to cover the pantry entrance in back.

Marko and his boys might be falling down drunk, but Lin assumed it only made them foolishly bold and more dangerous. An inebriated man might take the kind of stupid chances a sober man would never consider. And what was the old quote? May fortune favor the foolish.

In this case, Lin hoped fortune was on his side.

At the open front door, he pondered the silent siege, could almost smell the booze and Bay Rum perfume of his opponents.

One thing was sure. He tasted the salt of fear on his lips.

Yeah, fear.

With a trio of vengeance crazed drunks outside looking to put him in the ground, only an idiot wouldn't be afraid.

But only a coward would back down, and Lin was no coward.

Daring not to make a sound, not to even breathe, Lin edged closer to the front door, one quiet step after another.

His palm was slick with sweat around the butt of his Colt, and his blue shirt was soaked through. He knew the men were out there, likely just around the corner of the building. They were waiting, too.

But time was running out. Lin needed to move. Needed to force Marko's hand and make something happen.

If he charged out into the street, the gunnies would cut him down before he could get off a single shot.

If he continued to sit in here and wait, the devils might wheel in, triggers blazing.

If they took Lin out, Reece could get the first man. Stick'd take the second. But what about the third? And what if there were more on the way?

Feeling his skin crawl, Lin moved ever closer to the entryway.

A warm breeze slung packets of grit in from the street. At the wagon team, one of the horses again shifted its weight, stepped forward, anxious.

The wagon clanked, then shuddered ahead by two feet, despite the set brake.

That was the sign.

Lin took a step backwards.

The evasive move was just enough to save his life, but too late to avoid being tagged as a heavy club of solid oak swung around to slam into his arm, paralyzing his gun hand.

Enveloped in a blaze of hazy red pain, he fell back, gasping for air, only dimly aware of the boots pounding onto the boardwalk in front of the store. He felt his fingers let go of his gun and somebody tried to shove him over. Instead of going down with the push, he rolled forward, wrapping his arms around his attacker, driving both of them onto the walkway outside the store.

Together they stumbled off the boards, bounced away from the wagon and fell into a thrashing, cursing tangle, Lin's arms locked around his opponent in an iron embrace.

He opened his eyes to daylight.

In the middle of the street, Lin freed the stinking heap of a man from his bear hug. He cringed at the wave of pain and nausea rolling through his ribcage but managed to roll to his feet on instinct alone. He slapped his empty holster out of habit.

You lost your gun, he told himself.

Idiot!

In the street facing him, Marko was already on his feet, coming at him with a ten-inch long fighting knife. The blade was razor-honed iron and the grip, a polished maple with a light tiger striped grain. A beautiful way to die.

A crash of broken glass accompanied by a scream of pain from inside the store shook Lin's awareness. He could only hope Reece and Stick were holding their own against Marko's men.

———

THE SECOND LIN JARRET stepped back and got hit, Reece came around the counter with the scattergun. She'd worked on the old side-by-side British fowling piece at home and had carried it to town in the wagon on her lap, ready to fire with 40 grains of powder, fiber wad, and shot. When Lin and Marko cleared the doorway, a long-haired assailant dressed in fringed leather buckskins clomped in with a thick-handled machete. He took three steps toward Reece and lifted his sword arm in spite of the twin muzzles pointed at his chest.

Whether Buckskin saw the gun or not, it was clear he meant to separate Reece's head from her shoulders.

At the last second before Reece could pull the trigger, Buckskin's right foot went out from under him, kicking up a handful of round bullets from the barrel Lin spilled moments earlier. Slipping on the lead, he spun around backwards trying to right himself but instead smashed into a glass display case with a loud crash, his weight splintering a thin wood shelf filled with needles and pins.

He screamed out with pain as broken glass sliced into his bare hands and face.

Reece jabbed the gun toward him. "Move and I'll spill your guts from here to Sunday."

Bleeding and bleary-eyed, Mister Machete nodded his head.

Watching for any sudden moves, Reece squatted to retrieve the man's rusty, well-worn blade.

Stick made a loud gasp of anticipation. Reece swiveled on her heel in time to watch the ranch hand get a clear bead on a slender young man sneaking through the back door. It was one of the trio who had harassed her at the corral.

The Tejano wore a heavy sweater and floppy sombrero, and his mustache was waxed into wide looping curls on each side of his lip. He carried a small revolver, not unlike Stick's old-fashioned gun. As he made his way crouched along the wall of the pantry, he didn't realize he'd been spotted.

Reece fell back to a defensive position behind the big cash register, ready to unload both barrels of her shotgun. She recalled the man's words from this morning.

I know these Sinclair women. They like the whip. They beg for the wheeeeep.

Little rat bastard. Reece hadn't liked him this morning, and she liked him even less now. She decided—given the opportunity—she would enjoy putting this one in the ground.

But Stick kept true to his name. Without hesitation or unnecessary fuss, he aimed down the barrel of his revolver and waited with one eye closed until Mister Mustache was six feet from the pantry exit.

He kicked the partially closed door aside with his foot. "How about you drop the hardware, amigo?"

The intruder gave out an involuntary squawk and threw both hands over his head, inadvertently triggering his gun. Flame jumped from the muzzle as it spat two slugs into the ceiling.

Covering the distance between them in less than a second, Stick punched Mister Mustache in the face. With a wail, the intruder dropped his gun and followed it to the floor, fingers cradling his nose.

Stick kicked the little revolver away from the man's reach.

"Are you hit?" said Reece.

"I'm okay. You?"

"Unhappy, Stick. I'm real unhappy."

She turned to poke the heel of the first man with the muzzle of her gun. He winced as rivulets of blood seeped through the fringes of his leather and a thousand shards of glass littered the scene.

"Seems you cut yourself," said Reece. "You ought to get them wounds bandaged."

The hairy man slurred something obscene, and Reece prodded him again with the shotgun. "Get up, *chico*. I don't like it when people cause a mess and bleed all over my store. Now get out."

To his credit, the man tried, but kept slipping on pieces of glass, lead bullets, and his own blood.

Stick nudged the mustachio into a standing position and walked him at gunpoint to where his companion struggled to rise. The two intruders made a pathetic picture.

"How's Lin doing?" said Stick.

At the mention of the Ranger's name, a steel ball rolled through Reece's stomach.

Lin!

"Watch these two," Reece said and carried her gun to the door in time to see Lin and Marko square off in the street. The bearded redhead was breathing hard and staggering. Equally beat, Lin worried the air with a wooden club.

The Ranger's shirt was torn and the bottom half soaked with blood. A more dangerous cut had turned the leg of his trousers a bright red.

Reece's breath caught in her throat. She stepped forward, intent on putting a stop to the fight.

She couldn't bear to see Lin cut down.

She hadn't had time to figure him out, but for the almost seven hours since she'd met him, she'd thought about nobody else.

————

MARKO OUTWEIGHED Lin by twenty or thirty pounds and had the advantage of an inch or two of height, giving him an extended reach. As his fighting knife sliced through the air, he caught the weave of Lin's shirt, tearing it open to prick the Ranger's already-aching torso.

Lin jumped back, bleeding, and Marko pressed the attack.

With the grip in his left hand, he bent low for a fast jab. Lin pinwheeled away to the right, coming up on Marko's left where he delivered a hammer blow to the neck. Marko barely registered the hit, coming back around with the knife, fingers still wrapped tight behind the brass pommel.

Again, Lin had to dodge. Again, Marko came on.

"The girl had nothing to do with killing your friends," Lin told him. "Neither did I."

Marko wasn't listening. "You involved yourself in this. This morning at the corral you had every chance to walk away. Instead you said we could assume it was your business."

It was true, Lin thought, he had said it.

Bleary, bloodshot eyes tracked Lin's every feint, every dodge.

Marko was a natural fighting man, and hell with a blade. Lin had quickly come to the realization he was going to get cut more than once. There was no way to defeat his opponent without spilling some of his own blood.

The goal was to make sure Marko spilled more.

A gunshot echoed from inside the store, then another, but Lin didn't have time to wonder what was happening there.

He had to concentrate on every possible advantage Marko gave him.

There were damned few of those.

Marko flashed the blade sideways. Lin came in fast and hard with a picture-perfect parry of the knife, unleashing an elbow to his opponent's nose. Cartilage crunched, and Marko squealed. Lin danced back with a professional fighter's footwork, but instead of backing off, Marko continued to press.

"You Rangers act all high and mighty. I ain't seeing it now, Jarret. I ain't seeing nothing more than a slick young cowboy come sniffing around Reece Sinclair. You're no different than every other man in these parts."

His swings were insane zig-zagging affairs, ripping the air between them, landing mere inches away from Lin's throat, ribs, and groin.

Lin tried cranking around for a kick but Marko swerved at the last instant. He tried grinding his boot into Marko's shin, but any pain he inflicted only brought more rage and more taunts from his opponent.

"It's what you're doing, ain't it boy? Sniffing around like a stray dog after some bitch in heat?"

A weapon, Lin thought. If only he had a weapon of some kind.

Then he saw the club Marko had used on the boardwalk to hit him. During their initial scuffle, it had rolled to the edge of the planks and waited in the dirt behind the wagon.

Luck was with Lin then.

Marko's next jab went high and wild. Lin lunged beneath it, slamming into the ground to slide through the dust on his good shoulder. His knuckles brushed the club, but the impact left him breathless and weak.

Marko was already following up, hurling himself across the street, screaming obscenities.

"Gonna kill you, Ranger."

The knife soared down and bit into Lin's thigh, slashing through pants and skin, but not landing deep enough to stop him.

Lin wept blood like a stuck pig, and he hurt like fire—but he'd live.

Not for long if he didn't move.

Lin wrapped his fingers around the stick and crab-walked back against the wagon wheel. He barely had time to register the wheel was wet with mud when Marko came down with another chopping motion.

Lin used the length of oak to pop him under the chin —hard—clapping the big man's jaws shut, forcing him to chomp into his own tongue.

Marko screamed with an eruption of blood, jerking his hands up to his face.

Lin finally had some room to maneuver. Regaining his

feet, he clutched his weapon like a club and closed on his opponent.

Tired, breathing with considerable difficulty, far more effort than before, Marko squared off with him.

Behind the angry sneer, Lin saw the drunk confusion on Marko's face. It was clear he'd expected to take the Ranger quick and easy. Saturated with booze, and now tussling in the heat of the afternoon sun, he was losing ground. He needed to end the fight sooner than later.

Lin was willing to oblige him, but he was weak too, and his knees trembled.

Marko slashed out with the knife. Lin countered with a swipe of the club.

They circled one another, each prepared to strike again and again, neither willing to give an inch until his opponent was down.

Reece Sinclair walked onto the boardwalk, aimed the scattergun high and unloaded one of the barrels. His back to the store, Marko flinched at the booming concussion. Lin had seen it coming and rooted himself.

In the time it took Marko to react, Lin put everything he had into one last smashing blow to Marko's temple, and the bigger man dropped like a sack of wet sand.

CHAPTER 8

LIN STOOD OVER MARKO FOR A FULL MINUTE AS THE redhead rolled back and forth, groaning in a semi-conscious stupor.

At the boardwalk, Reece sidestepped to allow Marko's two men to slouch past, hands clasped on top of their bare heads, mingled blood and sweat leaking down both of their faces.

Stick followed them, his old 5-shooter in hand, Lin's lost Colt in the other. Both weapons were cocked and ready to fire.

At his urging, the two defeated men marched across the planks and out into the street.

Lin looked forward to hearing about what had happened inside.

With blue powder smoke still framing her slim figure like the devil herself, Reece delivered her ultimatum to the invaders. "Take your scruffy backsides home to the cantina and thank God you're still alive."

Slowly, Marko struggled to his feet and spat a bloody gob into the dust. He eyed the Carlyle shotgun Reece carried and dropped his hands to his side with a snarled oath. "This ain't over," he said, shoving his knife into a leather sheath on his belt. He swiveled his massive head from Reece to Lin and back again. "Y'all listening to me? I'm saying this ain't over."

Once his men joined him, Marko seemed unsure what to do next. He knew neither Reece nor Stick were bluffing with their guns.

One false move, thought Lin, and these three skunks would find themselves full of holes.

"Like I say, this ain't over," said Marko.

Dragging his shirt sleeve across his brow, Lin motioned toward a red-eyed albino in a single breasted vest and coat tramping up the street toward the store. The rawboned man wore a ruffled white shirt and a skinny black tie around his narrow collar.

"You maybe ought to ask your attorney whether it's over or not," said Reece.

Lin guessed this was Hollister Morse, the lawyer owner of the Muleskinner. He was a skeletal figure, with putrid strands of straw-colored hair falling from under a wide-brimmed hat. His jaw clicked when he spoke, and his tongue was an animated blue muscle playing across his brown teeth with each word.

"You boys been pickin' a fight with Miss Sinclair?"

"Nothing I can't handle," said Reece. "But I'd appreciate your encouraging these men to develop a more congenial disposition. We are, after all, neighbors, Mr. Morse. We wouldn't want bad feelings between us, now would we?"

Morse had a distinctive, jerking gait, and as he lurched directly into Marko's space, he shook his head. "Mister Hornsby will not be happy to learn about this."

Marko's response was cold and mean. "You seen what

their Indians did to Carlos and Rollie. If he was here right now, Hornsby'd pin a medal to our chest."

Morse poked his boney index finger into Marko's chest. "And Mr. Cardoza will pin you both to the ground with a stake if you foul up his chances at acquiring the Sinclair Ranch."

He sent a shivering smile over Marko's shoulder. "Hypothetically speaking, of course, Miss Reece. All legal and above board."

Reece offered a slight bow.

"Noted, Mister Morse," she said, "but I'll tell you again, Rancho de Jada isn't for sale."

"Yes, well...may be." Morse straightened his posture and cocked his head toward the cantina. "For the nonce, everyone's invited to the cantina for drinks. On the house."

"I'd enjoy a free drink," said Marko.

"I'll pass," said Lin.

Morse nodded his ivory skull. "Don't ever say I wasn't cordial, Mr. Jarret."

"You have me at a disadvantage, Mr. Morse. I didn't realize we were acquainted."

"News spreads fast in the valley, Ranger. You might consider catching up."

Marco and his men sluffed off toward the cantina without a backwards glance.

Morse directed his speech toward Reece. "I meant what I said, dear. And you heard Marko. The valley is changing. Alliances aren't what they used to be. The time might soon come when you'll need a friend like me, and my loyalties will be elsewhere."

"You best get on home, Mr. Morse," said Reece. "I hear tell your wife takes her supper early. You wouldn't want to keep her waiting."

"I hear things too, Miss Reece. I hear things about you and your sympathies. You're full of sass now but take my word for it. The balance of power is shifting. You'll need me in the coming confederacy."

Morse showed them his back and retired down the street.

Lin wondered what he'd meant about Reece's *sympathies?*

Because the balance of power was shifting all over the country. And talk of a coming confederacy carried all the ominous echoes of war.

———

BEFORE LONG, Lin found himself inside the store seated on a wood folding chair, a heavy dull ache pounding inside his ribs, a sharp pressure just above his knee. Only inches away, the face of an angel floated into his awareness.

Her eyes sparkled like emeralds. He leaned forward to kiss her.

And then grimaced with agony as he moved.

"Hold this tight," said Reece, jamming a wet towel onto his leg. He focused on his lap. The towel was spongy with blood. He pulled it away from a gaping tear in his pants to examine the open gash in his leg. It puckered around the edges and seeped blood.

"Oh, Lord," he sighed, feeling his head spin.

"You'll live," said Reece, "but I'm gonna put a couple dozen stitches in it before we leave for home."

With bone-chilling glee she held a needle up between his eyes, and Lin gritted his teeth. It appeared this was going to be more fun for her than him.

Stick crossed the room and handed him a bottle of amber liquid. "Have a slug of this, buddy."

"What is it?"

"Hell, I don't know. Picked it up behind the counter over there. It sure burned the calcium off my tonsils."

"Did you pay for it?" Reece asked.

"House pays," said Stick. "If Morse can afford to water his animals, you can, too." He turned his back and walked away slow. At the door he crooked an elbow against the jamb and watched the street outside.

"He's unusually reticent," said Lin.

"There's more to Stick than he lets on," said Reece. "We aren't all cut from the same canvas, Ranger."

Lin tried for a clever answer but came up empty. Instead, he swallowed some of Stick's liquor.

The booze gave him a warm, mellow feeling, and he wondered at her observation. He thought about the way she handled Morse, the comfortable way she had with the shotgun.

"I reckon I'm in debt to you for distracting Marko when you did."

"And I reckon I don't need minding like a child. I told you before."

"Reckon I never doubted it."

She picked up a clear bottle of fluid from the floor.

"This is gonna sting." Reece pulled the towel away from his leg and washed the wound with a splash of alcohol, then handed him the bottle. He put the bottle of clear fluid to his lips.

"Don't you dare," said Reece. "The stuff Stick has is bad enough. You swallow this, you'll have an open sinkhole where your stomach used to be." He breathed in deep and she handed him a fresh washcloth. "Use the liquor to clean the wound on your middle."

The raw juice stung badly, but pain was an old friend, and one or two more scars only added to a life well lived.

She stitched him up with practiced precision.

"Where'd you learn how to sew people up?" he said.

Without answering, she walked away to join Stick at the door.

Within a few minutes he was on his feet, joining them.

Gauging their expressions, something was wrong, above and beyond what they'd already been through.

"What is it?"

"More trouble," said Reece.

Reece led the way outside, and Lin put his hands on his hips. They watched seven horsemen pull up to the cantina, a trail of saffron dust spreading out behind them.

One of the men was Dub Hornsby, but he rode to the right and just behind a regal, narrow man with a head of midnight black hair and no hat. Dressed like Hollister Morse, but in an embroidered charro suit, he sat on an expensive Spanish saddle with inlaid ivory and silver. He rode a giant warhorse similar to Hornsby's, like a Percheron Lin's dad had once used for plowing. This horse, however, was pampered, with a custom trimmed tail and mane.

"It's Cardoza," said Reece. "We'd best forego loading up the rest of the freight and just head on out."

Lin took an accounting of the wagon's inventory.

Some cornmeal, plus three short barrels of bullets and powder.

"I'd rather not drive past them," said Stick. "Not if we want to make it home without causing more of a ruckus."

"We'll go home the long way," agreed Reece.

"Suits me," said Lin.

Reece turned to him with a proposition.

"This is your chance to cut out, Mr. Jarret," said Reece. "Between the two of us, we've agreed your services aren't needed."

Lin shook his head. "I'm riding a Sinclair horse."

"The blue roan makes a fair trade for the bay you rode in on."

Lin heard the catch in her voice even as she said it.

Regardless, he was already involved.

"During our scuffle, Marko said some personal things," said Lin. "I can't walk away and leave it."

It's what you're doing, ain't it boy? Sniffing around like a stray dog after some bitch in heat?

He climbed into the saddle beside Stick's palomino.

"I guess I'll stick for a while, myself."

CHAPTER 9

INSIDE THE MULESKINNER CANTINA, DUB HORNSBY had a headache. Right behind the eyeballs. Like somebody drove a rail spike through the top of his head.

Hollister Morse kept the wood-stove in the corner fired with hardwood year-round, and with all the windows closed, the temperature inside rivaled the July sun. Which only added to Hornsby's sour disposition.

As the evening stars winked on above a scarf of red-orange at the horizon, Morse turned up the wick on the bar's coal-oil lamp. Then he splashed a jigger of rye whisky into a tin cup on the counter.

In the corner opposite the stove, draped in shadows, Cardoza sat brooding. Watching. It was almost as if he were the director of a theatrical play waiting for the actors to begin reciting their lines. Such a man was Cardoza—moving people around this way and the other, all for his own amusement or benefit.

Hornsby knew it was all he and Marko and the others were to men like Cardoza. Pieces on an acres-wide stage to be directed on a whim? To be derided, maybe given the occasional sound of polite applause? To be killed off if and when the action demanded it.

Hornsby planned to give the old *Cortinista* a show.

He acknowledged his boss with a nod, then picked up his tin cup and drank. Rye was his current drink of choice, and it was good of Morse to remember it. Maybe it would help dull his headache.

Morse, at least, could be counted on. As long as the old cadaver didn't dry up and blow away.

Hornsby carried his cup to the foremost serving table and turned his attention to the three men seated there.

Never in his life had he seen such a bone-headed lineup of lice-infested idiots as these three. They mucked up the morning raid on the Sinclair cow herd, and Hornsby had lost a man as a result. Three men now, truth be told.

The fools should never have started taunting the girl. They should have expected those damned Indians would be protective. She was everybody's baby-sister on the Sinclair ranch.

"And this afternoon, you get all liquored up and go borrowin' trouble with the daughter again—this time in her own damn store," he said.

"Barb Sanchez owns the store," said Morse from behind the bar. "Don't give the usurpers any more credence than they deserve."

"Regardless, you know the girl's armed for bear up there. You know she works on guns in them back rooms. And don't you ever forget, she knows how to use them."

Felix Ruiz rolled his attention up from under his battered sombrero. His face was a skillet of mashed lips, broken teeth, and droopy mustache. "I didn't know what she did up there, *jefe*. I swear it on my mother's life. I didn't know she had this many guns."

"Because you're a damned idiot," muttered Hornsby. Then louder, "Guns are practically her stock in trade. But guns are worthless without men to fire them. There's nobody out at the ranch—unless you count those Jensen brothers, and they're sworn to peace. From what I hear, they don't even like girls. Sinclair is short on men these days."

"Short on water, too, eh, *jefe*?" said Ruiz with a snicker. "After we dam up the river last week?"

"Naturally," said Hornsby. "Short on water, too. Now, shut up. No need to go blabbering all we've done to anybody with a set of ears on their head."

Seated beside Ruiz, Saul Willats was glassy-eyed with shame. His fringed leathers, new and expensive-looking when he put them on in the morning, were torn and caked in sorry helpings of blood. The hair at his shoulders was knotted and carried sparkling remnants of glass.

"And you," said Hornsby. "Your face looks like the scratched up floor of a chicken coop. Was it worth it?"

"Close enough. We held our ground. Showed 'em we mean business," said Willats. "They won't dare go agin' us next time."

Hornsby had to laugh out loud. "You can't be so stupid as to mean it?" He bent over and grabbed Willats' mop of hair, snapped his face up. "Are you fool enough to not see what a sorry wreck you've made of this?"

Seated next to Willats, Marko leaned back in his chair, a chip on his shoulder the size of Missouri. "Aw... leave him alone, Dub," said Marko.

"You know what you boys are? You're an insult to *real* men. Do you know what's going on down in the valley tonight?" Hornsby risked a peek at Cardoza. "The *Cortinistas* are out there fighting. Honorable men standing up for our rights while you three get run off by a skinny little gal and her scattergun."

Hornsby pinched the bridge of his nose in frustration. The pounding in his head was back with a vengeance.

"Ain't a fair comparison," said Marko.

"Not fair? Why isn't it fair? Because it wasn't your idea to rush the store?"

Marko shrugged. "Maybe. And what if it was? It was your idea to roust the cattle pen this morning, and I saw well it turned out. Nobody's bawling you out because of it."

"The cattle pen was different. I didn't know the Ranger would be there."

"The Ranger ain't nothing. Two more minutes, and we never would've had to worry about him again."

"You didn't get two more minutes." Hornsby struggled to control his temper. Especially in front of Cardoza.

All his life, Dub Hornsby had been nothing more than a last-choice ranch hand. He'd carried water for drunks and old men on both sides of the river. He'd bowed down to rich snot-nose babies half his age. When Cardoza asked him to be foreman over his spread, he knew somebody had finally seen his worth. At the Diablo Flats, he was El Segundo. Second only to the big man himself.

He wasn't about to show weakness now, especially not with Cardoza looking on.

Hornsby signaled Morse for another shot of reassurance.

"We've got three soldiers dead in two days," he said. Morse handed him a fresh helping of rye and he drank it down in one swallow. "And you three certainly aren't in any kind of fighting shape."

Ruiz let his chin slump to his chest in defeat.

Hornsby slammed his cup into the table. "Are you listening to me?"

Ruiz jumped to attention. "*Si, jefe. Si.*"

Hornsby tossed the cup to the floor where it rolled through the sawdust.

Then he patted Ruiz on the shoulder. "I know you won't let me down again," said Hornsby. "Another week, the Sinclairs will leave. Rancho de Jada will belong to us."

Marko, the son-of-a-bitch, rolled his eyes and pushed himself back from the table.

"I don't care about the ranch, and I don't want to wait. It's the Sinclair gal I want. She looks to be a wildcat in the sheets. And the Ranger. I want him too—to plant his cold, dead hide. Nobody makes a fool out of me. I want them now—not in a week."

Hornsby took his time walking around the table. "What is you said?" He cupped his ear with curled fingers. "I don't think I quite heard you right."

"You heard me fine, Dub. Don't try to muscle me."

"What you want isn't important. What you—"

"No," said Cardoza from the back of the room. "No, Hornsby. Mr. Marko is right."

He pushed back his corner chair and emerged from the shadows, tall and graceful. Cardoza's expensive doubled-breasted suit was pressed free of wrinkles and decorated with mother-of-pearl buttons. Silver conchos with tassels glittered along the length of his trouser legs, and a gold watch chain gleamed in the lamplight. His polished boots showed a reflection.

Unlike Hornsby, Cardoza's hair and mustache were expertly trimmed. His manner and voice bespoke an education in the east, his accent was more Spanish-

European than south-of-the-border. He was undeniably vain.

And insanely fickle.

Hornsby wasn't sure what to say. "I don't understand, Mr. Cardoza. I thought you said the plan was—"

Cardoza held up his hand. "I have reconsidered my plan. In light of the unexpected turmoil experienced here in Jade City, I think it's better to move fast. To strike without warning."

Marko grinned, enjoying the spectacle of Hornsby being corrected. "We're going to take Rancho de Jada sooner than later? Just like I said."

Cardoza nodded in agreement. "*Si, si.* Yes, Marko, we've endured a personal affront. Not only the loss of life we've suffered," and here he paused to cross himself, "but the effrontery you men encountered from the girl, the audacious gall of the Ranger to step into something which doesn't concern him. Those types of affronts must be answered immediately."

Hornsby sputtered with frustration.

"With men like these? Today was nothing but an example of how incompetent they are. They weren't able to take over a penny-ante mercantile store and you expect them to subdue a ranch?" Hornsby snapped his fingers, and Morse poured him a fresh drink in a new cup. "You need to trust me."

He sipped, and the rye tried to dull the spike behind his eyes, slow his racing heart. It helped him breathe easy even as Cardoza looked down his nose at him. Hornsby continued, "We need to do it my way. Ruffle their feathers. Annoy 'em. Roust 'em like we did this morning. Make them fret. Like Ruiz said before, they're short on water, or will be soon—thanks to our work at the river."

"Fine, fine...but all of this is to what end?" said Cardoza.

"They won't be able to stand it. Sinclair's old and soft. His daughter...well, she's a woman ain't she? How long's she gonna stay around a dying ranch with me and the boys hectoring her every day or two?"

Hornsby appealed to Cardoza's ego.

"Give us another week. Maybe two. We'll find some additional men. We'll let Marko kill the Ranger. I'll deliver Rancho de Jada to you with a bow tied on it. You'll be remembered a long time for re-uniting the original Sanchez porciónes."

"I'll kill the Ranger anyway," said Marko. "No matter whose plan we follow."

Behind the bar, Hollister Morse cleared his throat. "What are you afraid of, Mister Hornsby? Sinclair isn't nearly as popular with folks around here these past few years. They've had a lot of hired hands quit. Their summer help is gone, and there isn't any winter help to be had. They've got a skeleton crew manning the place—two old Danes and a big-mouth toe-headed kid. They're ripe for attack, and they won't hold out long."

Cardoza reached into the pocket of his suitcoat and removed a pair of black lambskin gloves. As he put them on, he spoke with finality.

"Which is why we take the ranch now."

Hornsby let his enormous bulk drop onto a stool at the bar.

His job had been to take away Sinclair's claim to the Sanchez land during the fall while Cardoza helped Cortina press his case in Brownsville.

Why the change of plans all of a sudden?

Hornsby worried the inside of his lip.

Maybe the stories about a falling out between Cardoza and the more powerful Cortina were true. Maybe Cardoza figured securing the Sanchez land quick would be a feather in his cap. From there he could move through the whole valley, take some of the other ranches.

It would certainly make him a hero with the Tejanos as well as the Mexican people. Maybe it would be enough to challenge Cortina?

Across the river, they'd write ballads about his prowess for the next hundred years.

But Hornsby still thought it was better to wait.

"What about the other rancheros up river?" he said.

"Too far away to help—if you strike hard and fast," said Morse. "Also, as I said, Rancho de Jada is frowned upon by her neighbors."

"Help from the Apache?"

"Aside from the three working there, you ain't gonna hear from the rest of the tribes," said Marko. "I know Indians. Killing Carlos and Victor was personal retribution. Eye-for-eye over the cow raid. If it comes to a life and death defense of a white man and his daughter, they won't risk it."

Nobody said anything for a full minute.

Hornsby scratched his neck. "You oughtn't keep this place so damned hot and uncomfortable," he told Morse.

"Are we decided then?" said Cardoza.

"Hell, yeah," said Marko. "I didn't know there was any real debate." Ruiz and Willats nodded.

Cardoza didn't wait for Hornsby's assent. "Good," he said. "Then we take Rancho de Jada on Friday at dawn."

"There's a lot to consider," said Hornsby. "Horses, men. There will be food at the ranch, but we'll need to cart in our own water. Empty barrels we can fill from the river."

Cardoza spread his arms. "You are fortunate then, amigo. Today is Wednesday. You have all day tomorrow to make your preparations."

CHAPTER 10

Barb Sanchez finally came home late Wednesday night, and Lin spent most of Thursday fixing the corral with him, Reece, and Stick. After the previous day's trampling under hoof, nearly half the fence rails were splintered or completely done in, and a number of posts needed to be replaced.

Just as Reece had foretold, Barb and the Indians had gathered the herd to graze on the west pasture land called Defilement.

Ramon and the other Apaches had yet to return, and Barb didn't want to talk about them.

The old man made breakfast, then packed up his gear and set out to the corrals ahead of them. When Lin prepared to follow, he saddled up the bay he'd rode in on, giving the roan time to rest after her walk to Jade City the day before.

Reece and Stick each rode one of the brown mares from the wagon.

The sky was clear, but the land slept in a layer of clouds, and a turkey gobbled in the foggy distance.

"It's a beautiful morning at Rancho de Jada," said Lin

as he paralleled Reece along the shallow bank of the Rio Carlito. "Provided we don't have any more visitors."

"Humidity's high," said Reece. "Hard to keep your powder dry."

Lin stretched in the saddle, rubbing a sore spot in his back as he remembered unloading the barrels of black powder, bullets, and cornmeal into the livery barn's grain cabinet the night before.

At the time, he thought it an odd storage space, but he was too wrung out to ask any more questions.

He noted the powder flask she wore around her neck on a braided cord and the Carlyle in her mare's saddle boot.

"You fill your flask up from the new stash of powder we brought in from town?"

She nodded. "Like I said, hard to keep it dry," said Reece. "How's your leg this morning?"

"Nothing better for war wounds than a good night's sleep," he said, but his voice was tight.

"That's what I've heard."

"Too bad I didn't get a good night's sleep," Lin confessed. "I don't like going to bed hungry."

"You didn't like dad's cabrito stew?"

"I've never enjoyed the flavor of goat meat," said Lin. "I'm glad Barb was back on the job this morning. Best huevos rancheros I've had for a long time."

"We eat a lot of eggs here," said Reece. "Which is something, at least."

Again leaving the bank of the Little Carlito, they rode through a shallow dry resaca, an ancient oxbow lake. "Sometimes I think this ranch is the most beautiful place in the world. Other times, it is the most in need of repair."

Lin shrugged. "We all do the best we can."

"Not all of us," she said.

"Am I supposed to take it personal? Because I'm in too good a mood for sparring with you, Contessa."

He'd risked the nickname in jest, and it got the reaction he was looking for. Reece showed him a genuine smile.

"Contessa? Is that how you see me?"

"Why not? You're heiress to the most beautiful place in the world, ain't you?"

"And what are you heir to, Mister Jarret? Your uncle is a Texas Ranger, now you're a Ranger?"

She was fishing, which was fine with Lin. "Truth is, ma'am, I always wanted to run a stage line."

Her laugh was genuine. "A stage line? You're teasing me, now."

"No, ma'am, I'm not." He held her green eyes with his, and she didn't look away. "Well, maybe a little bit," he said.

Soon they'd turn off for the thorny woods surrounding the cow yard and rejoin the river near its fork. Reece knew a better trail through the persimmons than Lin had taken the first time he approached the corral. Today, following her lead, he was able to avoid stickers in his hat brim and scratches to his ears.

"The Ranger and the Contessa, huh?" said Stick, catching up from behind. "It's got a good sound to it. You might show up in one of them adventure-type stories like *Ivanhoe* or *The Three Musketeers*."

"Bite your tongue," said Reece.

"I don't take you for the bookish kind, Stick," said Lin. "I'm surprised."

"You spend a few winter weeks in a frozen line shack with nothing to do but count nails in the floorboards, and you'll get to be pretty bookish yourself. I've read just about anything worth reading. In fact, I can darned near recite the lines from Shakespeare's play, *Hamlet*. Give me a minute. Let me see how it goes here..."

While they rode through the trees, Stick recited more than one soliloquy, peppered with colorful metaphors.

When they cleared the trees and emerged into the clearing with the corral, Barb was waiting for them.

They hobbled their horses together in the deep grass and walked to the wreckage of split rail fencing. "Where are the Apaches?" Lin asked Barb.

"Hunting," said the old man.

Animals or men? Lin wondered.

When Lin asked about additional winter ranch hands, he got a similarly evasive answer from Reese. "If you know ranching, you know spring's the time to hire more hands. We always lose a some in the fall."

"How many do you have on the payroll today?"

"You'd have to ask Stick," said Reese. "He stays in the bunkhouse with the Jensen brothers, and Dad handles the books."

Except he had already asked Stick the same question the day before, and as far as Lin had been able to determine, there were no other hands.

"What happened to the young African I met when I first arrived?"

"There's nobody here today but us," said Reece.

Which was a pity, because it turned out Barb Sanchez was a tyrant on the jobsite. Lin would have welcomed the company. One day he was determined to get to the bottom of the mystery at Rancho de Jada.

For now, he worked and kept his questions to himself.

The morning passed with slow, steady, progress.

After Lin and Stick dug out the needed post holes,

they sawed and set three new hickory corners and braced them with *caliche* blocks from the smashed branding pit. Reece collected remnants of the ruined fence, dragging lengths of hardwood into a pile while Barb worked on the broken race and swinging crush gate.

"We'll bring in the cows tomorrow," he said. "Sort out the ones we already worked."

Again, the sun was high in the sky and the temperature unseasonably warm. Sometime around noon, Barb let them stop toiling long enough to choke down a cold lunch of molasses bread and lard cracklins. "Tonight we feast," he promised, pointing at Lin's leather holster and gun. "*El festival de balas, eh?*"

The festival of bullets.

"What do you mean?" said Lin.

"Barb thinks you're a better shot than me," said Stick. "He and I, we've got a little wager going. He's put the money on you. But he's an old man. He believes everything his hears. He thinks you Rangers are something special. Oh, I don't mean he admires you. Nobody around here really likes—"

"Stick," said Reece. "Why don't we finish our lunch in peace?"

Lin shared space on a cut persimmon log with the stable hand, and Reece sat across from them, finishing her bread.

"This bias against the Rangers," said Lin. "Your dad mentioned it. I'm not sure I understand it." He swallowed some coffee from a canteen and passed it to Stick.

"You would understand if you knew the Tejanos," said Reece. "Some of them have been deprived of their homes by government edict. All of them under suspicion from the immigrants. Conflicts occur every day. The Rangers haven't always been on the side of right. Or even the side of law and order."

"You sound like a *Cortinista*," said Lin.

"A minute ago, you're the one asking the questions. Now you know everything?"

"My uncle's mentioned a few things...," explained Lin.

"Your uncle isn't much better than the others," said Reece.

"Your dad seems to think so. They're old friends."

"My dad doesn't talk to the same people I talk to."

"And who do you talk to?"

Lin figured the question was honest enough, but Reece seemed to take it as a slight. She held her tongue but refused to turn away.

Stick emptied his canteen, then shook out the coffee grounds. "I've told your old man to put egg shells in his coffee when he cooks it. I don't know why he's pig-headed about it. Egg shells settle the grounds. Improves the flavor too."

Reece didn't take the bait, and Stick continued with his tirade. Deliberately changing the subject.

"I just think for a dollar a day and found, I ought to get a decent cup of coffee."

High overhead, a blue heron winged its way south to the Rio Grande, swooping low enough to be seen. Lin watched it glide on outstretched wings. It didn't have a care in the world. Could he be as lucky.

Stick slapped his thighs and stood up. "If you two want to jawbone over politics all day, don't blame me if Barb tans your hides. I got work to do." Lin watched him stride back across the sagebrush to where the old man was already back at it, installing a new iron hinge on the cattle chute.

"We were talking politics?" said Lin.

"He's right," said Reece. "We all have work to do."

They didn't visit much more until the sun was low and it was time to ride in.

————

WHEN LIN, Stick, and Reece rode into the ranch yard, the smell of roast pork and charcoal cooked beef was thick. Barb had abandoned the worksite a couple hours early, leaving them carefully assigned tasks in order for him to ride home and get started at the grill. If the rich, heady aromas at the livery barn were any indication, he'd found success. "It smells good down here, think how good it's gonna taste at the table," said Lin. "What do you say, Stick?"

"I say I haven't had a decent helping of grub in the past week, and it's a damn shame I have to share it with you."

"Says the man sucking down all the scrambled eggs this morning at breakfast," said Lin.

"I hardly got to eat my fill with you stuffing your face."

"I need to get to the kitchen," said Reece as soon as she left the saddle. "Barb will have potatoes to cook, and bread to slice. I can't very well expect him to do everything."

It was the first time Lin had seen her act like a girl, and he liked it.

He liked it a lot.

He wouldn't dare say anything for fear of losing his hat and head with it. Instead, he offered to tend to her horse. "I'll brush all three of these mounts down and meet you all shortly."

"Thanks," said Reece, dusting her hands. "Be sure to draw her some fresh water from the well."

"I'll do it...Contessa!" The men watched as she hot-footed it all the way to the hacienda.

"Aw, you don't have to take care of my horse, Lin," said Stick. "I was just needling you about sharing grub. Fact is, I'm awful glad for your company these past couple days."

"I said I'd take care of your horse, and I will," said Lin. "You go on. Get cleaned up for supper."

"You're sure?"

Lin swatted him away with his hat. "Go on, git."

"Listen, Lin. A word of advice. You be careful." Stick let the word hang in the air.

Then his full meaning sank into Lin's granite skull.

"Careful?" "You mean...with Reece?"

"It don't take Indian magic to tell you're sweet on her."

"Me? Nah," said Lin. "Didn't you hear? It's my job to watch out for her."

"If you say so."

After Stick was gone, Lin put each horse in its own stall, returning the bay to the pen next to the blue roan. The two horses made an ideal pair, one to ride, one to rest. "How about it, girl?" he asked the roan. "Shall it be you and me, tomorrow?"

After brushing down the horses, Lin gave them some hay and went to the well for fresh water. The bucket he cranked up was barely half full.

Once he finished with the horses, his nose latched onto the cooking again, but his parched throat led him back to the well. He dropped the bucket for a second helping.

The second bucket came up with less than the first.

This he poured down his face and shoulders, then mopped himself with a hand towel.

When he turned around, his uncle was pounding toward him in his big floppy boots and oversized hat.

He hadn't seen Oscar Bruhn for more than two years.

CHAPTER 11

THE OLD RANGER'S VOICE THRUMMED LIKE A BIG BASS fiddle and seemed to fill the entire outdoors with exuberance. Each yellow autumn leaf was just a little brighter, the water dripping off Lin's face, clean and cold.

"How's Lin Jarret today?" said Oscar as he grabbed his nephew by the back of the neck. The embrace was like a father for his son, and Oscar slapped Lin's back at least half a dozen times.

When he gripped Lin's shoulders, he said the same thing he always said. "You look more like your mom every day."

In point of fact, it was Oscar—his mom's brother—who favored the lady, thought Lin. The same thick gray hair, the same mischief in his voice. Affable. Loud. "I sure am glad you made it down here, boy. Just seeing you sets my heart to ease."

"It's good seeing you, too, Oz," said Lin, meaning it. He slapped his hat against the leg of his britches, and a ball of dust rose up. "Cap'n Bob sends his regards from San Antone."

Oscar thanked him. "Bob's a good owlhoot to serve under. But if you like it down here, you can serve under Steve Duncan."

"Duncan a good man?"

"There's worse." Then, he said, "You taking good care of Tom's girl for him?"

"I guess watching her is what I'm being paid for. But since I got here yesterday, it's been a pretty even trade. She's taken care of me—stitched me up after a little run-with with some local trouble-makers."

Oscar's voice betrayed a hint of conspiracy. "It's what I wondered. Pretty much how it was with your Aunt Lou and me. Maybe you and Reece..."

Lin tossed up his hands. "Oh, no," he said, swimming backwards through the air. "Not in a million summers of sunflower."

"It ain't' such a bad thing, son."

"I'd rather get hogtied and branded. At least I'd have my own head." Lin replaced his hat. "I'm gonna leave marriage to you old relics."

Together they walked toward the house. Oscar said, "Being serious, how you gettin' along with her royal highness?"

"¿*Quien sabe*?" Lin had no idea. Rather than admit it, he poked out his bottom lip.

"Fair to middlin, I s'pose."

"Then you're doing better than most of the boys around here."

"You gonna fill me in on Cardoza and Dub Hornsby tonight?" said Lin.

"Way Tom tells the story, you can fill me in first." Then his voice was somber. "It sounds like you handled some mighty big trouble yesterday." He reached out and brushed a knuckle against a yellowing bruise on Lin's chin. "Looks like trouble landed on you a bit as well."

"Nothing too much."

"You limping a little bit on your leg, ain'tcha?"

The long day's work at the corral hadn't done Lin's leg any favors, and now it throbbed even as it healed. "One more scar for the collection," he said, shrugging off the older man's worries. "Like I said, Reece stitched me up."

Oscar stopped, breathing in so long and deep Lin was sure the old man would bust. When he let it out, he wagged his head. "Don't try handling it all by yourself. That's all I'm saying."

"There's not much of anybody else here, Oz," said Lin.

Oscar sighed again and spoke under his breath. "Ain't it the goddamn truth?"

At the house, Tom Sinclair put an opaque bottle of beer with a ceramic stopper in Lin's hand, then walked him and Oscar into a grassy yard where Stick and Barb fried meat on the grill.

Lin saw the Jensen brothers nearby, each of them holding a beer bottle. He nodded, and they rosed their drinks in salute.

"We've got your uncle to thank for the steaks and bacon," said Sinclair. "The beer as well."

Before too long, the old men started remembering the Mexican War, putting themselves into a dozen outlandish fish stories. Barb encouraged Lin and Stick to shoot. Reece was sequestered in the kitchen, no doubt working culinary magic on the cookstove. Every now and then Barb would wander in to check in on her, and Tom would take over at the fire, eternally patient with Oscar's grilling advice.

Stick walked inside the house.

When he came out, he moseyed over with his Texas Paterson in a plain leather gunbelt. He took it out and showed it to Lin. "Now, it may not look like much compared to your heavy-duty rig?"

Lin was familiar with the No. 5 revolver. "Carried one myself for a while," he said.

Stick's gun had a nine-inch long octagonal barrel and a flared pistol grip at the butt. Lighter than Lin's big Colt the older gun had a folding trigger which deployed when the weapon was cocked. It was also missing the loading lever of Lin's later model.

Stick said, "You gonna show me your marksmanship now, or can we just assume I'm the best shot on the ranch? Because I've got no problem assuming I'm tops in the field."

Lin took a swig from his bottle and sighed. "Barb's got money on you, right?"

"He does."

"He the only one?"

Stick gave Lin a sheepish look. "Maybe. Maybe not."

"Who else?"

"We gonna shoot, or what? Give me a drink of beer." Lin let him take a good-natured swipe at the jug, then handed it to him. He drew his Colt sidearm from its place at his hip and sighed.

"You didn't say who else had money on the deal."

Stick wiped his mouth with the back of his hand. "Who else? Uh...let's say it might be the Contessa d'Mess."

"The Mess?"

Stick cocked his head back toward the kitchen. "She's got you messed up, boy."

Lin nodded slow, taking the taunts as they came. "I do believe I'm gonna have to show you up. I'm mighty sorry to take money from an old man and a woman, but it looks like you're leaving me no choice." He took back the bottle and drank. "What do you want to go for?"

Stick reached into the hip pocket of his trousers and removed a deck of cards. "Got just the thing."

Before they could go any further, Tom Sinclair called across the yard. "Supper's ready, boys. You all better come get it before the old men clean it all up."

Stick slapped Lin on the shoulder and palmed the cards while pointing an index finger at his nose. "We ain't through. This ain't over. The bets stand."

Lin said, "Sure, the bets stand." Racing to the house, Lin was first in line.

———

THE EVENING BREEZE carried a tropical heat in from the gulf, and Reece helped Barb set up a sumptuous spread outside on a long pinewood table behind the house.

It was the kind of meal Lin had first imagined when his uncle described Rancho de Jada. Casa Sinclair had been slow to rise to the occasion, but once the dust had settled from the previous day's perils, ranch life seemed more like the ideal Lin had expected it to be.

Oscar had carried in packages of beef and pork for grilling, and Reece secured round, golden potatoes from yesterday's trip to the store. They had bread with fresh butter and new beans with bacon and onions cooked in.

Lin couldn't remember when he'd eaten this well.

Barb carried out two heavy pots of coffee and cups. The Jensen brothers picked up their hats from the ground and shook their heads. "Bedtime for us," said Clyde, patting his gut. "We still have our evening Bible devotions to read."

Lin watched the brothers waddle down toward the bunkhouse.

Pushing back from the table with a ceramic cup of strong, black coffee with sugar and thick cream, Oscar picked Reece out for attention. "Are you still good with the numbers?"

"I expect so."

Tom said, "If you don't mind, show Oz your trick from the other day—the one with the three dice."

Reece didn't mind, and after stepping into the kitchen, came back with a trio of standard, six-sided dice. Lin and Stick stood up for a better view, and Oscar leaned in close.

Tom Sinclair relished the opportunity to show off his daughter's talent and explained the trick before Reece could sit down. "She's gonna have you roll the dice, then stack them up one on top of the other. Then she can tell you what all the hidden numbers add up to. Not the numbers on the side, mind you, but the top and bottom numbers—the ones covered up. The ones she can't even see."

Tom slapped the dice into Oscar's hand. Reece covered her eyes, and the old Ranger rolled. His fingers shook a little as he stacked the dice three-high, one on top of the other. The top number was five.

"Okay, Reece," said Tom.

Reece glanced at the stack and said, "Sixteen."

"Go on, now," said Tom. "Go on and check it."

Oscar picked up the top die. The bottom number was two. The top of the next die was a three. The opposite side a four. On the bottom die, the hidden numbers were likewise three and four.

"Let's see now...adding all them up...is...sixteen."

"Sixteen it is. Just like Reece said," said Tom with a big nod.

"Do it again," said Stick. "Let me roll this time."

Eventually Reece performed the trick five times, letting each of the men roll the dice and stack them up without her watching. Five times, she got the sum of the hidden numbers correct.

"It's a pretty good trick. Remind me to take you along the next time I play poker with the boys," said Oscar.

Reece reassembled the three dice into a neat little tower.

"Hey, speaking of wagers," said Stick.

"It's getting dark," said Barb, "*Lin y Stick necesitan disparar*."

"What's this you're talking about?" said Oscar.

Lin told him. "Seems like some of the folks here have a little wager going about which one of us is the best shot, me or Stick."

Stick hitched his thumbs into his gun belt. "You want to put a personal wager on it?" he said.

"What do you have to wager?" said Lin.

"I win, you let me have the big .52 caliber Maynard rifle you carry."

"What do I get if I win?"

Lin dug into his pants pocket and pulled out three gold dollars.

"Not exactly an even wager," said Lin. "But since we're friends...."

Lin brought his rifle out from the house and handed it to Reece. "Please hold this for us, Contessa?"

She poked out her tongue at him, and he grinned.

Then Stick pulled the playing cards out of his shirt pocket. "Let's go then...friend," he said.

The six of them pushed away from the table and marched a ways out into the sagebrush behind the house. "From where we stand, how far would you say it is to the short mesquite tree over there?" said Stick, pointing. "Fifteen, twenty yards away?"

"I'd say closer to twenty."

Stick held up the deck of cards and pulled out the ace of hearts along with the ace of diamonds.

"Go fix 'em up in the branches."

When Lin returned from doing his friends' bidding, the two cards looked like white birds fluttering in the wide reach of the boughs against the deep indigo sky. The red markings were barely visible.

Backed by a bright pink swash of color spread across an orange rimmed treeless horizon, Stick Carvell pulled his Texas Paterson with one fluid motion, cocked and fired. Cocked and fired. With each deafening concussion, the target card jerked away from the tree before fluttering to the ground.

"Damn good shootin'," crowed Tom Sinclair, and Barb clapped his hands with glee. Lin took a sidelong glance at Reece. In the golden glow of sunset, her face was mysterious, and neutral.

She caught him looking.

He turned away quick and ran to retrieve the cards from the base of the mesquite tree, holding them high for everybody to see. The cards were torn, but intact with the center heart and diamond shot directly out of each card.

Again Sinclair complimented him, "You've got a fine talent." Then he said to Lin, "How you think you can top it, Ranger?"

Lin gave the pierced cards to Stick with a friendly nod.

"Not bad," he said.

"Not bad?" Stick dealt an ace of spades and an ace of clubs from the deck. Then he took a stroll toward the tree. "Let's see you match it."

"How about this?" said Lin.

Without warning, he spun on his heel and dropped to his haunches, Colt in hand, looking directly into the semicircular blaze of the setting sun. The two shots he triggered seemed nearly simultaneous. Barely three seconds passed when he stood tall with the pistol back inside its holster.

The stunned onlookers stood stock still until Stick cleared his throat and cocked a thumb over his shoulder. "Uh, Lin...the target was going to be down yonder."

"With the sun over my shoulder helping me?" said Lin. "No, sir. I don't need the crutch."

"But we was shootin' at cards."

"I wasn't."

"I'm not sure, I understand...?"

Lin flashed a look at Reece and she caught it with a perplexed expression. Then it became clear to her.

"The dice," she said. "I left the three dice stacked up on the supper table."

As one, the six of them returned to the table. Only one dice remained.

Stick's eyes narrowed. "You're telling me you picked them two top cubes off while staring into the sun?"

"Like flies off the back of a bull," Lin told him.

Then he winked at Reece.

"I'll take my cash money," he said, and Stick paid him. As the tall man turned away, Lin called him back. Retrieving the Maynard from Reece, he tossed it to

Stick. "You go ahead and use it while I'm here. Do some target shooting."

Stick caught the gun and his face lit up. "You're not so bad for a Ranger," he said.

"You're catching on," said Lin.

CHAPTER 12

THEY MOVED A PAIR OF WOOD FOLDING CHAIRS OUT from the table, and Lin retired with his uncle while Sinclair carried a pot of coffee and three cups to the grass. Tom filled each cup half-way. After handing them out, he took a cup for himself and pulled up a chair.

Oscar opened his whiskey flask. "Coffee needs flavoring," he said, topping off his cup. He passed the flask around. The north wind held just enough of a chill to make Lin wish for a jacket, but there was warmth in the cup.

Barb had asked Stick to help him clean up the grill and scrape out the pit, leaving Lin alone with Sinclair and his uncle for a moment.

He sipped from his cup and tilted his head back to the sky. The pressing velvet void was buckshot with twinkling light, and a scurry of fast wings were a pair of bats snatching up a mosquito supper.

Lin set his cup down to the ground beside his chair.

Careful in the dark not to spill his tobacco, he rolled a smoke and lit the end. Then sat back, watching the older men puff cigars.

"I've got news about Cardoza. I thought it best to hold back until Reece and Barb weren't around," said Oscar.

Tom said, "Lin tells me he's in Jade City. The kids saw him at the Muleskinner the other day."

"He's in tight with that skeleton attorney," said Oscar. "Hollister Morse."

"You got more news?" said Tom.

"I do."

Lin could tell Oscar was struggling through his liquor for the right words. He'd been sipping from the flask all night long.

When he spoke, his words were slightly slurred. "Seems like Cardoza's relationship with Cortina ain't what-you-call true blue these days. I've got a reliable source says they're squabbling a lot. Fighting about what all this insurrection bullshit—whatever-you-wanna-call-it —means for the future of the valley."

"Is it good or bad having the two of them fight?" asked Sinclair. "Or does it matter?"

"Not good at all. Not good for any of us." He drained his cup and refreshed it with a splash from the flask.

"Sounds good to me, Oz," said Lin. "If they go after each other, kill each other off, what's wrong with it? Two less problems, is the way I'd see it."

Oscar wagged his head with force. "No, sir," he said. "It don't work at all."

"Why not?"

"If they went ahead and made war on each other directly, I'd be on your side. But they won't."

Oscar tried to explain it. "These two men *need* each other. They both know it. Their respective lands border one another, and their families have been neighbors down south since the days of Moses. They squabble.

They show off. They fight to be top dog among their followers." Oscar drank deep and pointed a finger at Lin. "Guess who gets caught in the backwash?"

"The Diablo Flats is a pretty piece of Sanchez land," said Sinclair. "Just imagine how it must've been once." Sinclair drank from his cup, and Lin knew the old man was thinking of Rancho de Jada and the Flats as one sprawling empire.

"Imagination don't matter," said Oscar. "What matters is the here and now. Word is Cardoza is looking to make a power play, show himself to be the stronger man, maybe bring a few *Cortinistas* into his own camp, start his own war against the Anglos." Oscar emptied his cup again. With a restrained voice he told them, "He's got a howitzer cannon. Maybe two."

"The hell," said Sinclair.

"From all accounts, the cannon is like the old 841 Gavin had during the local skirmish here. I don't know where he got it. Somebody said he stole it off of a river boat."

"What local skirmish? Who's Gavin?" said Lin.

"Gavin was a munitions officer me and Tom knew. It wasn't five miles as the crow flies from where we're sitting right now. We used the big gun to drive them Mex bastards back across a dusty arroyo out back, tails between their legs."

Sinclair nodded. "He's right, Lin. It happened not too far from the corrals you worked today."

"What a glorious damned time," said Oscar. "Made me feel good to be alive. Like you and me—we knew we were on the good Lord's side of things."

Sinclair was silent for a long time. Then he said, "You still believe it, Oz?"

"That I'm on the Lord's side of things? Hell, yes. Don't you?"

"I try," said Sinclair.

"Fart in a *fiesta*," said Oscar. "You've got to do more than try."

Lin finished his coffee and cigarette, then dropped the butt into his empty cup. He listened to its fading sizzle.

Then he said, "You think Cardoza will use this cannon? Maybe attack Rancho de Jada head on?"

"Sure, if he's lookin' to prove himself. Wouldn't surprise me if he tried to take over half the small outfits all along the river. Your place is situated well, being directly across the river from his. If Cardoza managed to occupy Rancho de Jada, he could use it as a base of operations to take out all the others. It was the kind of move designed to impress the locals. They'd write ballads about him for the vaqueros to sing to their señoritas by moonlight." Oscar snorted. "If I were you, I might think about making a deal with him."

"What kind of deal?"

Oscar leaned back in his chair. "Water rights. Grazing."

"Bring his damn sheep across on to my land?" said Sinclair.

"Why the hell not?"

Sinclair didn't have an answer, and the three men sat in silence, each one of them lost in his own thoughts.

For Lin, it meant figuring out what such an attack might look like. Would they hit the hacienda first, or pick off the cows and outer corrals again? Would they strike the livery or go right for the human inhabitants?

Or would Tom Sinclair make a deal?

"What about leasing out some of the pasture, Tom?"

he said. "If you don't mind me saying, most of your wealth is in livestock right now. The cows and the grazing land."

"Since you mentioned it, where are your cows right now?" said Oscar. "If you don't mind me asking."

"Small acreage to the west. Called Defilement. It's not too far from here."

"The old sheep station?"

"Matter of fact, it was."

It was clear to Lin Oscar knew the place.

Across from Lin, Sinclair was a pale blue ghost slumped in his chair. his craggy cheeks outlined by the dull crimson of his cigar. The talk of battles—old and possibly new—had taken the starch out of him.

It's almost like he's not even here, thought Lin.

Another part of the Rancho de Jada mystery, thought Lin. Because there was something about the place weighing on Sinclair. Something nobody was saying.

Lin wondered about Reece. The barrels full of bullets. Her comments about freedom.

Stick's reluctance to talk about the lack of hired men.

The African's odd disappearance.

Something was afoot.

Oscar leaned back in his chair and talked about the Mexican war. "Fifteen years ago now. You ever think fifteen years could pass by so fast, Tom? You and me sitting here, a couple old men? We're as old now as Muggins was then."

"Muggins?" said Lin.

"The old sonuvabitch, Mordechai Muggins. Our commanding officer. I swear to God, what a silly name. I haven't thought of him for a while."

Sinclair nodded. "Who could forget?"

Oscar dropped his cup in the grass and drank straight

from his flask. He wiped his lips with his fingers before continuing for Lin's benefit.

"Corporal Muggins had this idea of the slave states forming their own Republic. Like Texas—only bigger. One big cotton empire."

"Fifteen years ago already," said Sinclair. "There's a lot more talk today, especially since Dred Scott."

"Plenty of groups getting together to preserve our way of life," agreed Oscar. "Some of the boys favor the Knights of the Golden Circle. Others like the Ivory Compass."

By *boys*, Lin figured Oscar meant some of the Rangers.

"Plenty of groups opposing our way of life, too," said Sinclair. "Plenty of northern immigrants moving in. Abolitionists. There's a group called the Hellbenders."

Oscar stayed with the topic of Muggins. "Old Mordechai was the quintessential officer. Pressed wool, polished brass, yes-sir, no-sir, salute—all a bunch of military nonsense. You get the idea. Trouble was, the old bastard had a soft spot for the Indians. Always feeling sorry for them, offering them a handout. Muggins saw the Indian as superior to the African. His thinking was it made him more sophisticated than the rest of us."

The night breeze kicked up a chill while Oscar talked. The stars, magnified by the cold. Lin rolled another smoke just to keep warm.

"One day at the Fort," said Oscar. "This is over at Fort Texas, mind you. Muggins drives in with this team and a brand new four wheeled buggy. I mean you never saw such a fancy wagon. It's all polished wood and painted a glossy black and inlaid with gold leaf."

"Don't forget the upholstery," said Sinclair.

"Oh, yeah—the upholstery was nicer than most

people's parlor lounge. I mean, quilted and stuffed for comfort. The main thing was his fancy buggy had a retractable roof. A fella could go out on a sunny day and pull this roof back or put it up if he wanted shade. Or if it's raining or otherwise inclement weather, a man's got some cover. You see what I mean?"

Lin said he saw it as plain as day.

"Well, one day old Corporal Muggins, he's got this pretty Comanche squaw, nobody knows where he found her, and he's driving her around the prairie in this buggy." Oscar took a long pull from the flask, and his words slurred all the more. "An' pretty soon he's drivin' her off into the trees by the Rio Carlito."

Oscar started to giggle. "Hell, Tom—you and me, and all them dumb bastards back then—we knew what he was fixin' to do, didn't we?"

Lin swallowed hard, watching his uncle empty the contents of his flask and continue to giggle. "You know, it took him five or ten minutes before he really got down to business in there. I mean we could hear this Injun gal in there fussin' and cryin' and we're all standing around laughing. You 'member, don'cha, Tom?"

It sounded to Lin like the kind of memory a man might work hard to forget.

Sinclair didn't respond, but Oscar reveled in the telling of it, losing himself to laughter, unable to fit more than two or three words between snickers. "It's just...just s'damn...funny." He appealed to Lin, "I mean...can'tcha just see this prim old bastard...tryin' to work on this...this savage..."

Lin felt his stomach turn for several reasons. He waited for Oscar to catch his breath, then interrupted the tale.

"This man, Muggins," said Lin. "What happened to him?"

Oscar mopped tears from his eyes and did his best to quell his mirthful enthusiasm. Finally, he said, "He got a lead ball in the guts two days later."

Lin put his cigarette to his lips and inhaled.

"Good riddance," whispered Sinclair.

"Aw, he wasn't as bad as you think," said Oscar.

"I saw him beat a slave once until the poor devil couldn't stand up," said Sinclair.

"Well, it's not a reason to wish the man dead," said Oscar.

"I'm just glad to be done with it," said Sinclair.

"Best days of our lives," said Oscar.

For a while they listened to the night sounds on the range. The bugs and the owls and a distant coyote.

After a while, Sinclair said, "I'm gonna turn in." To Oscar, he said, "Barb's got a space for you down 't the bunkhouse."

The old Ranger waved him away. "I'm staying in Jade City tonight. Girl I know in there rents out a room."

"Suit yourself," said Sinclair.

In the dark, Lin listened to the old ranchero's steps recede toward the house.

A man burdened by time, thought Lin.

He looked at his uncle sucking the last drop out of his flask.

Both of them, burdened. They shouldered the load in different ways.

Lin decided to do better than either one of them.

CHAPTER 13

IN THE SADDLE OF A RESTLESS HORSE, DUB HORNSBY did his best to take stock of his situation. Behind him, twenty-seven fighting men let their horses shuffle around in the cool Rancho de Jada dust. The soldiers chewed tobacco, left their mounts to relieve themselves, mumbled one to another. The darkness was full but expectant, with a faint gray light growing up in the east.

Friday morning, and the hard men were getting restless.

He was, too, for that matter.

Ten of the men had joined Dub's own troop the day before, handpicked by Cardoza. Crossing from the Diablo Flats at Bolton's station on Spanish saddles and stallions wearing the Diamond-Crown brand, they followed Carlito into Jade City.

The Mexicans carried their own weapons, various long knives and modified percussion-fire carbines of mixed heritage.

They had all taken their supper together in the cantina.

For the most part, the Mexicans kept to themselves,

and to his credit, Cardoza kept his soldiers sober, sent them to their sleeping blankets early. Hornsby had to admit they were a good influence on his own men. There had been no trouble between the teams.

They woke early and rode out at four o'clock on Hornsby's ebony mustangs, gathering on the edge of Sinclair's ranch in the dry arroyo north of the hacienda.

They meant to storm the place with the first glimmer of the sun.

They meant to occupy the hacienda within the hour.

Hornsby, with Marko and Felix Ruiz flanking him, smelled Cardoza's approach before hearing him. His highness carried a twist of chew reeking of dry apples and bourbon, and his clothes smelled like sausage. Back at the cantina, where Hollister Morse waited for word of the morning's inevitable victory, Cardoza had fried breakfast for all the men.

Hornsby had been too nervous to eat.

"We charge soon eh, *amigo*?" said Cardoza. There was no need to whisper. Who would hear them out here?

But still Cardoza whispered.

He urged his stallion around Hornsby in a circle, then pulled in alongside, facing the opposite direction allowing them to converse easily. Everything about Cardoza's attire called attention to his wealth and power.

The Mexican was dressed in a canvas shirt with a vest and pants, his black leather chaparreras decorated with gold embroidered flourishes. On his head he wore a dark poblano with a silver band and chinstrap. Two Remington pistols hung at his waist in a pair of lush lambskin cross-draw holsters.

His saddle was a simple rawhide frame with a cinch fitted around the horn. Flat, round tapaderos of silver covered the stirrups. He wore fancy spurs inlaid with turquoise.

Hornsby's outfit was more conservative, better suited to the business of the day. Long leather duster, flat brimmed wideawake cap, a gun at his side. Marko and Ruiz were dressed in similar work clothes.

Cardoza pinned them down. "Are you excited, men? Maybe you're thinking about the good things ahead for you? Tonight we celebrate with wine. With the larder of Sinclair's home." He arced a stream of tobacco spit into the dirt. "What about you, Marko? Thinking about the woman?"

"The woman doesn't enter into it," said Hornsby.

"Doesn't she? Marko here said he has wanted the Sinclair *niña* a long time."

"She's an insufferable little thing."

"Then maybe she needs to be made to suffer. Maybe taught some manners," said Marko.

Cardoza seemed to agree. "She is...*hermosa*. What's the word?"

"Beautiful."

"Ah, *si*."

Hornsby was annoyed by Cardoza. Not only did he stink of sausage, but his breath reeked of stale coffee.

Hornsby was tired of the chiding.

"I want this thing buttoned down quick as possible," he said.

Cardoza patted the inside pocket of his vest. "I am carrying the legal papers Mister Morse had drawn up. Once Sinclair and Sanchez sign them, our empire is reunited." Cardoza's voice took on an air of menace. "Even if they don't sign them, it will be one again. As it was meant to be."

Hornsby wondered about it. Bringing together the

Sanchez land had been the original intent—reuniting two disparate properties rent asunder by an uncaring imperialistic document. But Cardoza seemed increasingly bored by the prospect of actually running the ranch, and more concerned about using the Sinclair place as a springboard to capturing the other ranches in the area. He mostly wanted to gain favor with his men and, most important, with Cortina.

More than the *spoils* of war, Cardoza coveted the war itself.

"All I care about is the job at hand," said Hornsby, "and not getting killed."

"Enjoy yourselves today, amigos." Cardoza held up a gloved fist. "This is *el gusto*."

"I'd enjoy myself a lot more if I knew where those damned Indians were," said Hornsby.

"I have a man watching the Sinclair cattle. He's seen no sign of the Apache," said Cardoza.

"If they don't want you to see 'em, you ain't gonna see 'em."

"I think you're overly concerned."

"Maybe. But the sooner we take care of those cattle, the better."

Cardoza agreed. "As I speak, my man is gathering vaqueros for a short drive to Rio Grande City where a buyer named Hutton awaits. For now, the beeves are in a grazing pasture by the old sheep station."

"Defilement," said Hornsby. He knew the place, not a far ride out of Jade City to the northeast.

"My hope is we'll catch the nativos here, today, by surprise, same as the Texas Ranger and the old man."

Ruiz licked his lips, let his eyes play over the far scenery of mesquite and sagebrush. "They could be here, right now, watching us. We'd never know."

Cardoza stroked his chin. "They are men, not specters. Believe me, *amigo*. They are out by the cows or sleeping in the bunkhouse. *No te preocupes*. Don't worry."

But Hornsby agreed with Ruiz.

He called up a picture in his mind of the Indians' victims, Carlos and Victor, as he'd last seen them on the boardwalk where they'd been dumped, their guts exposed to the autumn sky, their lips and chins and noses snipped and tweaked. Hornsby shuddered. They'd been murdered in the worst possible way.

He didn't blame Ruiz for feeling anxious.

It had been bad enough to leave Able's body after the altercation on Wednesday morning at the corral. The dead man's scarred face flashed through his mind's eye. Too impetuous, too cocky, a recalcitrant drunk—that was Able.

Hornsby hadn't been overly sorry to lose him.

But Carlos and Victor were good men. Capable men. They'd split off from the others on the way back to Jade City, and the next time Hornsby saw them, they were dead in front of the cantina.

Any man who wasn't worried about the Apache, was a fool.

"We have all the firepower we need to take care of Sinclair and his people," said Cardoza.

He meant the howitzer, of course.

The bronze, smooth-bore piece of artillery was Cardoza's newest passion. It lobbed nine pound balls more than a thousand feet, and rode behind him on a two-wheeled wagon. Cardoza had stolen the gun from a riverboat and had the cart and ammunition trunks built to specification.

Hornsby suspected he planned to use it as a bluff.

After all, what good would it do him to bomb the

buildings at Rancho de Jada to pieces if he didn't have to? Why blow it up and destroy everything?

They had already sabotaged the rancho's supply of water, damming up the Little Carlito in a secluded place off the main trail. Hornsby looked over his shoulder at the high-wheeled box wagon, grateful for the tall barrels of water they carried.

On the horizon, between two stands of persimmon and cedar, the gray bands faded to pink.

"Almost time," said Cardoza. "I can feel it. Can you?"

Hornsby could feel it all right, like a rumbling in the guts. It was clear the other men were equally eager to move and end the waiting.

Cardoza cheered the sun's crown slipping over the horizon and reared his horse in the first shafts of golden blaze. "Ay-yi-yi," he called. "*¡Adelante*"

The men's enthusiastic reply was like a hot wind, lifting Hornsby and his stallion into place beside his boss, driving the army forward with rapid acceleration. Dust rose behind the legion of pounding hooves like a mighty cape trailing the wind.

Bursting up from the old, dry riverbed, they took to the plain in pairs and groups of three, swinging around thorny arbustos, dodging badger dens and rocked outcroppings. Directly behind Cardoza, two men sitting ramrod straight in the saddle steered the four-horse hitch-team caisson as it rolled along with the howitzer.

After a while they found themselves at the foot of a long, sloping incline leading to Sinclair's stable. Here's where they had agreed to split into two groups.

Cardoza signaled his men to follow him the long way around to the house. He motioned for Hornsby to attack the livery barn.

The bunch of riders forked out, flowing like worker

ants to their task, and just as dedicated to the destruction of anything standing in their way. Hornsby glimpsed Cardoza burring off, low in the saddle, gun-hand held to the sky. He sashayed around a pyramid of split wood to disappear with ten men and the howitzer into a line of trees.

Hornsby's own raiders fanned out around the livery, and three men roared up and down through the center alley of the place, hacking at the stall doors with an axe and a shovel, shooting the glass out of two four-paned windows. Hornsby had expected to find a few men here amongst the equestrian population. It was early, of course, but he figured on surprising—Stick Carvell or maybe an Apache.

But there was no resistance. No return fire. Nothing.

Only the tiny remuda, a fair amount of tack, a dusty grain closet, and a solid buckboard wagon.

"Leave some men here to watch the animals," said Hornsby to his lead man after the echoes of gunfire abated. "We'll station our own mounts here afterwards."

Then Hornsby turned his sights on the bunkhouse.

It was a long, one story pole building covered in grey siding, windows on each side under the drooping eaves of a low-slung roof. There was one door in back, closed, and one door in the front.

Open, with a short old man dressed in long red underwear standing just outside the door, holding a black book in his hand.

Clyde Jensen.

Hornsby reined in at the threshold of the bunkhouse with Marko at his side and shot the old man through the forehead with a crashing roar from his pistol.

The noise sat Hornsby's stallion back with his front hooves kicking up the dirt. "Whoa, there. Be good boy," said Hornsby. The stallion shuddered and came down on the book, smashing it into the dust.

A Holy Bible.

Hornsby turned his attention to his men. "Careful, the old buzzard's got a brother around here someplace."

Marko agreed, and howled a warning before lobbing a few shots into the building's dilapidated facade. When no fire was returned and nobody emerged, he instructed Felix Ruiz and Saul Willats to skirt the length of the building on foot and come in from behind.

"You two leave your horses here with me and Dub. Edge down along the walls and peek inside. Could be we're catching them ranch-hands asleep."

Hornsby didn't think they'd find more than two or three more men, but one could never tell. When Ruiz and Willats looked at him for confirmation, he gave the go-ahead to Marko's plan. "Clear the place out," he told them.

Ruiz dropped from his horse into a crouch, arms akimbo, oily black hair jutting out from under his sombrero. Gun in hand, he duck-walked along the southern wall's rock foundation.

Willats was heavier and wore a possum fur cap over his glass-scratched face along with his familiar fringed buckskins. His gait was more lumbering and strained. Hornsby could hear his labored breath from forty feet away, and not for the first time, felt a tinge of regret for the whole damned undertaking. The damned fool would get himself killed, and somebody else with him.

Hornsby was so preoccupied ruminating on Willats' sorry performance he almost didn't catch Cecil Jensen's assault until it was too late.

The second Jensen had positioned himself just inside the door where he knelt with a long, flintlock musket. A loud clap and a hurried expulsion of powder smoke pushed Jensen back, kicking the muzzle of the rifle up, sending its cargo of death too high.

As it was, Hornsby felt the hot breeze of the projectile and cranked his Colt around to spit twin flames of death, cutting the old man down. Cecil Jensen tumbled into the dirt, face down next to his brother, his outstretched arm reaching for the mangled holy book.

From the side of the bunkhouse, Willats called to him. "Everything okay, Dub?"

Damn the man! Hornsby waved him way with a flurry of his hand. "Yes, yes." Hornsby shooed him along with a harsh whisper. "Get on with it."

Willats progressed down his side of the building, rounding the far corner where he disappeared.

———

A MINUTE PASSED. Then two.

Hornsby waited for Ruiz and Willats to clear the building and appear at the front exit. Waited for them with his Colt pistol in hand. Heart pounding, breath coming in quick, raspy gasps.

Taking down the Jensens had irritated him. He didn't mourn their loss, didn't feel the slightest tinge of guilt. But looking at their riddled bodies, spread-eagle on the ground reaching for the Bible, annoyed him.

He wanted more worthy adversaries.

He was prepared for a fire fight, dedicated to cutting down the next yellow dog who showed his snout. But nobody came. Ready to rain down hell, and all he was allowed were a few sprinkles.

His heart raced. Then slowed.

Silence. The place seemed abandoned.

"Coming out, *jefe*," called Ruiz before showing up in the open door, both hands visible.

"Empty?" said Hornsby, exchanging a look of frustration with Marko. The redhead too was chomping at the bit.

"Like a church on Saturday night," said Ruiz.

Hornsby sucked his front teeth.

"Well, damn," he said.

In truth, it was going better than he ever would've guessed. Rancho de Jada was open as a whore on nickel night. He should be pleased at the ease of the conquest.

Instead, he felt cheated.

"The real push-back will be at the hacienda," he told Marko.

But obviously Cardoza could handle it with his ten hardcase *soldados*.

More time went by. Willats had yet to show himself.

"Where's your partner?" said Hornsby. "Did you lose him in there?"

Ruiz's eyes betrayed the curiosity Hornsby felt. "*¿Que? I don't think—*"

In the open doorway, Ruiz half-turned, then went ridged before coming back around like a clock pendulum to face front.

Hornsby saw the gaping hole between Ruiz's collar bones even before a bolt of thunder rocked the air.

Ambush.

Hornsby fumbled for his gun, pulled it halfway, then watched as Ruiz smacked into the ground to die, twitching. With almost impossible speed, another blast tore a furrow in the ground next to him.

Rifle fire! But where the hell was it coming from?

Hornsby dropped his Colt back into its leather and called out "*Vamanos*!" His skittish horse reared again, this time with a violent neigh, and pawed the air with its hooves.

Marko's horse balked too, spinning like a child's top. As he regained his seat in the saddle and took control, Marko pulled his gun. Two more men reined in beside them, saw Ruiz's body and immediately drew their firearms. As one, the firing squad unloaded into the entrance of the bunkhouse.

Hornsby screamed. "Idiots! The shooter isn't in there."

Lost in a cloud of blue powder smoke, Hornsby tried to wheel around. Under the onslaught of the jangled men, lead smacked into the bunkhouse lintel and tore through the worn siding.

The men tossed everything they had at the lonesome wood shell, spending the balance of their powder, losing their balls to the wind.

Hornsby shouted above the din, "Hold up, dammit, hold up." But three more blasts roared before the men regained their senses.

While they waited for the smoke to clear, Marko said, "Whoever he was, we got him, Dub. No man alive could'a survived such a drubbing."

"I told you—"

Then a groan came from the corner of the bunkhouse and a bloody hand appeared. Fingers splayed in a scarlet death grip slid along the corner of the building down from shoulder height. Then an arm appeared, then Willats, his eyes strained, popping out like spring toadstools, his mouth a slobbering, bloody mess.

He gurgled a desperate warning, then fell to his knees.

At first, Hornsby worried they had clipped him with their wild fandango of lead. "Look what you—"

But then he saw the horrible truth and recoiled in anger and disgust. Only a high caliber long gun could do damage like that.

The entire back of Willats' skull was gone.

One of the shooters, a man named Anderson, crossed himself. "Mother of God," he said.

"Let's split up," said Hornsby. "Anderson, you take—"

But then Anderson's chest caved in with a grisly crack followed by a crashing boom echoing through the ranch buildings. He tumbled off his horse even as it veered away from Hornsby and the others.

"I tried to tell you, idiots," said Hornsby.

Somebody was picking them off, one by one.

CHAPTER 14

THROUGH A COLD GLASS WINDOW, UNDER THE insistent glare of a bright morning star, Lin Jarret struggled to get comfortable in his room at Rancho de Jada. He'd been sleeping outside on the ride here, and now he felt claustrophobic and pent up under low-ceilings and close walls.

Add to these annoyances, the excess of the night before—too much coffee, too much whiskey...far too many smokes.

Or maybe it was his uncle's news about the howitzer. The thought of Cardoza attacking the ranch with such overwhelming force pushed Lin's mind in a thousand different directions. His first inclination was to take charge with Tom Sinclair, fight back directly, and trade bullet for bullet.

But where did such a thing leave them when the big artillery started booming? He didn't know.

And wasn't Sinclair paying Lin to watch over Reece? The girl was his first priority. The sack of gold in his saddle bag was a shining, burning thing of pride he couldn't escape. His uncle had recommended him as best for the job. Getting Reece to safety would always be Lin's first order of business.

He was sure of it.

But after everything was settled in his mind, he still couldn't sleep.

What he lost in dreams, he made up for in wild thoughts about Reece Sinclair.

She was unlike any woman he'd ever known. There hadn't been so awful many women, he had to admit to himself. But still, there had been a few, and if there was one thing for sure, it was this lady carried a few secrets.

For one, she freighted around barrels of bullets. There weren't many women involved in such things. Truth was, Lin didn't know any. It stood to reason a Western town on the open range would have call to defend itself from any number of predators. Especially with the Cortinistas causing trouble. But Reese stocked enough firepower in Sanchez's store to outfit a small army.

What was it all about?

Part of the gunsmithing business?

Or maybe the girl was in cahoots with Cardoza, using the Tejanos to run stolen munitions. But stolen from who? And Reese seemed as loyal to her dad as Sinclair was to her. Plotting against him didn't make sense.

Next, he decided she was working for Cortina against Cardoza. Maybe she'd worked out a plan to save the Sanchez land for her family by outfitting the *Cortinistas* in exchange for their protection.

But if such was the case, who was her go-between? That didn't track either.

Then he considered her weird talent with numbers and decided the most logical idea was she was a *bruja*— one of a long bloodline of ancient Spanish witches.

This was more likely the truth, he thought, face-tiously.

Weren't all women devils of one kind or other?

If nothing else, spending time in the dark had given him an education in the nighttime voices of the hacienda. The house creaked a bit when the north wind came. The kitchen window near the stove rattled.

Somebody went out to use the privy and a door hinge made a sound like an ocelot kitten with its foot in a trap —a bestial noise learned from hard experience, and Lin rubbed the scar of a three-clawed scratch on the back of his hand.

There were sounds from the surrounding yards as well.

Chickens. The wind through the summer kitchen.

Down at the well, the creak of hemp against the old wooden windlass. The nickering of horses at the stable. A square of tin banging on the side of the haybarn.

Initially, the tin had brought him to his feet, and he stood beside the bed, taking in the night. From this angle, he had a clear view of the bunkhouse and could see dim candlelight there. Were the Jensen boys up late, reading their Bible? Was Stick Carvell similarly awake, stewing about the fate of Rancho de Jada?

Or maybe he slept with the lamp light on. Lin imagined him down there, curled up on his blanket, hugging Lin's Maynard carbine.

Lin crawled back into bed and pulled the light woolen spread up over himself.

He couldn't stop chewing over the mystery of the place.

And then all at once, it came together. The ammunition, the reason the locals shunned Rancho de Jada and wouldn't work for Tom Sinclair, the *sympathies* Hollister Morse had mentioned.

A line of gray showed at the edge of the earth.

Lin knew the answer and figured he might as well rest his eyes until dawn. There would be time to talk with Tom and Reece at breakfast.

An instant later, he was driven from the bed with dazzling sunlight and a hail of gunfire.

He'd slipped away, fallen into deep, dreamless morning sleep, and dawn had crept up on him.

Dawn, and something far more deadly.

The shots echoed from the bunkhouse, and a quick scan out the window showed him four men on sleek black stallions cantering around the front of the building.

Lin dressed without thinking. Foregoing his socks, he jammed his bare feet into his boots. He tossed on his shirt, not bothering to fix the buttons. He pulled his gunbelt from the top of the mirrored bureau, strapped it around himself, and flung open the hallway door.

The sound of more gunfire came from outside. This time it sounded like the roar of a heavy carbine.

Lin expected to find Reece's bedroom door closed. He expected to have to knock, maybe even rouse her from sleep. Maybe he'd catch her just waking up.

He should've known better. She rushed out into the hall to meet him, dressed in loose cotton work shirt, pants, and boots. A powder horn and leather pouch were slung over her shoulder on braided leather cords, and she also carried a rifle in her left hand.

Over her shoulder, Lin had a clear view into her bedroom. He saw her dressing table, covered with a crocheted doily and topped with small bottles of cut glass and a silver brush and comb set. Compared to the warrior who led him down the hall, it all seemed artificial somehow.

Far too feminine for Reece Sinclair.

No—feminine was the wrong word, because Reece exuded womanhood. The contents of the table were simply too soft. The person he raced to the parlor was hard, strong.

How hard, how strong—he figured they might both soon find out.

They met Sinclair and Barb Sanchez at the parlor's front window. Lin caught the warning look in Sinclair's eye, the worry as he glanced at Reece. "Give me the rifle," he said, pulling the gun from her grip. Then to Lin: "Get her the hell out of here. Before the whole place goes up."

As if on cue in a stage play, a monstrous concussion shook the windows of the house. It was an explosion like Lin had only ever heard under controlled circumstances with the Rangers. When the artillery fire hit the yard in front of the house, the fury was like a tornado. Strained timbers cracked and square nails screamed as they were partially wrenched from their sockets. The cacophony was immediately followed by a stream of men riding past on horseback. Yelling obscenities, they tossed off a blizzard of lead.

"I told you to get Reece away," said Sinclair as he brushed past a cushioned daybed with his six-shooter in hand. He tossed up the sash of a kitchen window and started banging away at the horses.

The angle was wrong, along with the range. He's not hitting a damn thing, thought Lin. Worse, he was wasting ammunition and time—reload time.

Reece pulled away to join her dad.

Lin reached out and grabbed her arm.

"No, Reece. Your dad's right. We need to go."

"I'm not leaving him."

Then Barb joined Sinclair at the window. He carried two extra rifles with powder and ammunition in a satchel. Together, the two men began loading, reloading, and pounding out a steady beat of gunfire.

"They can take care of themselves," said Lin. "We're going through your dad's office, out the back windows. Even if I have to carry you."

Another roar of the cyclone and the vinery behind the house exploded in a shower of wood and chaff.

Reece fell backwards at the shock and Lin caught her. They faced each other, inches apart, and both understood the gravity of what they faced.

The house could be smashed at any time.

Reece blinked. "All right. We'll go. But not out the back. I'll lead the way."

"We need to get away from the horsemen," said Lin. "Away from the cannon. We need to find Stick. He's down at the bunkhouse, all alone."

At least Stick had the Maynard. Lin thought about the loud, booming concussions he'd heard from the bunkhouse.

"This way," said Reece, taking Lin back up the hallway toward her bedroom.

"No," said Lin. "The house isn't safe. I've thought this out. We need to get to the bunkhouse. It's more strategically placed. From there we can protect the horses at the livery, make good an escape if need be."

"We're not leaving the ranch," said Reece.

He tried to pull her back by the shoulder, but she slipped out of his reach. Swinging around, she nearly clubbed him with her powder flask.

"I've thought it out too," she said. "Don't you think I know the ranch a lot better than you do?"

Lin ground his teeth together, feeling the anger well up inside.

Behind them came more bursts of rifle fire, and above it all, a man's voice barking orders in Spanish. Cardoza.

Lin gave in and shoved Reece ahead toward her room.

"I knew I should've started a stage coach line," he said.

"I wish you would've," said Reece.

Inside the lacey boudoir, Reece slammed the door behind them and dropped to the floorboards. "Crawl under the bed," she said.

"I don't understand."

"The bed. Follow me under it," she said.

Line complied and discovered a trap door inlaid in the floor.

"A hidey hole?" he said.

Reece pulled up the ring handle embedded in there and one side of the hinged door came with her, releasing a heavy, earthen odor into the room.

"A tunnel?" said Lin.

"Yes, it leads to the outside."

Another mortar careened over the property, slashing into the back patio and shaking the house.

"Follow me," said Reece, disappearing into the ground.

Lin followed, and the trap door fell shut behind them with a loud bang.

Under the floor joists, the battle outside with muffled and distant. Lin tasted a musty, metallic tang on his lips and the atmosphere was heavy and thick with the stink of age. Spider webs clung to Lin's face as he tried to orient himself in the blackness.

Then Reece struck a lucifer, and the walls of the tunnel were evident in the little flame's glow. Having turned around to face him, she rested on hands and knees, the match sparking out quick. She lit another.

The tunnel was three feet deep by the same number wide with thick clay walls held back by crumbling brick. The passage extended into the distance without end, running in a direction perpendicular from the rest of the house.

As the flame winked out, once again Lin asked, "How far will this take us?"

"Three hundred feet. It runs under the house to the back patio, then curves around to the line of jacals near the bunkhouse. There's a *bosquecillo* there we can hide in."

"Then I was right about you."

"What are you talking about?"

Lin recalled the conclusion he'd drawn from his early morning ruminations.

"The spare ammunition. The African man's disappearance. The reason some of the other rancheros in the area don't like you," he said. "I think I know why. You're an abolitionist, aren't you? One of those *Hellbenders*. You help slaves escape across the river into Mexico."

Reece didn't confirm nor deny his speculations. "The tunnel was put in when the house was built in case the Comanche attacked," she said. "Right now, we're the ones escaping."

"But you are an abolitionist," said Lin. "Do you understand there are people who would kill you for that fact alone?"

Scurrying ahead of him on her knees, she continued to be evasive. "You said it, not me. Seems like there's plenty of people who want to kill a body for just about anything these days. Depending on the people."

"I see why you don't have anybody working here. I thought maybe it was because cattle weren't welcome in sheep country. Or maybe it was just the off-season. The truth is word is starting to get around about what you all stand for."

"Everybody stands for something," said Reece. "Even if you think you don't. Even if you aren't sure what it is."

After a while, the tunnel narrowed, but Lin continued to blindly follow, his heavy Colt thudding awkwardly against the floor of the tunnel. The six-shooter was the only defense they had once they reached the trees.

Six-shots, and then—*No, dammit.*

Only *four* shots remained in the cylinder. He hadn't filled the empty chambers in the cylinder after last night's shooting match with Stick.

Lin's stomach churned at the greenhorn mistake.

He hoped those two missing bullets didn't sign their death warrant.

CHAPTER 15

Dub Hornsby's pappy was a no-good, shiftless drunk, and he never claimed to be a hero. On top of it, he didn't beat Dub across the head and shoulders all those years expecting to raise his boy to be a hero, either.

"Better a live loser than a dead winner," his dad would say, and Dub readily agreed with him. In his heart of hearts, Dub always knew he was a coward. And who cares, he thought. He certainly wasn't alone in possessing a healthy dose of caution.

Heroes got their ass handed to them on funeral parlor slabs.

In front of the ranch bunkhouse, as another rifle shot kicked up the sod, just missing his horse by an inch, Hornsby wheeled his stallion around and called to his nearest man. "Jenkins, fall back," he said. "Fall back."

Jenkins had gone down like a sack of wet grain, sliding off his horse slow and natural, as if having your heart shot out was nothing more than falling into a gentle slumber.

The next few blasts had been warning shots. Hornsby

got the feeling the aggressor was playing with him, could kill him at any time.

Where was the coyote hiding? And how did he reload so fast?

He gave Marko an order, and this time it wasn't questioned. "Take the men. Regroup with Cardoza near the well." Marko waved his arm high and sent out a gathering call. The men gigged their horses around and fell into line behind him.

Another carbine blast came from the scraggly line of foliage, and more lead whizzed past Hornsby with blistering proximity. The fat man gauged the angle of the shot. In the distance, behind the bunkhouse was a line of mud and thatched roof huts partially hidden by the sagebrush and mesquite. Jacals fallen into disrepair, dating back to the decades before the bunkhouse was constructed.

The gunman was in there. Somewhere.

But he would have to wait until later for another chance to kill Hornsby.

With the bunkhouse and livery cleared, there was no reason to root out this rat and take any more casualties. There'd be plenty of time to find the Indians and flush out the shooter after they had taken charge of the house and had it secure.

But rather than turn his back on the rifleman's sites, he backed his horse away from the bunkhouse. Slow and sure. The hairs on his neck stood straight up, and his skin squirmed with gooseflesh until he was well out of range. In the same way as he'd abandoned Able's corpse for the buzzards on Wednesday, Hornsby left Ruiz, Willats, and Jenkins in the dirt yard surrounding the bunkhouse.

He spurred his stallion for the white-washed hacienda behind his men, hell bent for leather, cursing Cardoza for his impatience, cursing himself for not trusting his own instincts. Cursing his spinelessness and the fact he hadn't stood up for those instincts.

Cardoza had counted on taking Sinclair by surprise. He was so confident in the raiders' numbers and all-fired sure of his damned cannon, he wasn't being careful. He hadn't considered any pushback at all.

Hornsby liked to think he was more shrewd. The new man, Jarret, was a Ranger. Where there was one, there was bound to be more. And hadn't the Apaches been there with their knives, just as he had predicted?

Then came a tremendous boom from up ahead, and a cloud of smoke rose up from the gathering of horses near the well. The yard in front of the house erupted in a pillar of twirling debris, like a *piñata* bursting out of the ground. Like a grassy mud volcano.

At the same time, rifle slugs poured out from the windows.

Cardoza's men were bunched up too close to the cannon. Rather than spread out and surround the house, they had all been overly eager to watch the mortar fire.

Now, just within shooting range of the house, they presented themselves as a massive target. Nearby Cardoza posed on his horse as if for a portrait.

Hornsby rode into the ranks and urged the men to break apart and step back, telling them to find cover behind the short retaining wall of bricks enclosing the hacienda's grass yard.

In the midst of his warning, two solid rounds from the house cut down one of the men. Panic took the horse as its rider slumped sideways in his saddle. Galloping through the array, it spread confusion like a virus. Two more horses spun in a circle, bucking their riders sense-less, tearing away across the open yard.

Another shot fried the air, and Hornsby directed Cardoza's soldiers.

"The big window. It's Sinclair and Sanchez. Concentrate your attention there."

Cardoza swung around to cut him off. "I'm in command here, Dub."

"Then by God—*command*!" said Dub.

It was a slap in the face, and Cardoza wouldn't forget it, Hornsby knew. He also knew they'd need to survive the next few minutes first, and it might be a miracle if they did.

But Cardoza had signaled his marksmen.

The chosen three dropped from their horses and squatted behind the retaining wall. They flung rifles to their shoulders and set off their percussion caps, punching holes in the wood siding, answering the opening charges of the men within.

More gunshots came from the house.

"They reload quickly," said Cardoza with a tone of respect.

"Or they have many arms, already prepared," said Hornsby.

Like everyone in the valley, Hornsby had heard rumors Rancho de Jada was a way station on the south-Texas path to African emancipation. Some stories said a runaway slave could get whatever they needed from Tom Sinclair before they crossed the river into Mexico.

If the stories were true, Hornsby thought, it was one more reason to shut the place down.

These people were traitors to the southern states' way of life.

Cardoza made a swirling gesture with his finger, sending the trio of gunmen around to the far end of the house on foot while three more men covered them with triggered carbines. "Everything is under control, *amigo*," he said, showing Hornsby his line of straight white teeth. "I told you before not to worry, eh?"

Once Cardoza was sure the men understood his intent to surround the place, he turned to the cannoneer with a determined look on his face. For an instant, Hornsby was certain Cardoza meant to set off the cannon again and blast his own men. The Mexican's attack had been so wild, so careless, Hornsby would've believed almost anything.

Instead, Cardoza signaled the artilleryman to ease off.

When Tom Sinclair called out from the house, he demanded their retreat. "This place is mine, you damn rotten bastards. You don't belong here, you understand?"

Cardoza responded with an obscene gesture and scoffed. "You were warned to leave, Señor Sinclair. Just the other day, *mi servador*, Hornsby, told you to leave."

Hornsby clenched his jaw at the cheap insult. Payback for Hornsby's entreating Cardoza to take command. A reminder of his place in the scheme of things.

Servador. Servant.

Not *Segundo*—second—but *servador*.

"I don't give a hoot about Hornsby," said Sinclair. "and I care even less for you."

Cardoza made an exaggerated flourish with his open hand. "Should I remind you, we are family, Tómas? Would our beloved wives want us quarreling like this? Or would they want us to unite for the common good of the Sanchez legacy?" He put his hand over his heart.

"You can kiss my ass," said Sinclair.

While they bantered, Hornsby backpedaled to where Marko crouched low behind the round well casing. He pointed to the quiet end of the house, past the wreckage caused by the cannon.

And the front door had been jarred open.

Sinclair was at the opposite end, positioned at the window.

"How many men do you think are in there?" said Hornsby.

Marko made a guess. "Sanchez and Sinclair. Maybe Jarret and the girl."

"Four then. What I figure too."

"Only a matter of time, ain't it?"

"Time," agreed Hornsby.

Because the conclusion was foregone before they gathered in the morning. Rancho de Jada would fall into their hands.

"There was no good reason for us to have lost four men," he said.

"Forget about it," said Marko. "Winning is what matters most."

Hornsby tried to take the advice. Tried to push the annoying thought away.

He watched Cardoza's horse prance back and forth just beyond the range of the defensive carbines. He certainly was enjoying himself.

Plenty of time later for recriminations.

Hornsby told Marko his plan. "If you and me was to rush the opening in the house, we could take Sinclair by surprise."

"Just the two of us?" said Marko.

"Just the two of us."

"*Señor* Sinclair?" said Cardoza. "*Hola*, Sinclair..."

No answer.

Neither were any more shots coming from the house.

Had Cardoza's men breeched the abode from the other side?

"You go in front of me," Hornsby told Marko. He stood up and used his revolver to lay down a steady rhythm of cover, allowing Marko to approach the house. Once there, he drove his shoulder through the door, smashing through.

Hornsby followed.

He stumbled into the open parlor, his revolver up and ready to fire.

There was nobody there.

Then he heard a scuffle from farther on, and he crossed the space in three steps. He led with his gun hand down the hallway.

The house smelled of gun smoke and rancid sweat. Ahead was the kitchen, where Sinclair and Sanchez had been holding down the fort with their carbines. He strode forward, and, responding to a muffled noise, smashed open a door on his right.

It was the girl's bedroom. Inside, two of Cardoza's men grappled with Sinclair while Sanchez cowered in the corner, doing nothing to help his brother-in-law. What a sorry excuse for a man.

Hornsby leveled his gun at Sinclair's chest. "Give it up, Tom. It's all over."

"All over? I'll say when it's over," said Sinclair, pulling free of the soldier.

He shrugged his shirt collar back into place and smoothed out his sleeves. "You don't know who you're dealing with, Hornsby. I'll have the Army down here before you know what hit you. Then you and Cardoza'll be high-tailing it across the river."

"Yeah, let's bring the Army into it," said Hornsby, not lowering his gun for a second. "Let's tell them how your girl's been ferrying Africans 'cross the river and defying Texas law. Let's make Rancho de Jada an example for all good, decent Christians. Let's talk about Hellbenders."

"You have no legal right—"

"You're wrong, Sinclair. Mister Cardoza's got all the legalities covered," he said. "He had Morse draw up the legal transfer-of-ownership papers. Papers you and Barb Sanchez are both gonna sign. If only as a formality."

Sinclair stepped up and spit in Hornsby's face.

Hornsby brought the barrel of the pistol up across the old man's cheek, then down on his forehead. Sinclair hit the floor in a stupor, and Hornsby sneered at Sanchez's woeful, unmanly sob. Wiping the saliva from his chin, he added, "God help you, you poor bastards."

Cardoza appeared in the hallway with a wrinkled nose and annoyed expression. He brushed the plaster dust from his shirt with contempt.

Then he barked a command at the soldiers. "Take them into the office."

The men trudged out of the bedroom, and Cardoza squeezed Hornsby's shoulder with a gloved hand. "The day is won, eh? We will celebrate tonight."

Hornsby gave an affirmative nod, and an old soldier came from the bedroom across the hall. He carried a leather saddle bag in one hand, and a canvas sack in the other. He held the sack up to Cardoza, and it jingled conspicuously. "*Jefe*, looook," said the gray-haired man, his face full of joy.

Cardoza clutched the sack and three gold dollars spilled out to bounce on the floor. "The celebration gets bigger and better, eh, Hornsby?" He threw his arm around the soldier and kissed the man's head. Then he handed the sack back to him. "Gracias, señor," he said.

"Hold this for me, Manuel, and there will be much reward for your family."

Bowing away in reverse, Manuel carried the sack back into the other bedroom. Once out of his comandante's view, he spun around and began tossing the room apart.

Searching for more.

Cardoza rolled his eyes. "It takes little to please them," he said and assumed a regal air as he walked down the hallway. "Have some men ready the kitchen. Perhaps Señor Sanchez will prepare a magnificent dinner."

He strolled into the office.

Sanchez and Sinclair had been forced to sit on the floor amidst a pile of books. Cardoza pulled out the leather upholstered chair behind the broad desk and sat down. Then he removed his black lambskin gloves and laid them down beside an ink blotter, one on top of the other. He told Hornsby, "Start a fire burning in the fireplace, won't you?"

There was plenty of kindling in the *caliche* block hearth and Hornsby had it smoldering in no time.

"Here we are," said Sanchez. He breathed in with satisfaction. "A Sanchez family reunion." He leaned back and raised his eyes to the portrait of Jada Sanchez.

From across the room, Tom Sinclair said, "I never considered you a part of my family."

Cardoza ignored him and reached into his vest to the pocket sewn there. He removed a length of folded paper, put it on the flat surface of the desk, and opened it. With great care, he smoothed out the three creases.

Then, again reaching in, he pulled out a pen and a short bottle of ink.

Again, Cardoza took great care in the positioning of things, lining the pen up parallel with the long edge of the paper, setting the ink down on the opposite side. Slowly he unscrewed the cap and laid it aside.

He parked his elbows on the desk and laced his long, narrow fingers together in front of his face. Then he addressed the old men.

"I control this ranch," he said.

"I doubt it very much," said Sinclair.

"Rancho de Jada is mine. My men and I will occupy it for the foreseeable future, and from this place here, I will construct an empire."

Sinclair screwed his mouth into a defiant frown. "Like hell you will."

"As stubborn as your *esposa*." Cardoza's eyes traveled from the painting to Sinclair and back again. He clenched his teeth in a maniacal smile. "*Mi esposa* was stubborn too, *amigo*."

He nudged the bottom of the paper toward Sinclair. "Sign this and live. It's a simple proposition." He spoke to Barb, "This goes for you as well, *primo*."

"I won't sign it," said Sinclair.

With a casual manner, Cardoza let his hand fall to his holster. When the hand came back up, it held a pistol. Relaxed, he again told Sinclair what he wanted.

"Go to the devil," said Sinclair.

Cardoza shrugged. "You have called my bluff, amigo." He nodded, as if finally coming to the end of some inner argument. "As it happens, I don't need you. Only your signature. Or somebody who can make a good copy."

Cardoza laid the gun aside and turned the paper around. He dipped the pen in the inkwell and handed it to Barb Sanchez.

Sanchez took the pen with a node, pressed it against the paper, and signed on the bottom line, *Thomas Sinclair*. Then he blew across the wet signature.

Cardoza said, "Now you sign."

Sanchez put his own name down under Sinclair's.

"*Muy bien*," said Cardoza.

"Barb?" said Tom.

Cardoza picked up the revolver.

Overly casual, he shot Tom Sinclair through the chest. The ranchero slumped sideways.

"I had hoped he would go along with you," said Barb.

Cardoza nodded. "But I am grateful for your help. *Gracias, primo*."

Sanchez smiled at the thanks. "*De nada*."

Cardoza motioned Hornsby around to the back of the desk.

"You'll act as our witness, won't you Dub? Before his untimely demise, you saw Mister Sinclair sign the ownership papers over to me, didn't you?"

Hornsby was getting tired of Cardoza's theatrics. He looked at the scrawl of letters on the document. Glanced up at Sinclair. "Seems to me it's done."

"Oh, it's far from done," said Cardoza, laughing as he kicked the chair off into a lazy spin. "This is just the beginning."

Barb joined in the laughter, too.

Then Cardoza wheeled around and shot him through the head.

Barb tumbled out of his chair, dying at Tom Sinclair's lifeless feet.

"You saw how quickly he betrayed his *hermano*," said Cardoza. A man who is untrustworthy to his family..." Cardoza shook his head. "Such a man is better off dead."

CHAPTER 16

THEY CRAWLED IN THE DARK UNTIL LIN THOUGHT HIS elbows and knees were scraped raw. How far could it be between the house and the trees behind the bunkhouse? Three hundred feet, Reece told him. Three hundred feet was instantaneous by horse, a short jag by boot leather.

On hands and knees, in the dark, it was an eternity.

The knife wound on his thigh was a thudding agony and his pestering damn holster had a tendency to prod at the sore space with every push forward.

Twice he was convinced the walls of the tunnel were caving in on him, and he struggled to breathe. In through the nose, out through the mouth. Each time, the cold dirt under his palms and the sound of Reece inching along ahead kept him moving, kept him continuing to put one hand down in front of the other. The muscles of his neck and shoulders bunched up and complained, the stink of vermin waste roiled his guts.

When they finally came to the end of the way, the graveyard silence inside the tunnel raised goosebumps on Lin's arms and neck. Reece squirreled around to face him and lit another match, striking it on her boot. "The door is here, above me. I'm going to crack it open, slow. Otherwise, the daylight will blind us." She stood on her knees with her arms above her and pushed up. A sharp snap followed by the sound of wood rubbing on metal hinges. A three-sided crack of blinding light in the tunnel's black ceiling made Lin squint.

Thumb-sized clods of topsoil, curled leaves, and nests of grass rained down on Reece as she jostled the door. Holding the trap open with one hand, she sought a rock with her fingers to prop it into place. Then she crouched back down beside Lin, and they listened to the pitched battle back at the house. For a while the shooting was constant, then sporadic, then it stopped and there were no sounds at all.

They waited some more, but all Lin heard were the sounds of nature. A soft breeze, the chatter of a squirrel.

An odd sense of finality washed over Lin as the door on the forest floor swung up and away with a flurry of chaff. Lin saw the silhouette of a tall man framed in the daylight against a thick snarl of trees.

He reached for his gun, stopped himself as Stick Carvell's reassuring voice said, "Thank heavens, Reece, gal—I thought you were done in for sure."

Stick perched on the edge of the hole, offering his slender arms by way of escape from the pit. Reece clamored up and over the edge.

Lin gripped the mouth of the cave, slippery with leaves and underbrush. He hoisted himself out.

Careful to avoid bumping his sore leg, Lin dusted his arms and hands before adjusting his holster.

"How bad is it?" said Stick.

"As bad as you can imagine. Worse. They've taken the hacienda. Tom and Barb are inside."

"What about you, Stick?" said Reece.

"They showed up at the bunkhouse not too long after sunrise. I went out the back with your gun. They rode in hard and fast." Stick held up the Maynard rifle, and around his neck was a leather pouch. "I managed to keep 'em busy for a while."

"All by yourself?" said Lin.

His voice was dark. "One of them was the same little skunk with the waxed mustache from the store yesterday. Pegged him between the collar bones."

"I heard rifle fire down here this morning. Was it you?"

Stick nodded. "After I got the first two troublemakers, I got some distance, and—pow—took a third one right through the sternum. They weren't too eager to stay around down here afterwards." He shrugged. "O'course now, I'm out of bullets. Caps, too."

Lin scratched his head.

"They'll be back," said Stick. "Once they've secured the house, they'll come back looking for you."

"For us," said Reece.

Lin nodded. "They're not about to let the heir of Rancho de Jada run loose. They need to tie you up almost as much as they need your dad. Cardoza won't tolerate you out here, living, breathing, and on the loose."

"I can't believe Cardoza would go this far," said Reece. "If nothing else, he ought to honor the memory of my mother and also my aunt, his wife."

"He's not a man of honor," said Stick. "No matter what the locals think. He's a hypocrite—as dirty as Hollister Morse and Cortina and all the others of their ilk who prey on decent men. They tramp through, doing dirt to innocents in order to get power. Then they turn around and pretend they were honor-bound to do it."

Reece agreed, then said what they all were thinking.

"To get what he wants, Cardoza might well kill my father. Or Barb."

"Your dad won't give up without a scrap," said Stick.

"He might not have much choice," said Reece. "Cardoza and Hornsby hit us with a lot of men. I didn't have time to count, but my impression was more than twenty."

"At least a couple dozen," said Stick. "Down three or four now. They're a mixed lot of Anglos and Tejanos following Cardoza. For the time being, they're all up at the house."

"Which way from here?" Lin asked Reece. "You must have an escape route, for when you bring slaves out this way?"

"Miss Reece?" Stick stepped back, clearly alarmed. He said, "Lin knows about the Hellbenders? You told a Ranger about your work here?"

"I figured it out," said Lin. "You're not the only emancipators I ever met."

Stick pushed his rifle up between them. "Okay, but we just might be the last. Is there gonna be trouble between us?"

"No trouble," said Lin. "I'm on your side."

Stick held his grip on the gun high for several seconds, then studied Lin's face and relaxed. "Fair enough."

Lin turned back to Reece. "Like I said, where do we go from here? The bunkhouse is the first place they'll look."

"I've got a spot in the livery barn," she said. "It's a hidden space at the far end of the grain closet where we left the barrels last night. When the livery was built, it was the original tack room, the first bodega. We had it walled off two years ago. It's not evident—even if you look inside the grain closet—not unless you know it's there."

"Problem is, it's not very big either," said Stick. "The three of us can't hole up in there too long without gettin' to know each other awfully darn well. Maybe better than we might like."

"What about Ramon and the Apache herders?" said Lin. "What'll become of them?"

Stick said, "When it's cold they stay in the bunkhouse. Mostly they sleep outside, wherever they want. Oft-times, when they're out night-hawin' the cows, they'll make camp on the other side of the corral where we worked yesterday."

"We ought to get together with them, coordinate a defense," said Lin.

"Maybe not. They show up wherever and whenever they please. I haven't seen them yet today." Stick looked off into the distance. "My guess is they'll want to keep track of the cow herd. Probably they'll stay with them out at Defilement."

"I'm low on ammunition," said Lin.

"There's some supplies in the grain closet," said Reece. "The bullets we brought home from town. The small batch of powder."

"All right," said Lin. "We re-load in the grain closet. From there, we saddle up a couple horses and pound hell to leather for Jade City," said Lin. "Maybe I can find Oscar. Get some help."

"I'm not leaving the ranch," said Reece.

"It's not worth your life to stay," said Lin.

Reece answered him straight-away, "Maybe you don't think so. Maybe you've never had anything worth standing up and dying over."

"I've had folks I cared about."

"This is more than just my dad and Barb. This is about pride in a piece of ground. The only way of life I've ever known. It's a connection between the years of work I've put in a place and some piss-ant strolling in on a whim thinking I'm going to hand it over to him." It was clear her mind was made up. "This is my ranch, and I'm not running away. They'll have to kill me first."

"Amen," said Stick.

Lin chided him. "I appreciate your support, *amigo*."

The look on his companions' faces told Lin there was no two ways about it. They would stay and figure out some way of reclaiming the ranch.

Or, as Reece said, they'd die trying.

"Our first stop is your grain closet, then." Lin pulled his Colt and backed up the others, careful not to make any noise. "Lead the way," he said.

CHAPTER 17

LIN, STICK, AND REECE CREPT BEHIND THE CORNER OF the bunkhouse with a clear view of the livery.

While they watched, Cardoza's force of fighting men corralled twenty stallions in the weed-infested stable of pens outside the barn. Some of the animals were frothy and blowing, still on edge from the morning's action, some of them stood alone, silent.

All of them deserved the attention of water, food, and a brush.

Especially water.

The two soldiers left standing guard in the open alleyway weren't giving it to them.

Instead, they stood inside the door beside a parked wagon drinking from big dippers full of water carried from a barrel on the wagon's tailgate. They imbibed and were wasteful, pouring their helpings out onto the ground while still half full. Then they lit cigarettes in a chain and smoked. Both of the men were dressed in light grey trousers and embroidered sarape's. One of the men wore a sombrero. One was bare-headed, and bald.

After a while, one of the men walked to the barrel

again with two dippers of water sloshing over the rims. Lin watched the men drink their fill.

"If we could get past them, we'd be set," said Stick. "But if we start any shooting, we'll have the rest of the army back down here."

"How about one of us makes a distraction, draw them off?" said Lin. "Something like this."

Before Reece or Stick could stop him, Lin sauntered out into the open between the two buildings and waved his hat. "Hello the horse barn," he called. "Any of you sap-sucking coyotes care to outrun me?" He jumped high, clicking his heels together twice, then cowered low in the grass, moving out to the north as one of the men brought up his long gun.

The muzzle flashed and a curtain of smoke carried off into the stable, but Lin kept dodging around, laughing as he ran deeper into the scrub of trees.

The man who fired on him, followed at a gallop with the second man in tow.

Lin took cover in the prickly forest, waiting with his gun in hand.

Hopefully this would give Reece and Stick the chance they needed to reach the grain closet.

The first soldier's approach was telegraphed by the crunching of dry brush underfoot and a heavy, grunting breath. If the second man was standing back, covering the first man's approach with a raised rifle, Lin was dead.

But he took a chance it wasn't the case. He bet these mule-heads would be falling all over themselves in a race to see which of them could get to him first.

His wager was correct.

When Lin sprang out from behind the patch of cenizo, the first man continued to charge straight for him, rifle pointed straight at the sky. Lin cocked, fired, and missed.

Dammit!

He shot again, this time a hit, but barely had time to turn his attention to the second man, even as the first windmilled straight into the ground.

The second runner, seeing what happened to the first, had dropped to one knee and hoisted his weapon. Lin's Colt cracked blistering fast, and the man fell forward on his face.

Through the trees, Lin saw two more soldiers running toward him from the livery barn. He cursed again. They must've been inside the door, out of view.

From the tattered way they dressed, he could tell these were Dub Hornsby's men.

Lin didn't need Reese's uncanny power over numbers to figure out how grim the next few minutes appeared.

Only one shot remained in Lin's cylinder. Up against two primed and ready rifles.

He could only hope Reece and Stick had made it to the barn safely. Could only pray they were sequestering themselves away in the secret, walled-off room at the end of the grain closet.

Lin's one advantage was the men hadn't located him yet. They had slowed their incursion into the tree line and were picking their way through the brush. Lin ducked behind a waist-high rocky outcropping, edged along the leaf-littered base, and startled a pair of canyon wrens who madly took to the air.

He tensed every muscle.

One of the pursuers appeared on the scene, coming to a halt less than twenty feet away, holding a Springfield rifle.

Hornsby's man was little more than a boy.

Hell, he couldn't have been fifteen years old.

What was Hornsby thinking bringing a towhead barely ripe with peach fuzz into a man's world of powder-charged lead?

Lin looked around the immediate area, found a good sized rock, and palmed it.

The boy spied Lin, opened his mouth to shout a warning—

With a strong arm and a good eye, Lin pitched for all he was worth, landing the rock square on the kid's knuckles, making him drop his gun and fall to the ground.

Lin pointed his Colt straight at him. "Button your lip or die," he said, pushing a growl of menace into his throat.

The kid immediately wrapped his arms around his knees and started sobbing.

The next adversary was a dirt-encrusted old rum-guzzler with ten pounds of flab on his gut and an evil menace in his eye. Distracted by the kid, he ran onto the scene and said, "What's your pea-pickin' problem?"

Lin wasn't taking any chances with this one. He pressed finger to the trigger, aiming to blow him to kingdom come.

Then eased off.

What if this was the boy's father? Was Lin ready to shoot him down? In front of the kid?

The vision would haunt a man his whole life.

And a vengeful son could bird-dog Lin for all his remaining mortal days.

Rum-gut half turned as Lin bolted from behind the rock like a wild mustang. Unprepared for Lin's iron fist, he threw his arms up, dropping his gun. Lin cranked a second set of knuckles into the soft midsection, then finished the man with a crashing blow to the chin.

Rum-gut toppled down and rolled over onto his back, woozy.

Lin bent over the whining kid. "Get up," he told him.

The trembling towhead climbed to his feet, stood in too big boots at sloppy attention.

Lin pointed at Rum-gut's senseless form. "Is this your dad, brother, cousin—any relation to you at all?"

The kid shook his head.

"You see what happened here? I spared your life, you understand?"

The kid's nod was vigorous.

"You and me are square. You agree?"

Again, the nod.

Lin's fingers shot out, balling up the kid's collar into his fist. With one swift move, he spun the kid on his heels and planted a flat boot on his backside. The kid rocked forward and fell face first to the ground — hard.

"That's for trying to kill me in the first place. *Now* we're square." Pain made the kid agreeable. "You quit this outfit, you understand me?" said Lin. "You get up on your feet and run as fast and as far away as you can, or next time I see you, I'll kill you. *¿Sabes?*"

The kid nodded again and climbed to his feet. Before Lin could stop him, he picked up both of the fallen rifles and ran away like a deer, through the forest, toward the far pasture.

For now, at least, the kid was traveling in the right direction. Lin hoped he hadn't made a mistake not killing him or his potted friend.

Lin shoved his spent six-shooter into his holster and ran for the back door of the bunkhouse.

He only had one bullet left.

———

IN THE OPEN ALLEY, Reece led Stick to the grain closet, a walled up section taking up most of one full side of the livery barn. She moved the wood latch and the door popped open.

It was hard to tell in the murky, grain-dust covered darkness, but the room was smaller on the inside than the outside by at least three feet. She and Tom Sinclair had constructed the back wall around a central pivot so it revolved open, allowing access to a hidden space between it and the outer wall. Cramped quarters to be sure, not much more than 25 feet square, but it had served its purpose in providing rest for almost a dozen young men and women seeking emancipation.

Rest, and munitions.

They had unloaded powder, lead, and some percussion caps into the closet earlier in the week. Hopeful Cardoza's men hadn't discovered the cache, she was about to climb inside when another guard walked around the corner of the barn, past the water wagon.

Whistling, the unarmed man busied himself tying up the drawstring of his pants. Startled when he saw Reece, he sputtered out the beginnings of a warning.

Stick dropped him with one shot of his pistol.

The soldier kicked twice and died with a gurgle in the center of the barn.

"Poor hombre doesn't even have a gun. I'm sorry to have had to do it. Wish I could tell him."

"You'll have all day to talk to him. We've got to bring him along inside the closet," said Reece.

"The dead man?"

"If they find him there, they'll tear the place apart looking for us."

"I could drag him outside?" said Stick.

"No time," said Reece. "They will have heard the shot, they'll be coming."

Together, they hauled the corpse into the feed room and pulled the latch closed from the inside. Then Reece pushed on the back wall and it turned on its center, making a crack just wide enough to slip through. Reece went inside the hidden room first, then with Stick's help pulled the body in behind her.

Finally Stick joined her and pushed the revolving hatch shut.

Not a moment too soon.

Reece watched through a crack on the outer wall as a half-dozen men galloped into the barn in response to the gunshots.

Whether Stick knew it or not, his pistol was empty. Reece had been keeping track.

If they were found out now, they were dead.

CHAPTER 18

IN JADE CITY, MICAH LEMAY KEPT TO THE LONG
stretch of the late afternoon shadows. He'd been cautious
for a long time, religiously careful, and now he barely had
to think about it. An African in south Texas, freed by his
own undertaking, had to be a man of shadows. He
remembered the words of his pa. A runaway *must* be a
phantom—or he'll soon be a ghost. Words he'd lived by
for more than a week since breaking away from the
Landers spread upriver and making his way south toward
Mexico...and freedom.

Keep to the shadows. Don't let them see you.

If they do see you, don't meet their eyes and say
you're on errand to Rio Grande City. Or Brownsville.
Above all else, don't mention Rancho de Jada or Reese
Sinclair.

Never, ever, say the word: *Hellbenders*.

Not even if your life depended on it, because
someone else's life will depend on you keeping your
mouth shut.

And a black man using the word would be suspect for
sure.

On foot he'd made it as far as Emberville, the Overland Railroad station serving runaways in secret. The kindly old woman there had allowed him the use of a simple buckboard wagon and one horse, a mousey dun grulla, provided he leave the rig with Reece Sinclair at her Rio Grande spread.

Thus far, there hadn't been any indication of being missed by his keepers, or sign anybody was on his trail. The Landers gang boss was drunk most of the time, and if Micah was lucky, his absence had been overlooked for a while. Despite the wagon's lack of springs and a rough-hewn seat, the ride had been swift and without incident.

Now he faced his next challenge.

All he knew was his goal—a name and a pair of destinations, first whispered to him by his dying dad. "Find Reece Sinclair at the Jade City Mercantile or Rancho de Jada." At Emberville Station, the lady said to go to the Mercantile first. If there was any other help to be had, other than the good Lord above, Micah didn't know about it. He wasn't privy to any other safe havens except the one he was aiming for.

It had taken a week of riding through thorns and splashing through water and mud. It had taken a week of living in shadows. But he was here, now, in Jade City, having left buckboard rig parked in a secluded clearing at the Carlito river.

Here he was, behind the mercantile.

And there was nobody inside.

The midmorning sun was urgently climbing in the east, revealing a main street increasingly busy with wagons, mules, and foot-traffic along the boardwalk. Heedful to stay out-of-sight, he huddled behind the building, beside a stack of apple crates piled next to the rear entrance to the mercantile.

He rapped the door once more, pressed his ear to the painted wood.

It seemed odd the place wasn't open for business on a fair Friday morning.

A square window allowed him to see inside the dark interior, allowed a glimpse of his own reflection pressing against the edges of the pane, too big to fit inside the wavy glass.

At twenty years old, Micah was still growing up, and out. His shoulders were broad and wide as a timber cross-beam, his hips narrow and agile. The fear threatening to cut loose inside him wasn't evident on his face. His pate was clean-shaven and as smooth as his cheeks. His jaw was resolute and steady, his deep brown eyes confident. He wore a gray railroad cap with an over-sized bill he could pull down and hide behind, and his clothes were in good repair. Neither too flamboyant nor too shabby, he dressed to blend into a crowd. He moved naturally, with no sudden jerks or maneuvers, nothing too slow or lingering, nothing too fast or nervous.

Then the steady cadence of hoofbeats and clattering wagon wheels warned Micah of impending discovery. Somebody was coming along the outer road behind the mercantile building.

Quick, he shoved his hands in his pockets and took a few steps along the length of the store's wall, pretending to be a pedestrian on errands, hoping to become a part of the civic scenery, hoping whoever it was driving the wagon wouldn't notice him.

A flaxen wheel team rounded the corner pulling a high hay-carrier with a gritty dust exhaust and a crashing of springs. The determined buckskins were going hell-bent for leather and if the old teamster with the four-in-hand noticed Micah, he didn't let on as he turned again to follow a perpendicular dirt path away from town.

Micah breathed a sigh of relief and hurried back to the door.

He didn't like it, but he only had one option. The longer he stood around outside, the greater his chance of being discovered. The greater his chance of capture.

He gripped the thin shank of flat steel wire he carried in the cuff of his gray flannel coat. The door had a standard knob and cast iron latch. With practiced dexterity, Micah fit the wire into the keyhole, closed his eyes, and took a deep breath. With a few practiced twists and turns, he had the door unlocked.

Stealing a last glance around to make sure nobody saw him, he pushed open the mercantile door and let himself in. Only when the door was closed behind him did he breathe a sigh of relief. Only after re-locking the door from the inside and blocking the way with a nearby barrel of molasses did he start to relax.

As his eyes slowly adjusted to the light, he saw he was inside a back pantry room, the adjoining door, partially open. His first order of business, he decided, was to edge the front pantry door closed. There were too many people in the street and on the boardwalk today. If somebody happened to walk past the front of the store, look inside and catch a glimpse of him...

Micah shuddered and made his way around the inventory of storage crates and boxes.

He had a strong hand on the pantry door, when he heard voices from the front stoop. Curiosity had him peeking around the edge of the door where he saw two men sitting on a bench outside the shop's front window, passing the time of day. They were both heavily invested in the conversation, the brims of their hats brushed together.

One of the men was quick and animated. The other was equally intent, but slow in his mannerisms. The slow man was a living skeleton with hair like loose spun yellow yarn and his cheek seemed rude with a noticeable twitch. He was talking about cattle and somebody named Herby. Or Hornby.

With the background noise in the bustling street, Micah couldn't hear the men clearly.

At any rate, it was none of his busines, and he began to push the door closed. As he did, both men stood up and shook hands.

Then Micah's stomach lurched like a gut shot cat. The animated man mentioned Reece Sinclair. He distinctly said something about Rancho de Jada.

But what? Micah's heart slammed against his rib cage. What had he said?

Almost immediately he wondered if the urgent business had anything to do with him? Could word have spread to watch for an escaped slave from the north? Were these men watching the street for him?

If only the man would repeat himself. His tone of voice had held some kind of urgency, and the Skull-man replied by nodding under his pancake-brimmed black hat.

Sweat dripped from under Micah's cap and ran down the length of his jawline. If something was happening at Rancho de Jada, he wanted to know about it before he blundered into trouble he couldn't get away from. Trouble might get him killed.

The sound of Micah's heart was a steam hammer roaring in his ears, and he told himself to slow down and breathe easy. Nothing was sure. Not yet.

Outside, the two men stood watching the street traffic, continuing to gab. Micah needed to find out what they were talking about. It could mean a change of plans for him. It could mean life or death.

Wary, deliberate, he got down on his hands and knees and slipped out from the pantry into the front of the mercantile.

With a precise economy of movement, he slid behind the cash register station, then continued with prudent progress, duck-walking along the back of the display cases.

"I appreciate your time, Mister Morse," said the bigger fellow.

"You'll find Hutton to be an agreeable type," said the Skeleton, whose name was Morse. "They've handled Sinclair cattle before at the auction house in Rio Grande City. You should have no trouble."

"As it turns out, I know Hutton quite well. The auction house is a like a second home to me," said the animated man. Micah leaned over to look between the cabinets and up through the window. Standing with gloved hands in motion and his back to the store, the man related what he knew about the longhorn market. "Last week a lot of 26 sold at 10 cents a pound, and I've heard higher is the norm. Generally he's dealing in them long-legged critters from up north, some more'n three years old. I got a hunch he's ready for some grass-fed animals."

Morse agreed. "Only thing—it's important he makes payment to the Rancho de Jada, not to Sinclair. Until we get the papers filed at the capital, the ranch will still be in Sinclair's name."

"I understand."

"Of course, cash moneys is always welcome," said Morse. "When will you leave?"

Micah watched as the man turned to the sun, and now he could see the man's face. Under a heavy hat rode the features of an experienced cowboy, knowledgeable and strong. But there was something shifty there too—the nervous twitch of the eyelid or the way he licked his bottom lip.

"I've got a team coming in from the trail tonight. We'll ride out to the ranch in the morning and talk to Hornsby. Then set out from Defilement, get a headcount on the cows. It should be a routine drive to the city."

"We're agreed as to percentages then?"

"Agreed. I ain't fixin' to get rich on this run, just make a tidy sum to help me along."

"You help us now, there's more for you in the future. Under her new management, I expect the ranch will be more prosperous than ever before. Won't be long and cattle will be big business here, maybe as big as sheep. Maybe more. One thing's for certain—there's a lot of money to be made."

"I'm glad to hear it."

"Sinclair and his daughter had the right idea, just too bad for them, they ran out of time."

"Timing is everything."

"Mister Cardoza has more than 1000 head of sheep on the Diablo Flats. When we move over, we'll need men to oversee them here. Same when we bring in the new cows."

"It can be arranged. There's always men willing to work for a decent, god-fearing spread."

After a few more minutes, Morse said, "I suppose I'd better get back to the cantina. I was hoping to get word from the ranch this afternoon."

"Cardoza shouldn't have had any trouble. They don't have spit for munitions out there." The man motioned over his shoulder with his thumb. "Miss Reece keeps all the powder here in the store."

Finally, Morse shook hands with the man. "Good luck," he said.

"Good luck to you."

Micah watched the two walk away in opposite directions.

He stayed low, snuck back to the pantry room and closed the door. Once there he hunkered down in the dim recesses of the crates and drums, pondering what he'd heard.

What was all this about new management for Rancho de Jada? And the remark about the Sinclair's time running out? What could it mean? Was Reece Sinclair still at the ranch or not?

A sense of calamity washed over him, and Micah started to tremble like it was January with a cold cook stove. If the Sinclairs no longer owned the ranch, Micah would have to ford the river and cross into Mexico alone. But even if he made it there without being stopped, out in the open, in front of dozens of white folk...even if he made it across the Rio Grande, he knew no one, had no idea who he was supposed to contact or where such people were to be found.

Reece Sinclair had the information.

The only thing to do was go to the ranch and find her.

He had a fair knowledge of the region's geography, and at Emberville Station they'd told him to stay with the Little Carlito until he came to a hacienda with three out-buildings.

Micah was determined to prevail.

And yet...

They don't have spit for munitions out there.

Micah let his eyes travel over the labels on the casques surrounding him and once again, he thanked God his father had been able to teach him how to read when he was a boy. Because now he could at the boxes and read—*Eley Brothers, Foil-covered Percussion Caps, Quick Loader, American Powder Mills, Colt.*

He decided it might be best to arm himself.

CHAPTER 19

THE BUNKHOUSE WAS DARK INSIDE, AND COOL. THE ordered composition of the place rankled Lin. The musty smell of tired linen, the sour stink of boiled out socks, the rank sweat of men who toiled for days at the dung-plastered backsides of fly-bit bovines—it was all baked into the walls, sealed over with too many coats of paint. Ten beds, five on each side of the place were made up tight as a schoolmarm's collar, but only three of them looked recently used. Stick's bed, Lin guessed, and the Jensen Brothers.

Filtered through smudged glass, the daylight had a cold side to it leaving everything gray and forlorn. Or maybe it was the ghosts who inevitably haunted a bunkhouse. A hand of cards, forever face down and unplayed on a footlocker at the footboard of a bed. A candle, only half-spent. Toward the front of the long, narrow barracks, Lin found a coal-oil lantern and some lucifers. He found coffee, a tin pot, and a lonely cast-iron cookstove.

He resisted the urge to fire it up and cook a pot. Lord, what he wouldn't give for a cup of coffee.

To fire up the little stove with the small logs and kindling piled beside it. To stride out to the well, only forty feet away and fill the pot with fresh water. Lin cracked open the tin cannister of rich, loam dark coffee and smelled the grounds. Heaven.

He'd have cooked a pot on the spot.

If only nobody were watching the smokestack.

He didn't so much as hear the buzzing swarm of flies out front with his ears as know with some kind of warning sense of death.

Gun raised to spot beside his chin, he looked out the front window.

A more grotesque display of man flesh Lin couldn't imagine. He'd heard a few gruesome stories from the Mexican war from Oscar, but nothing in his imagination was like actually staring at five blood-soaked cadavers, the nearest one a salt lick for one of the tiger-striped barn cats.

The Jensens brothers were sprawled out next to one another, but instead of the peaceful repose of the faithful, their broken bodies lay twisted, the purple features of their face contorted by violent death. Lin caught a glimpse of a torn Bible mashed into the sod just beyond Clyde's reach.

Lin didn't know the other three men, but he supposed they were the bad owlhoots Stick had surprised with his rifle. Hornsby left his men to rot in the field, just as he had done earlier in the week. Lin's throat was bitter and hot.

He couldn't stop looking at the mangled Bible.

He thumped his chest, stomping down the rising bile there.

Lin wasn't much of a church-goer, but he figured the Jensen's wouldn't have much truck with revenge.

"Doesn't matter," he told himself. "Vengeance is for the living. It's me needs to rest in peace," he thought, "them two won't know the difference anymore."

Lin wrenched his gaze away from the grisly mess, forcing himself to pay attention to the livery barn.

The place was idle under the mid-morning sun, content with its new guest roster of horses, inside and out. Lin didn't see anything walking on two legs. Once more, he crossed his fingers, hoping Reece and Stick had made it to the grain closet.

For five more minutes, he monitored the barn. Then five additional minutes went by without a sign of humanity. All clear.

At the hacienda, everything remained quiet. The first wave of the commotion was over, but experience told him there would be more. A second wave of men, cleaning up around the ranch, picking off strays like him and Stick and Reece. For now, the initial wave of warriors were breathing normal again and taking stock of their gains. No doubt they'd be raiding the hacienda's liquor cabinet and telling tall stories.

Counting coup, as the Indians say.

Lin decided to make a run for the stables. Before the invaders got riled up again.

Once he joined Reece and Stick, they could decide on their best course of action.

Then a furtive movement caught Lin's eye. A quick dash across the yard and somebody was at the well.

It was a lone member of Cardoza's troop wearing a sweater and a wide tooled leather belt and holster. His handgun was compact, with pearl grips, and the man didn't wear a hat. Without it, and with his sparse crop of hair, his gray beard untrimmed, he looked sixty years old. As he crept along the side of the well, wary, ducking down, and looking over his shoulder, Lin got the impression he was a few years older. But he was definitely trying to avoid being seen by the house. A deserter?

The old man carried a small, familiar sack under his arm. Lin didn't have to see what was inside to recognize it. This was Lin's sack of gold, probably scavenged from his guest bedroom. The nervous way the oldster kept looking over his shoulder toward the hacienda said he was on the run. It was clear once he'd made his discovery, he set out on the prod, deserting his comrades.

Typical, and under normal circumstances Lin would have applauded the gray-hair's daring. But there was no two ways about it. As long as Lin was still on the job, the gold belonged to him.

He wasn't sharing it!

After crouching behind the block base of the well for a while, the thief chanced a peek over the rim. Sensing no pursuit, he dropped the bag at his feet and set to work retrieving some water. The pail hung from the winch at a tilted angle. Dry.

Frustrated, the old man loosed the pail down into the earth, cranked it back up fast, and applied the tin dipper to the bucket.

Apparently there wasn't any water to be had.

He loosed the bucket again, sending it down a second time.

Lin made his move, stepping out from the front door of the bunkhouse. "Toss the sack over here, *amigo*."

To his credit, the thirsty man's reaction was calm, and more calculated than Lin had expected. Rather than grab for his gun, he simply turned his head, took stock of Lin's Colt and nodded his head. With deft economy of motion, he scooped up the sack and tossed it into the air.

The load landed three feet from Lin with a metallic

plunk. If Lin didn't know the sack, with its drawstring cinched shut, was full of double-eagles, he might've thought it held iron chain links. As it was, the closer he got to the sack, the more familiar it became.

"I warn you," said the man. "I am Manuel Pierce. I am known across Rio Bravo for my gun."

Lin answered. "I am Lin Jarret. I am known for not giving a shit."

The sack was content to sit between them. Tempting as it was to run after it, Lin held his ground.

"I am keeping the gold for Cardoza," said Manuel.

"No, you're not." Lin toed the dirt, pushing the barrel of his gun gently toward his opponent. "Give me credit, senor. I've dealt with greedy men a time or two in my life. I know them. Know the look in their eye. I'm looking at a greedy man right now. You'd like nothing better than to hightail it out of here with the gold. But it don't matter a hill of beans. Because it turns out your sack belongs to me. It's payment you see, for keeping Miss Reece safe from hombres like you."

The old man's eyes darted back and forth as he licked his lips. Scheming. Plotting.

"You and me, *amigo*...we share the gold?"

Lin took a single step forward. "After everything I've been through today, I ain't in a real generous mood. How about instead, you turn around, walk away, and live to see the sunset?"

"I won't."

"You stole the sack from the house. I'm stealing it back. Real tidy bargain, considering you get to walk away with your life." Lin showed him his pearly whites. "I could'a killed you ten times already."

After another few seconds, the man spoke. His voice

was strained, but his intent was clear. "You who die," he said.

Lin took it as a prophetic long-term fortune rather than an immediate threat. Still, he kept his gun level as he approached the sack of gold. When he bent to pick it up, he kept his chin raised and never let his eyes wander.

No matter. The instant his fingers brushed the canvas, the old man pulled his revolver and fired.

Surprise! Lin had never seen a man as fast on the draw.

Fire spat and the sod erupted in front of the sack, spewing grit into Lin's face.

Thanks be—the fast ones were seldom the most accurate.

Cognizant of his single bullet, and not wanting to throw it away on a half-assed shot, Lin clutched the top of the sack. Instead of returning fire, he rolled back for the bunkhouse as two more thundering tugs of the trigger sent lead screaming past.

Inside the building, he put the cookstove between himself and the door. Not only was the damned old coyote fast with a gun, but he was fleet on his feet.

And fearless.

Already he nipped at Lin's heels.

Framed in the doorway, Manuel swung his gun hand around to land point blank on a vector line intersecting Lin's forehead. His long-nailed stub of a thumb cocked the hammer, his shrivel old finger pressed the trigger, and Lin ducked.

The bunkhouse coffee can exploded in a violent lurch as lead tore through the tin.

Lin kicked at the stack of wood beside the stove, one hand clutching the gold sack, one hand still holding his gun. He grunted, kicked again, sending up a meager shower of twigs. A couple more kicks sent logs into Manuel's path, causing him to stumble.

Lin pitched the sack of gold onto Stick's bed where the string let go and gold coins spilled onto the comforter.

The old man dove for it, his gun arm outstretched in Lin's direction.

Lin went into a crouch and his leg throbbed with the effort, but he cocked the gun and fired his last bullet at the same time another shot tore from the muzzle of Manuel's gun.

The old man folded in half and crashed into Stick's bedpost.

Lin felt hot lead blaze across the base of his neck, and the back of his skull caved in.

And then there was nothing but darkness.

CHAPTER 20

THE NEXT THING LIN KNEW WAS A CONSTANT churning pain running around the rim of his skull like a marble in a tin can, rolling, rolling, rolling. The second thing was the sense of being dragged.

The strong grip under his arms threatened to tear his shoulders apart at the socket, and the pulling, the haul of his heels against the sod, nearly yanked his blistered feet from his boots. The pain kept him from caring too much about the dragging, and the hazy cocoon he floated in tempered the pain. For long periods of time there was simply...nothing, and then he'd awake in a dreamy land-scape with one outlandish nightmare after another.

Hornsby and Tom Sinclair, Reece and Stick, they all drew him up into the clouds on a ghostly stage coach, bouncing over a washboard road. He sat atop the swaying spring seat, gently nursing the six-in hand, a half-dozen devil steeds breathing fire. Tossed up and down on a pass to purgatory, he dreamed the afterlife had an awful smell of human sweat and horse manure.

He always wanted to be stage coach driver.

Then there were moments of lucid understanding

when he saw Stick against the backdrop of horizontal slivers of light. There were moments of anguish when the pain was a purple, sweltering thing gnawing at his backbone, reaching up into the place between his ears and constricting his throat. There was day, and then there was night.

His eyes snapped open, and Lin was awake.

Staring into the face of a dead man he'd never seen before.

The skin of the corpse showed a blueish hue and the twilight made its eyes glow white. Lin caught a bittersweet stink of sour mash whiskey about it, and there was root oil in its hair. He recoiled by reflex, and his back came up against a solid wall covered in oats dust.

His nose tingled, he sneezed, and white pokers of hot agony lanced through him.

"Hush. Stay still."

A shadow leaned over in front of him. Lin tried blinking the girl into focus, but the light was too dim.

"Reece?"

Where was he?

Lin fought past the pain, struggled with the darkness. The last thing he remembered with any clarity was the faceoff with Manuel in the bunkhouse. The two guns going off at the same time. Had the old man's final bullet blinded him?

Now there was a purifying outside breeze sifting past, and the horizontal slivers of light were the dim cracks siding of the livery barn. The light was the dusk after sunset, and Lin Jarret was alive.

He breathed deep, past the smell of the corpse huddled next to him and took in as much night air as he could. His fingers slid on a rough-hewn wood floor. He brushed the girl's fingers, reached for her hand. She took it and squeezed.

With the corpse on one side, Reece on the other, and Stick hunkered down across from him between two stacks of crates, Lin made up one side of a grim quartet.

He could only assume they were tucked away in the cramped hidey hole behind the livery barn's grain closet. In the half-light he could see Reece sitting nearby. When she saw he was awake, her voice was casual and soft.

"Welcome to the land of the living."

He wanted to reply, but the marble inside his head kept spinning through its painful track, and words were hard to form with a thick, wooden tongue. "W-where..."

"Inside the livery barn," she whispered. "In the grain closet space I told you about."

Relieved, Lin felt his body relax against the sturdy wall. His leg wasn't throbbing near as bad as it had been, but his bare feet were raw inside of his boots. Sockless feet raise blisters, he thought. Nothing new. He'd been trail-bit before. If only his damned head would clear up...

"How...how long?"

"How long have we been here? About eight hours," said Reece. "But you're a relative newcomer. Stick found you about an hour ago, sneaked you in past the guards."

The guards.

"Cardoza's men are back?"

Stick nodded. "They're over beside the well right now," he said. "They can't hear us from there as long as we keep it down." He pulled a piece of beef jerky from his shirt pocket and tugged on it with clenched teeth.

The spicy aroma made Lin's stomach rumble. A good sign.

He pushed against the fog behind his eyes. "You...found me?"

"In the bunkhouse with one of the invaders. Looks like you had quite a shootout. The other fella was dead. You were not. I brought you here." Stick's words came through the wad of dry beef. "And you ain't all I found."

Stick reached into the small space behind his back and withdrew a short canvas sack. He slid it across the floor to Lin. "Gold dollars. Is this what you were fighting over?"

"It's my...uh...retainer," said Lin.

"It's his pay for watching over me," said Reece.

"Manuel wanted it, but I didn't feel inclined to share." Lin pulled the sack close to his leg and secured it there with his left hand, struggling to fit the pieces of memory together. The dreams were true. He and Manual had both fired their guns. And now it was fast Manual who was dead.

Lin addressed the corpse beside him. "But this isn't the man I shot."

"Naw, his name's Lefty," said Stick, tearing off another corner of beef. "My name for him. He sorta dropped dead —inconveniently at the last minute."

"We brought him along to make sure we wouldn't be discovered," said Reece.

"I've kinda taken a liking to him," said Stick. "He doesn't talk much. Of course, there's nothing wrong with talking. Just in our present circumstances, we need to be more careful about carrying on too much. I mean, a whisper here and there is okay, but the way I see it, with so many men around—"

Lin stated the obvious. "We've got to get out of here."

"We've been waitin' on you, pard."

In the dark, Lin's hand brushed his empty Colt. "I need to reload. The powder we brought in from Jade City the other night, the bullets..."

"Tough news," said Stick. "The freight we brought in is gone."

"Gone?" Lin rubbed his temples. "How?"

"Don't know," said Stick. "But somebody got to it."

"The Apache?"

"You can't think they are a part of this?" said Reece. "Ramon and the others would never betray us."

Lin's mind was moving fast. Judging from the tone of Reece's voice, maybe too fast. "All right, all right. But where are they? Can we count on them for help?"

Reece chewed on the question, then said, "Like Stick said before, they will stay with the cows. They probably aren't aware of this attack."

"Cardoza may go after the cattle, next," said Lin. "He's a sheep man. At some point, it figures he'd try to get the cows to market in Rio Grande City, pocket some cash before moving over his sheep."

"I don't envy him if the Apaches decide to get in his way," said Stick.

Reece couldn't agree. "Even our three *amigos nativos* will have difficulty against a wild bunch of Cardoza's tough *vaqueros*," said Reece. "In the past, I have instructed Ramone not to risk his life over the herd."

"You...*instructed?*"

"They're my cows."

"I don't think Ramone ever listens to you, anyway," said Stick. He finished off the jerky, swallowing hard.

As they conversed, the fuzzy thick wads of cotton at the corners of Lin's awareness started to dissolve. His mouth worked better to form words. "It's soon dark," he said.

With a sigh, he pressed his brow against the wall and saw the evening star on the violet horizon.

They were caught like possums in a trap. No ammunition, and nobody to help.

He needed to get a pair of socks.

For a brief time, he slept. When he woke up, Reese was still there beside him, holding his hand. "Tell me something," he said. "How did you do the dice trick?"

"What do you mean?" she whispered.

"I mean, how do you do it? How do you calculate what the hidden numbers will add up to?"

"It's not much of a calculation. Not if you know dice."

"Tell me anyway."

"On any standard cube, the opposite sides add up to seven. One and six. Two and five. Three and four. All you do is glance at the top number and subtract it from 21."

Lin smiled at the simplicity of the trick and relaxed into the wall of closet.

More stars appeared over the distant hacienda and a crowd of five or six men stood at the well, smoking.

Lin had never been good at sitting around, never content to wait.

Likewise, the men outside didn't seem overly patient.

They smoked cigarettes and talked loud, laughing like they were drunk, but there seemed to be something pestering them. Their conversation grew ever more animated. Their oaths louder and more blasphemous.

Every now and then one of the men would crank up the bucket and slosh a cup or two of water into an iron milk can. There wasn't much water to be had.

On a whim, Lin asked, "How is this place fixed for water?"

"We're not," said Stick, "and damned if I didn't just chew the saltiest beef ever."

"I had kept two crocks in here filled with water," said

Reece, "but they both cracked and drained out. I was a fool not to check on them."

"Maybe the cold weather had something to do with the crocks breaking," said Stick.

Even as she said it, the temperature around them seemed to drop. But Lin pressed on.

"I wasn't talking about how the three of us were stocked for water here in the closet," he said. "I was thinking more along the lines of the rancho itself. The well out there."

The crowd around the well was more animated now. One of Hornsby's boys was jittery, practically jumping up and down, and another was pounding his fist on the edge of the well casing.

"I've been watching the well all day," said Lin. "Since we first emerged from the tunnel. It's got me thinking."

"Got me thirsty," said Stick.

"When I first met you, remember what you said? You said to understand the valley, a man needs to understand the Tejano."

"Sure, but so what? You better explain it to me."

"It reminded me of something my uncle told me once. He said, to understand the west, you need to understand water." Lin turned to Reece. "How many gallons a day is your well good for?"

She told him. "It's fed by the same springs feeding the branch off the little Carlito." Then: "The last week or two it's been decreasing in volume. Maybe a crack in the bedrock."

"Hornsby and Cardoza brought in close to 30 men. And an equal number of horses, plus a wagon team. I assume the horses have been watered?"

"I don't think so," said Stick. "Cardoza brought a few

barrels of water along, and the men seem to have them emptied."

"Figure they've still got nineteen or twenty men to occupy the place," said Lin. He spoke to Reece. "You're good with numbers. You do the math."

She already had. "Our well won't produce near enough water to sustain an occupying force."

"Not even for another day," agreed Stick. "They'll have to carry their barrels to the Carlito at some point to fill them. Nobody's going to be happy."

Lin recalled the lean inventory he'd experienced. "Figure they're in for a disappointment when it comes to grub as well."

"I hope they like chicken, because chicken's about all there is," said Reece.

"You told me you weren't leaving," said Lin. "You wanted to stay."

"I won't be driven from my own home. I will fight."

Lin nodded with understanding. His headache was fading, he was thinking clear. "I've got a feeling Cardoza's men aren't nearly as loyal."

CHAPTER 21

THE EVENING WASN'T GOING WELL FOR DUB HORNSBY.

The night ahead promised disaster.

Cardoza's men, disciplined and mature on the eve of battle, were making up for it tonight at the Sinclair hacienda.

Hornsby had stopped two fights and was on his way behind the ranch house to break up another. Bellows of rage mixed with giddy, mocking voices of encouragement told him all he needed to know. He rounded the house to the clatter of broken crockery and the lantern-lit spectacle of two men, stripped to their waists, circling each other with knives.

One of the men was part of Hornsby's clan, an imbecile called Travis who wore a flat-brimmed kepi. The other's name was Phillip, one of Cardoza's troop. They were both bleary eyed drunk, and their cheeks twisted in rage as they sputtered profanities at each other.

"*Cerdoooo*..." hissed Phillip. "*Gran cerdo*."

Travis lunged with his blade, missed, and pinwheeled into a trio of enthused spectators. The friendly wall of arms pushed him back into the fight, "Go get 'im, boy."

Travis stumbled sideways into Phillip's wild haymaker, catching the fist on his shoulder, only to rebound into a solid stance. A lucky uppercut put Phillip back on his heels.

Again, the two men squared off.

Hornsby had seen enough. He pulled his sidearm and fired a shot into the air.

It was the only way to get their attention.

"You boys got nothing better to do than fight, I'll give you some work," said Hornsby. "You," he pointed at the combatants, "and you." "Get the water wagon and take it out to the Carlito. Fill a couple barrels with water for morning. You wanna fight, do it away from the house. But I'm warning you...if you don't both come back, the one of you who does, I will personally turn over to Mister Cardoza."

The men could barely contain their rage. Phillip's closed mouth moved like he was chewing or maybe biting off mad protests. Travis pulled his kepi down over his eyes and spit on the ground in front of Hornsby and turned his back to him. The onlookers cheered.

A definite sense of mutiny filled the evening air.

The afternoon had been a revelry of song and celebration for a battalion of twenty men. They had taken turns watching the horses. Traded off getting drunk and playing card games. They told jokes, and—after finding a violin—made a lame attempt at song.

Hours later, they could barely stand to be in the same room with each other.

When they cracked open the larder outside in the spring kitchen, they had discovered six bottles of mulberry wine, a half-empty bottle of whiskey and a bulb of thick, strong liqueur with smells reminiscent of three-month-old underwear. Now, as the sun slumped below the horizon, it was all gone.

Every last drop had trickled away down the hedonistic gullet of one man or another.

Leaving nothing but water to drink. And precious little.

The men were bored. And hungry. And thirsty.

Hornsby experienced a moment of grim satisfaction. He'd warned Cardoza about these idiots.

Amidst a continued chorus of atta'boys and back slaps from their comrades, Travis and Phillip broke Hornsby's gaze and shuffled away around toward the wagon at the side of the house. A wave of relief washed over Hornsby as he watched them crawl onto the wagon and set out for the river.

Next time it wouldn't go as well. Next time, there would be open betrayal.

He went to Sinclair's den where Cardoza sat behind the desk.

"If only there were more to eat," said Cardoza when Hornsby walked in. "What kind of house is this? I'm surprised at Sanchez. I thought he kept a better pantry?"

All afternoon, two of the men had butchered and fried chickens as fast as they could clean them. The air inside the house was thick with the smell of hot grease and burnt feathers.

But it hadn't been enough. Now all the birds were gone.

And without birds, there would be no more fresh eggs.

"I thought Sanchez brought up some supplies from the livery barn for us?" said Cardoza.

Hornsby smirked. "Black powder, some lead balls. A bit of cornmeal." He motioned toward the stash in the corner of the room. "We'll have cornbread for breakfast." Then added, "If somebody makes it."

Marko appeared in the office. The jerked a thumb over his shoulder. "I was in the privy taking care of business. Next thing I know the boys are all riled up. What went on out there?"

"Tell you later," said Hornsby.

"We were discussing the lack of edibles," said Cardoza.

"We can always make a stew from what's left of the chicken bones," said Marko. "Anyway, stew's about all we're gonna get. I took the outside shed apart. We've got a scrap of salt pork. Nothing else."

"Nothing more to drink?" said Cardoza.

"Nope." For once, the big red-head's face was devoid of its usually smug arrogance.

Hornsby knew what Marko was thinking.

Another hour, maybe two, and the remainder of the men would ride back to Jade City, surrendering all they had gained today.

After seizing the place from Sinclair, the plan was to push on to the next ranch up the line. And the next. And the next.

Now, they were stopped before they even got started.

With the daughter and the Ranger still out there, somewhere.

"There's been no sign of the Sinclair girl?" said Cardoza. "You've searched for her?"

Marko's face showed the frustration he obviously felt. "Some men just return from the search," he said. "All they found was one of our men, Manuel, dead in the bunkhouse with signs of some kind of struggle. But nothing else. No Ranger. No girl."

"Old Manuel...tch." Cardoza clicked his tongue with

sympathy. "I'm not surprised to have lost a few soldiers, but still..." he said. Then he leaned back in his chair. He was visibly irritated, his fingers pressed together in a steeple. His jaw twitched and the veins at his temples pulsed.

Hornsby had to admit—he enjoyed the sight.

Cardoza wasn't used to being foiled.

He assumed an early morning attack would capture the entire family in one fell swoop. He assumed the Rancho de Jada would be well stocked, and he refused to carry anything along, other than water, even when Hornsby had suggested it.

He knew he'd need water because Hornsby and Marko had dammed up the Little Carlito upstream. But he scrimped because water was heavy and hadn't carried along enough, and his lazy men wouldn't volunteer to fetch any from the river.

Amateur mistakes, thought Hornsby, but not entirely out of character.

Cardoza was one of those men who thought as long as he wore the right clothes and trimmed his hair in the current fashion, courted the most powerful friends and commanded men beneath him, all of life would magically line up. Cardoza always knew fate would work with him and not against him.

Tonight, he was momentarily perplexed by the unexpected turn of events.

But he wasn't altogether indecisive.

He stood up behind the desk and patted the pocket of his jacket. "With victory in our grasp, I shall retire to Jade City and deliver these legal documents to my attorney at the Muleskinner."

"I expected as much," said Hornsby.

Safe in town, Cardoza could eat and drink his fill

while Morse flattered him. Messengers on horseback could ride to Cortina with word of the day's conquest, and Cardoza could begin his life as heir apparent to this side of the Rio Grande.

What Cardoza didn't seem to yet understand, is total victory still relied completely on his men.

As long as the men held their positions here, Rancho de Jada was secure. But if they went rogue, if they decided on a different course of action, there was nothing Hornsby or his boss could do to stop them.

Hornsby joined Cardoza at the door. "I'll go with you," he said.

Together, they walked outside and around to the rear of the house where Hornsby had found the fighting men. The patio was littered with broken glass. Sand and sod had been kicked across the inlaid stones, and a nearby chair was turned over.

Cardoza walked into the darkness and retrieved his tall horse. Holding the bridle in hand, he appeared thoughtful and serene. Not the face of a conquering hero, thought Hornsby. The ramrod could only imagine what was going on inside Cardoza's mind. There was no way to read through the stoic face.

"I'd like you to stay here at the ranch," said Cardoza.

"There's no reason."

Cardoza put a hand to Hornsby's shoulder and petitioned his loyalty. "There's every reason for you to do it," he said. "I'm not asking you for myself, Dub. I'm asking you for the men. For the sake of the cause. We need to take a long-term view of these things. These men are going to need your good example tonight. They'll need to see your strong arm at the plow."

"Marko can take care of the men," said Hornsby.

"He's always bucking for a leadership position of some kind. I'll ride back out first thing tomorrow morning."

Cardoza lowered his voice and led Hornsby back around to the front of the house. Lantern light spilled through the windows. They could hear a trickle of cursing and restless laughter from the men.

"Until we have the daughter and the Texas Ranger, we need a strong presence out here, Dub. We need to tighten the noose."

Hornsby tried one final appeal. "Give me an hour. I'll take some men. We'll find Jarret and the girl."

Cardoza denied him. "Stay the night, Dub. Hunt this couple down at your leisure. Our man will be coming for the cattle in the morning. You need to be here when he arrives with his team of vaqueros."

"What time's he coming?"

"He will be here with the sunrise. You'll need to ride out to Defilement with him. Then, as you suggested, Marko can watch over the men here."

"I'd rather ride with you. Now."

"I know, Dub. But right now, your service is more important than your companionship."

There it was again. Your service. Not your friendship. Not your comradery.

Service.

Hornsby held his tongue.

Cardoza grinned. "Haven't we always faced adversity together?"

A glass bottle shattered in the other room, and somebody yelled. The drunken shout was returned and a fight seemed imminent.

Hornsby felt a cold river of sweat drip down his back. By morning the men would rip the hacienda apart.

And him too.

"If I stay, we hunt for the Ranger and the girl tonight. It will give the men something to do," said Hornsby. It was the only thing possible to keep the men at bay, but he didn't think it would be enough.

"Also," said Hornsby, "as soon as you hit town, you send a rider back out here with a wagon full of supplies. Take 'em from the old man's store."

"Of course I will," said Cardoza.

"Make sure there's plenty of rye."

"There will be."

"And the girl? What do you want us to do if we find her?"

Cardoza waved his hand, giving his assent. "If it's the kind of distraction the men need, then by all means, let them do what they will with her." Cardoza's voice was husky and low. "I'm sure she would be a most amusing way for them to spend the night."

Dub's mouth was dry as he thought about the night ahead. He didn't have much hope they'd find Jarret or the girl. If those two knew what was good for them, they'd be miles away by now.

"I'll bid you good-night, then," said Cardoza.

Hornsby watched as his boss got comfortable in the saddle and cantered away, down past the bunkhouse and livery barn.

Then Hornsby turned back to the house. He looked through the front window and into the parlor where Marko fidgeted close to the door.

Hornsby remembered the redhead's lust for Reece Sinclair.

He went to the house and called Marko out.

"I sent Travis and one of the Mexicans off to the river for water. Run catch up with them. After you've filled the barrels, I want you, personally, to search for girl."

Marko couldn't have been more pleased. "Right away," he said, ducking into night.

If only the rest of the men could be so easily placated.

"Aye, yi-yi-yi," came a cry from the far end of the house together with the sound of more broken glass.

And what if Marko found the girl? If he brought her back here, what then?

Then, if necessary, Dub Hornsby would saddle up his own horse and ride the hell out of here himself.

Let the wolves tear the girl, and each other, apart.

———

LIN WATCHED as a water wagon trundled past, one man steering the horses, another in back, propped up by three barrels. A short time later, Cardoza himself rode away from the house on a lively horse trotting past the livery barn.

When there was silence, Lin carefully slipped out of the grain closet.

One sleepy guard sat cross legged on the ground with his back to the alleyway, his cheek resting on his chin. Lin padded up behind him and dropped the butt of his gun against the back of the man's skull.

Whistling an all-clear, Lin opened his bay's pen and led his horse out. He had a blanket and saddle on the horse in no time, but Hornsby's stallions made a fuss at his presence. It seemed like Reece and Stick took an eternity to saddle up.

"Let's go, let's go," said Lin, not trying too hard to mask his impatience.

Once the three riders were secure, Lin rode down the line of square stalls inside and out to the gated fences.

One by one, he opened the pens holding Hornsby's Diablo Flats steeds.

At first the animals held back, ears pinned back, blowing and hesitant.

Then, as if a signal had been given, there was no holding back the cavvy of black horses.

Lin warned Reece and Stick clear of the whirlwind.

There was nothing they could do but follow the charge in a backwash of thudding hooves and churned up earth.

Eventually, the three caught up and began riding herd.

"Get that bangtail in line," said Reece, and Stick grabbed for the bridle, led one dark horse in next to his bay, then another.

The three of them sat high on their mounts, tall in the saddle, but twisting to the left and right, keeping track of the enemy horses. Atop his favorite bay, Lin finally felt more in control.

Even if he was wearing a dead man's pair of socks.

Lefty didn't mind, he told himself, still sitting upright and glassy-eyed back in the hidden room of the grain closet.

Cardoza's string of black beauties slowed as they moved away from the ranch and became more orderly—a testament to both Reece and Stick's natural ability with the four-legged beasts. He had to give himself some credit as well. Wrangling close to three dozen steeds over territory unfamiliar to them wasn't an easy thing to accomplish if the horses didn't want to go.

Especially in the dead of night.

Fortunately, he, Reece and Stick led the critters in the direction of the Little Carlito, and the thirsty devils smelled water.

"Without horses, those men in the house are stuck," said Lin. "It's a two hour walk to Jade City."

"With no water to drink until they hit the river," Stick reminded him.

"I wish I could see the look on Dub Hornsby's face when he realizes he has to walk to town," said Stick.

"His gut is half the size of San Antonio. He'll never make it," said Lin.

Together they rode with the stallions, galloping up and down the line, steering the ebony column toward the river's fork in the direction of the newly refurbished cow corral. The night was clear, if colder than Lin liked, and the crease in his scalp where Manuel's bullet parted his hair was still sore. As was his leg. And his blistered feet.

Who would have thought keeping tabs on an heiress would get him all banged up?

Before long all of the horses were drinking in the shallow waters of the Little Carlito and there was time to smoke a cigarette.

"Once they quench their thirst, we'll house them in the pens we repaired yesterday," said Reece. "There's a stack of hay there."

"Or we could just let them run wild," said Stick.

"I'd rather not risk them coming back to the ranch," said Lin. "Cardoza and Hornsby wanted to occupy Rancho de Jada. Let's give them what they asked for."

"Only until I return," said Reece. "Then I'll kill them with my bare hands."

Lin took a lungful of smoke and let it out slow. "Yeah...about this talk of killing."

Reece gave him a curious look.

"Let's walk," he said, and took her by the hand.

CHAPTER 22

UNDER A QUILT OF SHIMMERING STARS, LIN SCUFFLED along the banks of the Carlito, listening to the night sounds of the stallions quenching their thirst, the wail of a coyote in the distance. On such a clear Texas night, it was easy to believe all his problems were pretend. All he had to do was breathe the crisp air, scented as it was with cypress leaves and hints of sage, listen to the soft footsteps, the easy breathing of the girl by his side...

If he closed his eyes, he could almost forget about Tom Sinclair, probably murdered in his own hacienda, and now his killers drank his wine and ate his food. Could almost imagine he had never seen the Jensen brothers splayed out in scarlet puddles mud.

He could just about ignore the fact somebody had stolen the black powder and ammunition he'd helped bring from the mercantile earlier in the week.

The one thing he couldn't forget was the job he'd been hired to perform.

"About this talk of killing," he said.

Reece seemed to sense the disapproval in his voice

and let his hand drop away from hers. "Call it revenge," she said. "You know as well as I do my father is dead."

"Maybe, maybe not." Lin considered building another cigarette before discarding the impulse. He'd smoked far too much since coming to Rancho de Jada.

"Either way, I know all about revenge," said Lin. "The recipient pays the price, fair enough. But it's a burden to the avenger, too. I don't want to see you go through such horror."

She kept her distance as he strolled up to a tall tree.

"How do you know so much?"

Lin hooked his arm around a low branch. He didn't like talking about himself. When he did, it came out stilted and felt awkward.

But there was no other way to explain it.

"After my parents died, I was on my own, working at a sawmill. A young woman my age was killed." He'd never talked about that day with anybody, not even his uncle.

With Reese, talking felt natural, almost obligatory.

Besides, it was necessary to prove his point.

"She was coming to see a man I worked with. These two had been sparkin' a while, and the gal had been fortunate enough to land a half-bushel of shiny new red apples. She was bringing a sample to her beau. Crossing the street from the mercantile."

Lin paused, pulling his thoughts into line as a wave of emotion washed over him. Finally he told her, "A drunken teamster with a wild four in hand rounded the corner, came straight at her. The horses were out of control, the wagon nearly tipping over. She was in the middle of the street. She..." He clenched his fist against the bark of the tree. "She dropped the apple."

For a full minute Reece didn't say anything. Then she said, "She was killed, wasn't she?"

Lin said she was. "She was busted up inside. It took her four days to die."

"I suppose now you're going to tell me how her beau wanted revenge. How it weighed on him night and day until he finally took it, only to realize it didn't bring back the dead?" Reece's tone of voice was still defiant. "Save it, Ranger. I've heard it before."

Lin watched as a shooting star curved down from space then winked out low over the far horizon. "You bet he wanted revenge. Hell, we all did. Nothing I would've liked better than to see the old drunk hang."

"What happened?"

Lin spread his hands and shook his head. "Nothing happened," he said. "The old man stayed a single night in jail and sobered up the next morning. He blubbered out a string of apologies to the kindly old sheriff who let him cross the street for a cup of coffee in the diner. Naturally, the old teamster never arrived at the diner. Instead, he very promptly, and very efficiently, disappeared forever."

"Your friend never found him?"

"Nobody ever did," said Lin. "But searching for the old boy consumed my friend. He couldn't forgive. And he couldn't forget. Every day for more than year he fretted and fussed and talked non-stop about nothing else. He was like a pot constantly on the boil. He changed from being good at this job to become a hazard to everyone around him. He went from being a big, strapping boy, to a shrunken husk."

"It wouldn't happen to me," said Reece.

"The thing is, gal—once you set foot on the vengeance trail, I don't think it's up to you anymore." He tried to find the words. "It's almost like a fever."

"The difference is your friend didn't ever find his man. I know where Hornsby and Cardoza live."

"Reece, honey, it won't make any difference."

She flinched as if struck and stepped away from him, tense and on guard. Her voice hissed like a snake. "Don't you ever *Reece-honey*, me you bastard."

Immediately taken aback, Lin stood up straight. "Hey, what'd I say?"

"What did you say? I'll tell you what you said. Back at the corral last Wednesday, when I had Dub Hornsby dead to rights in the iron sites of your rifle, you said, *Let it go for now*."

"Had you shot him, it would've been murder."

"Nobody would have been the wiser, and we'd be better off now."

"I'd have been the wiser—if I lived to reckon it. You do understand, it might've been us murdered. You might've been right about Hornsby's men being short on ammunition, but they still outgunned us."

Reece pulled at the braid behind her neck until her hair shook loose around her shoulders. "You told me a story, let me tell you one."

Lin pulled his tobacco pouch from his shirt pocket.

One more cigarette couldn't hurt.

"I'm listening," he said.

Reece hugged her arms around herself and looked at the moon for inspiration.

"When I was eleven years old," she said, "we had a cat on the ranch named Otter. He'd started out as a gray, tiger-striped kitten living in haystack outside the livery barn, but soon grew to be a sassy, big Tom."

"How'd he come by his name?"

"One day at the little river, my dad saw him from a distance lounging on the bank all stretched out, long and sleek."

"Like an otter," said Lin.

"Like an otter. If he'd stayed down at the river, or gone on to live someplace else, everything would've been fine. But he didn't. He lived on the ranch. He stayed around the livery barn with the other cats."

Lin slipped the rolling paper in his mouth, wetting it and twisting the ends to hold it tight. Then he struck a match on his boot. "Otter was a pet."

"A pet is precisely what he was *not*," said Reese. "He was wild and ornery. He dominated all the other barn cats, making a fuss, picking fights at all hours of the night. He especially liked to fight with a friendly white Tom whose name was Catfish. Finally, Dad decided to take care of Otter, to shoot him."

"Sounds like Otter asked for it."

"But I was eleven years old, you see."

"And you didn't want your dad to kill off the kitty."

"I did not."

"Even though he was tearing up the other cats."

"I caught Dad walking toward the livery with his rifle one morning, and I stopped him. At first he wouldn't hear me. But I begged him not to hurt Otter. I cried and pleaded."

"What happened?"

"Dad gave in. He put his arms around me and praised my sense of charity." Her laugh was cold and ironic. "He told me he was proud of my gentle heart. Two months later we had a fresh litter of kittens from Catfish and a gray female."

Lin sucked in the smoke, watched the ember flare.

He let her take her time.

He had a pretty good idea where the story was going.

"I must tell you, Ranger, I loved those little kittens.

There were four of them, two gray tigers and two were pure white. The mother was a tiger like Otter, but she had these two little snowflakes with blue eyes."

"A rare blend," said Lin.

"I loved those two white kittens. They were…They were so cute. So…innocent." Her voice caught in her throat. "One day I went down to the barn with a bottle of milk for them. When they didn't come running out to meet me…"

"You knew something was wrong."

"I did," she nodded, and Lin could see her tears in the moonlight. "I did, and I looked everywhere."

"And when you found them?"

"It was too late. And Otter was there, licking the blood on his lips, and this feral, evil glare in his eyes. He looked so…satisfied…with himself."

Lin pinched his cigarette between thumb and forefinger.

"Sure must've been hard for you, gal."

"It's nature's way sometimes." She shrugged. "Toms can be cruel." Then she turned her face up into the moonlight. "He killed four more cats, including the other two kittens, before Dad finally put him down."

"Some cats are just mean to the core."

"And some people are the same way," said Reece, brushing the tears from her eyes. "Do you understand?"

"I'm not sure."

"If I wouldn't have interfered the first time, if I would've gone ahead and not interfered, Dad would've killed Otter early on. All those other cats would've been saved."

"People aren't all-knowing," said Lin. "We can't fore-tell the future."

"My dad could. He knew from experience Otter was a menace. By not killing him when he had the chance, he had a hand in those future tragedies."

"Maybe."

"No maybe about it. Let me ask you, what would have happened if he never would've shot Otter?"

"I suppose Otter would've lived to be a fat old cat."

"And he would've killed how many more kittens?"

She had Lin there.

"A man's not a cat," he said.

"If we let Cardoza and Hornsby go, they'll go on killing. Not today, necessarily. Maybe not tomorrow. But eventually they will, because it's what they know. Just like Otter, it's in their nature."

"I can't argue with you."

"Some men can't live without hurting others. Without *enslaving* others. Some men only exist to subjugate other people to their will because it makes them feel powerful. And they enjoy watching other people bend."

Lin saw what she was driving at.

"And I can't live with it," said Reece. "When bad things happen to the other families on the Rio Grande because I failed to act, I won't be able to live with myself."

"Hellbenders," said Lin. Then he made a guess. "Hellbenders is you. It's you started the group."

"There is no group," said Reece. "There's just me."

A few of the horses were restless at the water. It was time to move them on.

"And maybe you," she said. "Will you help me?"

Lin thought about the eleven year old Reece finding her beloved kittens murdered on a sunny, Sunday morning.

"Yes," he said. "I'll help you."

"Will you help me kill them?"

"Yes," he said, flicking his cigarette into the water. "I'll help you kill them."

CHAPTER 23

MICAH LEMAY WOKE UP IN THE DARK OF THE mercantile building. The street in front of the store was quiet, and there were only one or two lights showing in the buildings on main street. Hunkered down in the back pantry, he felt safe for the first time in more days than he cared to remember. He felt safe for the first time in years.

Sleep had wrapped its arms around him like his grandma's heavy quilt, and he'd passed the late afternoon and evening in a dreamless slumber.

Then the memory of the overheard boardwalk conversation came back to him. The Sinclair ranch was under new management. Reece Sinclair might be gone. Any safe passage she could offer in Mexico would disappear with her.

He had to get to the ranch, but first he had to load up on supplies. Judging from the peaceful nature of the slumbering, moonlit town, there would be no better time to do it. He looked around the store, inspecting each barrel, reading the labels of every crate. He was careful not to make any noise.

Practiced determination kept him on the job, judiciously choosing the most pragmatic defenses, the most utilitarian gear. He picked up a big bore English shotgun, a pair of Remington revolvers, percussion caps and lead balls to fit, and four small barrels of black powder. He took towels and rope to use for tourniquets and bandages. He stashed sugar candy and dried fruit in his pockets. Finally, he chose between a ten pound sack of coffee and a quart of corn-mash whiskey.

He took the coffee.

After Micah had gathered his stockpile at the mercantile back door, he swept out into the night after his horse and buggy. Finding the rig just where he'd left it, he made a wide arc around the edge of Jade City and came in quick and silent. As if sensing the surreptitious nature of their mission, his sweet horse kept her head down and her tread light. It was almost like she was walking tip-toe, thought Micah, and the springs and bearings of the wagon were well-oiled so there was no problem there.

In Emberville, the station-master had apologized for the grulla mare, calling her a two-reign horse, suggesting she wasn't yet ready for the bridle, foreshadowing trouble for Micah's buckboard journey. But nothing could've been farther from the truth. The critter had been steadfast and obedient, the perfect companion on a fugitive's lonely flight.

Micah had almost made it to the back side of the mercantile when a light came on at a house across the street, and the sound of raucous laughter made his blood freeze. He pulled up tight on the reins and prayed the wagon didn't rattle in its quick stop. Parked in the open, less than a stone's throw from the store, Micah knew he and the wagon were clearly visible if the residents of the little apartment looked outside.

More laughing. A woman's giggle. Flirtatious and dirty.

Then Micah heard a man's voice. "How about a little bit more," he said. Mean sounding, lusty and hard. "Get back to the bed, and I'll give it to you."

The light went out in the window, but Micah dared not move. For almost five minutes he held his ground, measuring his breath, keeping to his prayers. The voices didn't return, and after another short wait, he coaxed the horse over to the rear entrance of the mercantile.

His shirt and hatband alike were soaked with sweat.

The voice he'd heard belonged to the man from the boardwalk. The one who was coming for the Sinclair cattle the next morning.

―――――

A FRAGMENTED SERIES of clouds played hide and seek with the moon, and Micah was glad to have a coal oil travel lantern to drive by. The open Texas grassland passed by in orange flickers and shadow. The close encounter in Jade City left him nervous and on edge. The sooner he reached the Little Carlito River, the better.

At least the trail away from the upper river was clear, he told himself. When the moon appeared, the wide open land offered a view of the far horizon's thorny bosquecillo―a scar of darkness across a swash of twinkling of stars. Those brushy trees marked the little river and the way to Rancho de Jada.

He couldn't get there soon enough to satisfy him. Still, he didn't dare push the grulla too hard. She'd lugged him and the wagon halfway across Texas in less than a week's time. He fought against impatience with remembered psalms, but they only left him more jangled.

The valley of the shadow of death.

Valley of shadow. Shadow of death.

Tonight, scripture was not a comfort.

He kept the big bore English gun across his lap and thanked God for the lantern.

When he emerged from the trees, the Little Carlito stretched ahead and to the left, and he steered the buckboard along the shallow bend. He was surprised to find the creek nearly dry with only a pittance of water coursing along its lumpy floor.

Odd.

The season had been unusually wet.

The horse balked a bit then, unsure of its footing. She flung her head back, and her nostrils flared. Did she smell danger?

If so, there was nothing in the night air Micah could detect.

She was a good horse, but she was tired.

And despite his day-long sleep, Micah was, too.

Which might have been why he didn't see the strange wagon with its butt end hanging precariously off the bank of the Little Carlito until he was forced to steer around it. Showing their surprise at Micah's arrival, the twin ebony steeds on the bigger box-spring rig pulled against the wagon's brake, snorting and blowing.

Micah reigned in just past the big freighter as a blob of walking paste with sagging britches and a kepi flat-billed cap stumbled out around front.

The big wagon's team of animals was sleek and powerful. Round and shirtless, the man who shushed them was not. After he cursed the horses, he started complaining about the river.

"There ain't no damn water here, you idiot. You got us on the wrong side of the dirt. I ought to—"

When the man saw Micah, he tugged a gun from his waistband more from instinct than reasoned thought. He closed one eye and fired.

The muzzle popped with sparks, and Micah heard the bullet slap the side of his wagon.

He only had a second to react, and the shotgun on his lap was primed and ready to fire. Without wasting a move, Micah jerked the barrel around and triggered off the powder.

The explosion of shot plowed into the pasty man's chest, putting him flat on the ground without grunt or groan, and the horses beside him pitched to the left and right. Fighting against the resistance of the heavy freighter behind them, they blew through wide open nostrils and their rolling eyes reflected the moon.

Micah's grulla reacted to the blast in similar fashion, making a mad sideways lunge, cranking the high front wheels of the buckboard around. The steel of the wheels dug at the edge of the wagon box, threatening a pile up.

"Whoa, whoa," said Micah. "Whoa, girl." But before he could straighten things out, fresh gunfire returned to split the air.

"Lord-a-mercy," he said, ducking down flat to the bench, while at the same time whipping the reins in a frantic attempt to drive the horse clockwise away from the scene.

Instead of distancing itself from the tumult, the scared, confused critter pulled around in the opposite direction, taking Micah back toward the source of the shooting.

Another shot whizzed past, and rather than roll straight into hell, Micah leapt from the wagon with both hands holding tight to the shotgun. He slammed into the ground hard enough to lose his wind, and the buckboard rolled on past and away.

He came quickly to his knees, struggled to rise. "Damn the luck. And damn the no-good son-of-a-bitch who started it." The oaths rolled off his tongue and pushed him on. "Don't you give up, now," he told himself. "Don't you by-God-give up."

Micah got his feet under him in time to see another man come toward him from the creek bank, this one taller than the first. This one was a Mexican with a wide sombrero. Again, he was shirtless but this one's hairless chest was a trail map of puffy scars. Instead of a gun, the attacker held a long knife, it's well-honed, steel blade glinting in the moonlight.

Micah held the shotgun out between them, poking the muzzle toward the man. "I ain't got no fight with you," he said.

"Maybe not. But maybe I got a fight with you, *chico*."

Micah tightened his grip on the shotgun, risked a glance at the dead man on the ground nearby. "That was self-defense, mister. You can't blame me."

"Oh, you did me a favor there," he said with a jerk of his chin.

The way the man kept coming, the way he kept running his knife back and forth through the air as if over an invisible whetstone, Micah sensed the truth. The man had witnessed the shotgun blast. He knew Micah's gun was empty.

"I don't understand. If I did you a favor, why should we fight?"

"Because I've got to fight with everybody." The Mexican sneered. "It's in my nature."

"If I did you a favor, you ought to repay me," said Micah. "Only the fair thing to do."

"I'll repay you by splitting your guts wide open."

The Mexican feinted, then came in with a straight jab, easily deflected off the shotgun's steel. Micah secured his grip, jammed the wood stock into his attacker's mouth, heard the crunch of bone and backed away fast.

The Mexican was staggered, but not out, and his white teeth glowed in orange like a circus jester. Instead of backing off, he roared with pain and rage, pressing the attack.

Micah crouched into a solid defense, planting his heavy boots on solid ground, griping the shotgun like a club. His attacker came in fast like a wild dog, whipping his knife in and out, trying to nip at Micah's defense.

They circled three times, and each time the Mexican lunged, Micah parried. Each swipe of the blade bought only the night air. Truth be told, the Mexican wasn't much of a fighter. Clumsy with the knife, his moves were derivative and weak.

He imagined himself a fighting man but was far from it.

"You think because you're bigger than me, you will win," said the Mexican. "You think maybe because of your skin color, I'm scared of you. Nobody scares Phillip Juarez."

"Mister, the only thing I think is you've had too much old fire water to drink." The damn skunk's breath could curl the toes of a honey badger, and the longer they scuffled, the more winded the Mexican got.

"I've killed bigger men than you."

"Maybe it's not something a Christian man ought not to brag on," said Micah.

Juarez rushed in again, and Micah cranked his right arm forward, mashing the butt of the gun into his attacker's lips. And again—double tap—and a front tooth snapped.

Micah followed the success of his blow with another to the chin, and once Juarez was reeling, he kicked out with his boot, catching him behind the knee.

Juarez went over backwards, landed hard, bounced back into a hunched over stance.

"Who says I'm a Christian man?" he said.

Micah had to admit it. "You've got a point."

Juarez was bleeding hard now from the mouth, and he wiped his chin with the back of his hand. "I ain't afraid of you."

"You've already said as much."

With a mad scream Juarez raised the knife over his head and sprinted forward.

Micah ducked away from the blade and smacked the Mexican flat on the side of the head with the gunstock.

Juarez hit the ground with a whoosh of sour breath and Micah stood over top of him, waiting for him to flinch. Seconds ticked by.

Juarez was out like a candle.

Micah scratched his ear. "Told you we had no reason to fight," he said.

"Sounds good to me, *amigo*," said a rough voice coming up from the river back behind him. "But how's-about you go ahead and drop your scattergun anyway?"

Micah heard the warning. Heard the tell-tale click of a hammer being pulled back.

Up until now, he'd been lucky.

He let go of the gun. Watched it land with a clatter next to Juarez.

It seemed his luck had just run out.

CHAPTER 24

AFTER THEIR CONVERSATION, LIN AND REECE HELPED Stick round up the horses and drive them the short distance to the corrals. The bunch was compliant enough, and before long all of them were safe behind the fences, nosing through the hay.

Lin secured the final gate pin and pushed back the brim of his hat. The night air was cool, but he was sweating. "We'll need to get back out here in the morning to take care of 'em. For tonight, they should be all right."

"What now?" said Stick. "How are you fixin' to pry those owlhoots out of the house? It's gonna be quite a chore without cap or ball. No powder, neither. Nothing to use but rocks." He raised his eyebrows. "But on the plus side, I guess we're still carrying the sack of gold from the bunkhouse. Maybe we should try and buy those devils off, Lin? Hell, I've seen wilder plans in my time. There was this once when I was around 14 years-old, when—"

"Okay, Stick...okay," said Lin, gently tamping down his fire. "We'll...think of something."

Lin pulled his hat down tight and was about to mount up when a gunshot punched through the night air nearby, followed immediately by another. He removed his foot from the stirrup and stood quietly beside the bay, listening to the echoes die away.

"Who the heck?" said Stick.

"Downriver a way, back toward the place," said Reece.

"Let's go see," said Stick.

"I'll go see," said Lin. "You two stay here."

"Horse apples," said Stick. "Last time we split up, you 'bout got your head blown off."

"Stick's got a good point," said Reece.

Lin knew when he was licked.

"Okay but stay back a ways. Go slow."

The moon continued to guide the three of them as they crept along the banks of the Little Carlito, moving in the direction of the gunfire. Occasional clouds obscured their view, forcing them to vary the speed of the progress.

Like the crevice where they tended to the horses, the water here was deep Lin recognized a wide spot in the road as the place where they would normally burr away from the trail when traveling to the hacienda.

"I'm in unfamiliar territory," he said.

"The course of the river dries up a great deal farther along," Stick whispered.

"Something's got to be damming up the Carlito," said Reece. "I'll bet it's why our well's belly up, too."

"That's the way I figure it," said Lin. "Didn't your dad ever ride out to look into it?"

"It just got to the point we noticed a few days ago." Reece's voice cracked. "There have been many things to get done each day. Hornsby's kept us busy with guerilla attacks, and it's been a strain trying to keep up with everything."

"The old spring ebbs and flows," said Stick. "The little river, too. I hadn't really figured on a dam."

"If the river's dammed up, Hornsby's behind it," said Lin.

They continued on, pressing through the tall grass and thistles, ducking the low branches of thorn trees, lead trees, and ash. Around a narrow bend, they discovered a wide, flat basin. The river current was practically non-existent here and the still water was stale with whiffs of rotting moss and rancid mud. A barrier wall of mud and rock heaved up on the water's far side, fortified with uprooted cedars and intertwined hardwood branches.

Lin forged through stands of sticky weed and butterfly leaf to the edge of the dam where the channel narrowed to a trickle and the Little Carlito befitted its name more than ever. Reece came up behind him. "The sons-of-bitches," she said.

"Hell of a *presa* to be built in such a short time," said Lin. "It's not permanent, of course. There's no decent foundation, and those few branches won't help much once the pressure builds up a little more." He pointed out the flaws as he spoke. "Still and all, it's a hell of a job."

"I didn't take you for an engineer," said Reece.

"You smell horses?" said Lin.

Reece rubbed her nose with vigor. "After bringing in Cardoza's herd, what else would I smell?"

"I meant here, nearby. Smells like a different bunch. And cigar smoke, too."

Reece tilted her head to listen, and Lin could just make out the sounds of a forced conversation, then steel on steel. The strenuous rough and tumble of a fight.

They crept along the dry side of the river bank to a grassy clearing. Less than a hundred feet away, a wagon with four horses was backed up to the river, and half-again the distance away, a pair of men were doing their best to finish each other off.

The contest was woefully one-sided, and when the big man stood over top the other, Lin pulled his Colt from its holster. "Stay here," he told Stick. "Keep watch. Don't come out until I tell you to. Even if it looks okay. I want to be sure."

"You know me, Lin. You can count on me. I always stick to it. Yes, sir."

"Good."

Lin's Colt was empty, but the strangers didn't know it. With his gun in the lead, Lin took Reece with the other hand and crept up slow.

As they approached him, the big man was talking to his downed opponent. "Told you we had no reason to fight."

Lin stepped in close.

"Sounds good to me, *amigo*," said Lin. "But how's-about you go ahead and drop your scattergun anyway?" He pulled back the hammer on his Colt.

The big man let his gun drop to the ground.

He held up both hands.

"I ain't otherwise armed," he said.

Lin was impressed with the fellow's delivery. His stance was rock-solid without trembling, his voice didn't quaver in the least. "You got a name, mister?"

"Micah LeMay," said Micah. "Who are you?"

"Lin Jarret," he said. "Texas Ranger."

"I'll be go to the devil," whispered Micah.

"What'd you say?" said Lin.

"Just cussing my guardian angel," said Micah.

"Cussing your——?"

Lin walked around, caught sight of Micah's face in the moonlight and grinned. "Oh...I see."

"You see a black man standing over a man flat-out on the ground next to four horses and a wagon," said Micah. "Why don't you just save yourself some time and shoot me now, Ranger?"

"Nope," said Lin, punching his gun back into its leather. "Nope, ain't gonna shoot you."

"I sure as hell prefer shooting to a rope."

"Ain't got a rope," said Lin. "You got a rope, Reece?"

Micah swiveled his head to look at the girl. "Reece Sinclair?"

"I don't have a rope either, Mister LeMay."

"You are Reece Sinclair?"

She nodded.

"You sure?" said Micah. "I mean, you aren't trying to pull one over on me?"

"I'm not," said Reece. "We're not." She greeted him with an outstretched hand. "You're welcome at Rancho de Jada."

"Are we there now? I mean, am I here? Or...there?" Micah momentarily worked to straighten out his words. "What I'm traying to say, is this the Sinclair ranch?"

"You're standing on it."

"Oh, thank God."

"I can imagine why you've come."

"I been running all week, Miss Sinclair."

"Call me Reece."

Micah's big chest collapsed as he let out a lungful of air.

"I imagine you've been holding your breath more days than you care to count," said Lin.

"You're telling me." Then his voice was wary again. "True you're a Texas Ranger?"

"Yeah," said Lin. "I can't deny it."

"You'll understand if I say I don't trust you, sir."

"No offense, LeMay, but we've got no reason to trust you either."

Reece began, "Lin..."

"No, Miss Reece, he's right." Micah took a step back. "I got a feelin' you all might be in trouble out here."

"What makes you say so?" said Lin.

"Earlier today I heard two men talking in Jade City."

"You've been to Jade City?"

"I was at your store, Miss Reece. Looking for you. Two men were out front talking about cattle."

Reece walked in between the two men. "What did they say?"

Micah did his best to recount as much as he could recall of the conversation between Morse and his companion. Before he could mention his wagon load of ammunition, the four horses on the high-wheeled spring wagon started making a fuss.

"Looks like he was loading up with water," said Lin, meaning the man on the ground.

The horses strained against the wagon brake, pulling the rig sideways. A chunk of sod fell away from the bank and splashed into the river. The shirtless man groaned.

"We'd do well to bind him before he wakes up," said Lin.

"Ought to lead the team away from the water, too," said Micah. "Them burr-heads don't seem any too tame."

"They're from Cardoza's cavvy on the Diablo Flats. You know Cardoza?"

Micah said he didn't. "Should I?"

"You know Dub Hornsby?" said Lin.

"No."

"Hornsby and Cardoza hurrahed the ranch today," said Lin. "We're lucky to be alive."

Micah took in the information, mulled it over. "Let's get the rig pulled away from the water," he said. "Then maybe I can help you."

CHAPTER 25

TOGETHER, THE THREE MANAGED TO TAKE THE HORSES in hand and lead the big wagon away from the edge of the water. Once they had it parked a way away, Micah dragged his shirtless, dazed opponent into the clearing and hogtied him wrists to ankles with a slender length of hemp. "He called himself Juarez," said Micah. "Am I supposed to know him, also?"

Lin said no. "He's another one of the Diablo Flats knot-heads from across the river. I don't know what Cardoza is paying him, but it's not enough." Together, they hoisted Juarez into the back of the wagon where he groaned once, then lightly continued to snore.

Then Micah walked back toward the river, put his hands on his hips, and whistled like a songbird.

After a few seconds, he did it again. Like he was calling somebody.

"This better not be a trick of some kind," said Lin.

Lin was grateful for his foresight in having Stick stay back and keep watch over them.

"No trick, Ranger."

Lin tensed, ready for anything.

Within a minute, a dark horse pulling a short buck-board with a lantern perched on a forward post rounded a bend in the river.

"This rig was shared with me in Emberville," said Micah. "It's from the Overland Trail station."

When Micah had the horse in hand, Lin peered over the side of the sturdy buckboard wagon. "Hand me your lantern, will you?"

Micah turned the latch holding the glass-enclosed, iron lantern in place and handed it over to Lin. In the spotlight were at least five wooden barrels, three long crates, three short crates, and a several tied gunny sacks.

"Unless I miss my guess, you've got an arsenal tucked away here."

"After I heard those men talking, I was worried about the ranch," said Micah.

"You're a God-send, Micah," said Reese.

Micah's voice carried a sheepish hint. "I have to tell you true, Miss Reece. I wasn't thinking about you as much as myself. I need you, need this ranch, to get me across the Rio Grande. Without you, I have no idea who to go to, who to see."

"I wanted to ask you more about this emancipation business, too," said Lin. "When I first rode into the ranch with you the other day, we met an African man. Next thing I know, he's disappeared. I'm guessing you drove him across the border when you came into town ahead of us."

"I did," said Reese.

"And where'd you take him?"

"There's a place there, just across the river, and just on the other side of the Diablo Flats. A cantina called *El Pato Borrocho* where you'll find a man called Lash."

"Lash runs The Drunk Duck?" Lin said.

"I don't think so. But he is always there, at a table in back." Reece turned to Micah. "No matter what happens to me, you find Lash, tell him I sent you." She put her hand on his arm. "He will lead you to your people."

"All well and good enough for him," said Lin. "I'm a little more concerned about us making it through the night. Hornsby's gonna be getting thirsty before long. He's gonna be looking for these two and the wagon."

"We need a plan," said Reece.

"I'll do all I can to help," said Micah.

"What about your friend across the border? What about this man, Lash? Surely if he's neighbor to Cardoza, he knows full well what the man is capable of. Can we get help from Lash? Maybe raise enough of a force to take the hacienda?"

Reece was shaking her head before Lin finished speaking.

"Lash works alone." Again, she touched Micah's arm. "I'm afraid there is no grand society. Just a few imperfect people trying to do the right thing."

"We appreciate it, ma'am."

"You know something, Mister LeMay...," said Lin, tapping his chin. "Just a wild idea here, but..."

After a quick jog, he was at the edge of the river, holding the coal oil lantern high. "I admit, I'm no engineer," he said.

Micah looked at him, then at Reece, then back. "What's on your mind, Jarret?"

"Before we saw you, I was telling Miss Sinclair about this presa's weak spots. There, and there at the foundation." His arm was a giant's shadow on the flickering orange floor of the river.

"Did your people build it, Miss Reece?" said Micah.

Reece explained. "These vermin who attacked our

house—sometime during the past week, they dammed up the river, hoping to drive us out."

"They got impatient and attacked us this morning rather than wait us out from lack of water," said Lin. "The plan backfired and has ended up hurting them more than it hurt the Sinclairs." He kept to the bank of the Little Carlito and pointed upstream. "There's a lot of pressure built up there. The right amount of force on this side might open the river back up."

Reece said, "What are you thinking, Lin?"

"LeMay's brought enough powder to blast open the dam."

"And bring every one of Hornsby's men down on top of us. I'm sorry if I don't think this seems like an overly good idea," said Reece.

"I think it's the perfect idea." Lin asked Micah to draw the buckboard up close to the river where the rock and sod had been piled to hold back the current. "We'll concentrate the powder in one big blast, there at the base. I'll bet the pent up water on the other side will do the rest."

"Why now?" asked Reece as Micah hurried up onto the buckboard. "Why not wait until after we win back the ranch?"

Lin counted off the reasons. "Now, because we have the opportunity. LeMay's here with enough powder to bend the river. Enough powder to bend hell itself." He grinned at his wordplay.

Reece wasn't having it. "Answer the question," she said.

"Second reason? Just what you said. It's a distraction. It will get Hornsby and his men out of the house. Scatter them outside, confuse them. Remember, they don't have horses and we do. Slowly but surely, we pick 'em off." He jerked a thumb over his shoulder. "There's two less men right there. How many more are we actually talking about?"

"Eleven," said Reece, automatically. "Not counting Hornsby."

"Based on Stick's first count of 27," said Lin. "You've been keeping track?"

"Not consciously, but yes."

Micah steered his wagon into place and Lin jumped to the box. He walked to the tailgate and helped Reece climb aboard. Using a long bar from the bed of the wagon, they opened two a box of percussion caps and a small barrel filled with bullets.

"We need to get our sidearms loaded. Prime the shotgun and the Maynard, too."

Lin shoved one of the powder kegs toward the back of the wagon. "First, I'll lift the powder down to you, LeMay. You carry them over to the water."

Lin almost called to Stick for help with the manual labor, but a tingle at the back of his skull held him back. It was probably driving the poor fella crazy to stand guard, but Lin liked having an ace up his sleeve.

He didn't like to take chances.

The powder barrels were heavy, but LeMay handled them as if they were empty paper cartons, setting them down gently to the moon-washed sod.

Once they were done, it was Reece's turn to ask about Stick. "It seems like we should've heard from him by now." A wave of guilt ran through Lin. He had been positive Stick could take care of himself. He'd been focused on Reece's safety, and he hadn't considered...

"I'll call him," said Lin.

He cupped his hand around his mouth, was just about

ready to get Stick's attention, when Micah hollered out a warning. "Watch out, Ranger!"

Lin spun around in time to see somebody charging him from the edge of the river.

He reached for his gun, had it halfway out when, at the last second the heavy assault took him down to the sod and a rock hard fist drummed into his skull over and over and over...

CHAPTER 26

LIN'S ARMS WERE PINNED UNDER THE WEIGHT OF HIS attacker and at first all he could do was take the furious drubbing like a man. Somewhere far away he heard his Uncle's voice, "Good thing you got a hard head," then he bucked like a bronco, kicking at the sod with all his might.

When he finally got an elbow free, he jammed it into flesh and bone.

"Gaaugh!" The mass pulled away and Lin rolled free.

He got to his feet in time to catch Marko's second onslaught on his raised forearm, a pounding haymaker that nearly broke the bone. Furious, Lin snapped out a fast book, catching the bigger man off-balance. Marko crashed face-first into the dirt, buying precious seconds for Lin to scurry away.

When Marko heaved up his heavy frame, he came face to face with the muzzle of Lin's Colt.

"Stand tall, you rotten bastard," said Lin, the bells ringing in his brain finally starting to subside. He shook his head in disbelief. "I've had more of you than I can stand."

Marko pushed back a filthy strand of rust-colored hair and looked around. He looked at Reece for the first time, was surprised by Micah LeMay. His attention lingered on the big African before he turned back to Lin. "Got yourself some help, did you?"

"None of your concern." Lin pulled his Colt from its holster. "Now you stand down."

Marko shook his head. "Nice bluff. But I heard you talking. I know you're lolly-gagging around here without ammunition. How else do you think I took out your fair-haired boy over there?" Marko motioned to the edge of the river where Stick had stayed behind.

Lin saw red. He seethed, "By god, if you've hurt that cowboy, I'll tear your heart out."

"Don't know if I hurt him or not. Could be the lights went out too fast for him to feel much of anything." Marko made a pounding fist gesture. "Lights out."

Then he laughed, and a line of drool dropped from his lower lip. "You're a fancy talker, Ranger. I'd enjoy you trying to tear my heart out. You better ask young Reece about it first though. My heart sorta belongs to her."

Marko batted his eyelids toward the wagon. "Don't your heart belong to me, missy?"

Lin struggled to control his temper. He wanted nothing more than to flay Marko's flesh from his bones but rushing headlong into things might only get him killed. And then what would happen to Reece?

Lin stomped on his fury, brought a measure of control into his voice.

"For all your tough talk, you don't look too good, son. I've seen more healthy stuff hanging from the back end of a cow."

Lin was baiting him, but it wasn't far from the truth.

Marko was drenched in sweat, and even given the recent scuffle, he was breathing too hard.

Lin laughed in the bigger man's face. "You had to walk all the way out here, didn't you? I'll bet you enjoyed it."

"What'd you do with our horses?" said Marko.

"You boys can't keep track of your animals, it ain't on me," said Lin.

"You all act like you're the cat swallowed the canary," said Marko. "Well, you ain't. You've got nothing."

"We got you," said Lin.

"Not hardly." Marko spread his arms. "Like I said, you got nothing."

He puckered his lips toward Reece and told her, "You especially, sweet thing. You've lost more than anybody today. Your home. Your legacy."

His cheeks spread wide and the laugh-lines around his eyes deepened.

Lin stepped into the redhead's face faster than he could react. Without a word he used the butt of his pistol to hammer Marko's nose back into this skull where it exploded with blood and an audible pop. Then he cranked a powerful blow into Marko's guts, his fist like a steam driven piston, shoving the man back, driving him away from the others.

Marko bent at the waist, putting his hands flat on his knees, trying to breath as a steady stream of sticky blood drained from his face to the ground. "Gonna...make you pay..." he said.

"I've been hearing it all day and all night," said Lin. "Been hearing it from you all damn week. Nothing but a swelling gas bag of threats. Well, it works both ways, hoss. I've been wanting to take you apart for the last couple days, myself. Seems like you're giving me the excuse I've been waiting for."

Marko's reply was a succession of obscenities involving Reece, and Lin took the bait.

He tossed his Colt to the ground, then fired off a fast kick meant for the face, but instead got his boot caught between Marko's big hands. A hard twist sent shards of agony through his ankle and up into his leg, forcing him to the ground.

Right where Marko wanted him.

Again.

Lin had only just recovered from the big man's series of skull-drills. There was every chance he wouldn't survive another beating. And if he did, he'd spend the rest of his days wrapped in fuzzy cotton gauze.

Marko hurled himself down, and Lin caught him with the flats of both feet. Levering his assailant up, there wasn't enough momentum to carry Marko over. Instead of knocking him away, he only succeeded in putting off the man's next attack.

Again, Marko threatened to pin him to the ground. Lin somersaulted backwards, buying himself precious seconds. Once on his feet, he dodged toward the river, putting Micah's buckboard between Marco and himself, giving himself a chance to catch his breath.

"I can help, Ranger," said Micah, but Lin shooed him away.

"Thanks for the offer," he said. "Get Reece out of here."

Micha nodded, and Lin went back to the fight.

Enraged by Lin's evasive run, Marko was a cauldron of fire, his piggy black eyes sinking back between the folds of flesh on his face, his hair a blood-matted halo. "Gonna cut you up, little bug," he muttered. "Gonna tear your filthy scalp loose with my teeth."

Lin backed away as Marko came for him, hooking his

fingers, in a come-along gesture, enticing him forward. "You want me? Come get me. We'll see who cuts up who."

Marko lunged, and Lin slipped aside, catching him across the back of the neck with the edge of his hand. Smooth as the velvet night, he spun on one heel and hammered two crushing blows to Marko's kidneys. Then he crashed the heel of his boot into the small of his back.

Marko flew toward the river, crossing the distance uncontrolled, slamming into the space between two heavy powder barrels.

From the corner of his eye, Lin saw Micah hustling Reece back down along the shoreline. Hopefully they'd find Stick with little more than a headache.

Again, Lin closed on his enemy, only to be caught short when Marko produced the big iron knife from his boot. It was the same blade from their Jade City fight. As if in harmony, the cuts on Lin's stomach and leg started to thrum with pain.

"Surprised, Ranger?" said Marko. "Maybe you overestimated yourself?"

Lin's hand shot out and caught Marko's wrist in a rigid grip. He squeezed with all his might, hoping to twist the knife free, but Marko's free arm came around, unleashing new torment to Lin's ribcage. Then the knife came around, skimming the tendons in Lin's arm pit, forcing him backwards. A quarter-inch closer and his right arm would be bleeding out, useless forever. Lin couldn't afford another close call.

He tried to pivot, but Marko was all over him. Just as in the earlier fight, the taste of blood on his blade seemed to fuel his frenzy.

He had Lin backed against Micah's buckboard now and swatted the air with the flat of his blade as if killing flies. In the flickering orange light of Micah's lamp, Marko was like some fiery demon from the pit, snorting, roaring, teeth gnashing. The blood pulsed hard through the veins in his head. "Gonna gut you, Ranger," he rasped. "Gonna pull you apart and chew you up."

The knife came in straight and overhanded then, in a chopping motion.

Lin moved at the last possible second—a small, smooth sideways gesture, and the knife was embedded in the wood of the buckboard halfway to the hilt. Marko tugged at the blade, realized it was stuck. Too late.

Both hands pulling at the hilt of the knife left Marko's bloody face defenseless. Lin butted his forehead into the sore, smashed remains of the nose. Followed up the screaming agony with a solid punch to the soft tissue at the fissure between Marko's rib-cage and stomach.

The barrage left Marko gasping for air, apoplectic and raging, but unable to do anything but fall backwards into the barrels of powder with all his dead weight. The barrels tipped, then tumbled over the edge of the river bank to burst apart on the rocky bed. Marko tripped, lost his footing and went over too, reaching out at the last second to grab the rim of a third barrel and carry it down where it landed on top of his with a sickening crunch before breaking apart, spilling black powder in every direction.

Lin spun fast and grabbed up the lantern from where Reece had set it on the seat of the buckboard. With two bounds he carried it back to the edge of the river and, with a big overhand arc, sent the fire down on Marco with all his might.

CHAPTER 27

THE BLAST WAS INSTANTANEOUS AND DEAFENING.

And Lin was too close to the edge. A fist of force slammed him over sideways even as the ground under his feet buckled and gave way. In the riverbed, structures of dirt and tree branch begrudgingly shifted, carriage-sized moons of mud and boulders rumbled and moved. Lin caught himself on a fragmenting, muddy slope, sore arms absorbing the awkward impact of his weight, lungs choked for air in the strangling black cloud.

Then a second explosion tore through the weakened corner of the dam and water broke through. Deaf to all but an endless whine and blinded by powder smoke, Lin was caught in the spray of heat and mud, pelted with rocks and wet, sloppy debris. Fighting to hang on to the slippery side of the riverbank, he lost his foothold and was pitched headlong into the chasm.

He'd been right about the shoddy engineering of the dam. His plan to set the river to rights had worked too well. He hadn't counted on being caught up in it.

Lin had the sense of being turned over onto his back, then crushed beneath a roaring cascade of freezing dark.

That much he could hear—the mad rage of the pent-up river punching through the eternal ringing, the snarl of foaming water tearing at the earth. He gagged and tried to inhale, took a lungful of water and was slammed into something hard and unyielding.

When he opened his eyes, he saw swarms of popping sparks, pin-pricks of red and orange light—fiery echoes of the explosion. Or maybe he was already dead, floating among the stars of heaven.

Even so, Lin scrambled like hell for life.

He shook off his initial delirium, realized he was moving. Pummeled by rocks and chunks of driftwood, shoved around like old linen in his grandma's wash tub, he had the sense of one single, powerful push. The presa had collapsed, the rushing current was free. Numb below the chin, Lin was drowning in a mad torrent ironically called the Little Carlito.

There was no way to tell how far into the river he'd been carried, no markers in the coal black dead of night to measure his progress. His eyes seemed spotty anyway, half-blinded by the white-hot intensity of the hot powder, but he knew he was lucky to be alive.

Instinctively he'd been kicking the entire time, rioting against the heaving elements, pushing to keep his head above water. His entire body was wracked with pain, and in memory the brawl with Marko was a blur. In the after-shock of the dam-burst everything ran together. Spitting water, slapping against the surface foam, Lin felt more in control.

Slowly he began to relax.

Working with the water, rather than against it, he sensed a slowing of the tide. His feet hit bottom and he bounced up. A long, gnarled tree branch gouged his neck from behind, and he floated to its side and grabbed ahold. The branch kept him upright, and once again his boots scraped the river's floor.

Suddenly, the river's stench filled his lungs, and he retched at the smell of ripe rot and decay. Powder burns to his face were an itching sting, and the rush of water was more even now, less demanding. Lin sensed the channel had widened and the water level dropped to his chest. Then his waist.

Before long, he was on his feet, sloshing through the flow, staggering into the side of the riverbed. The branch he clung to rolled on away, death waving a boney hand.

Until we meet again.

The fear of oblivion replaced with the burden of pain.

"Good...god almighty," Lin wheezed, and the sound of his own voice was half-choked and raspy. He cleared his throat over and over and floating in memory was the image of Tom Sinclair at the lunch table, coughing, coughing, unable to catch his breath.

We have to assume my dad is dead.

Reece's voice, crystal clear.

Lin figured she was right. By now, Sinclair might be gone, along with Sanchez too.

If he didn't get a handle on himself, Reece and the others would figure he was lost too, caught up in the blast with Marko, another casualty of war.

The Cardoza war.

Part of Cortina's bigger complaint.

Both campaigns were leftover shreds of the Mexican-American War. Or were they portents of a war to come?

A war promising to rend the United States in two.

His back flat against the wall of the river, the current flowing past his knees and shins, Lin decided he was done with war. His squalling leg wound was enough, his bruised and twisted frame had taken all the punishment he ever cared to feel. He figured he would rest here forever.

But Reece's voice kept nagging him, kept urging him on.

The story of that damn cat.

The fact of her home torn out from under her.

She needed him.

Reluctantly, he forced himself to walk on. One foot in front of the other, until he found an access up the rim of the confluence, a path to solid, dry ground. For her sake, he'd find it.

Because, if it was up to him, he decided he'd just as soon lay back down and die.

———

REECE FOUND Stick Carvell in the grass beside the Lower Carlito not too much the worse for wear. She ran her fingers over the back of his head, tender and attentive to any cuts or contusions. A lump half the size of a hen's egg sat behind his left ear, and when she touched it, Stick grimaced.

"Shhhh," she soothed him. "You're fine, now. Everything's okay."

Brushing his hair away from his brow, she felt his cool forehead and noticed his breathing was slow and regular. "Find his hat, will you please?" she said.

In the distance, Reece could hear Lin and Marko fighting. She whispered a silent curse and not for the first time prayed Lin Jarret wouldn't end up dead.

Micah handed over the hat, and Reece worked to set Stick into an upright, seated position, his shoulders reclining against her. She whispered into his ear. "Wake up now, Stick. We need to be on the move."

His head lolled to the side, and eyelids fluttered. "What happened?"

"Marko caught you from behind."

"The dirty skunk."

"Can you get up?"

"I...I think so."

Reece turned to Micah and asked for help. "Let's get him away from the river back and into the clear. Micah nodded, bent to get his arms under Stick, and the world went sideways with an enormous boom.

Perched at the river's edge, Reece caught the fireball from the corner of her eye, and the wave of heat scorched her eyebrows and pushed her and Stick backwards. Micah hurled himself in front of them both, absorbing a scatter of dirt and debris across his back.

The tumult stole all the air from the river region, then dumped it back into place when a second thunderclap split the night. Reece turned inland as chaff rained down on them, and she pointed back toward the clearing.

As the massive wall of dirt and mud gave way behind him, Micah picked Stick up with surprising care, making sure to keep him level, prudent to support his neck and head. Reece took the lead, hurrying toward the wagon and the last place she'd seen Lin and Marko.

Both men were gone as were the barrels of black powder.

At the river, the presa had split at its weakest point. Halfway out into the channel, water was bursting through and the nearest bank had collapsed entirely. It was as if some kind of immense river creature had taken a bite out of the earth. Lin's assessment of the dam had been correct, and now he was caught in the aftermath of a plan too hastily enacted, perhaps unavoidable.

While Micah braced Stick up against one of the

buckboard wagon wheels, Reece waved away swirls of smoke and searched the churning river for Lin. There was nothing. No sign of Marko either. If the men were caught in the explosion, if they'd fallen into the raging channel, then they were gone.

Reece walked back to the wagon to rejoin the others. Half-way there, she picked up Lin's Colt revolver. If only they'd been better prepared, she thought. But she bit off the recrimination even as she made it.

They *had* been prepared. They had carried back powder, caps, and lead from the store and stashed it in the grain closet's hidden room.

Somebody had betrayed them. But who?

"I trust you two got acquainted?" she said. Then, squatting down next to Stick, she said, "How are you doing?"

He rubbed the back of his head and offered a weak smile. "I got a hard head, Miss. I'll be fine. Mighty glad you all pulled me away from the river though. I sure didn't like the noise of the explosion. Looks like the ranch ought to have water again, but Lord-a-mighty, what a racket."

Reece glanced up at Micah. "He's just fine," she assured him.

"I guess he talks like this all the time?"

"Sorta like our river out there," said Reece. "Get him going, it's hard to stop."

"I just sometimes got a lot on my mind," said Stick, "and it all tends to come right on out of my mouth."

"I've got a lot on my mind too," said Reece. "Like where we go from here. They'll have heard the powder explosion back at the house. I expect Hornsby will send men out to investigate. Especially when Marko and these other two men go missing."

"I've got to apologize," said Micah. "I surely didn't set out to kill anybody tonight."

"I've had first-hand experience with these devils," said Stick. "I'd wager the bastard didn't give you much choice in the matter."

"We sure didn't sit down and smoke a pipe over it."

Stick, continued to rub his neck. "I sure could wish I had a swig of something strong for this headache, though. Maybe a cup of hot coffee."

Micah clapped his hands together. "Coffee, I got," he said. But then he said, "A fire we don't."

Reece turned the idea over in her mind. Could they chance a fire? It had been ten minutes since the explosion. How long would it take for the men to get here? Without horses, certainly more than a half-an-hour. Closer to 45 minutes. Maybe more depending on their ability to navigate in the dark.

A fire would be good. For coffee.

For Lin.

If there was one chance in a million he was out there, the fire would be a signal. And a way to stall for time.

"A fire would be good," said Reece. "But let's be quick about it. It won't be long, and they'll be coming for us."

CHAPTER 28

BEFORE REECE COULD OFFER TO HELP, MICAH HAD A campfire blazing and with a tin pot of bubbling coffee overtop. "Got warm beer, dried meat, and hard rolls along too, if you'd like."

Reece declined anything to eat, but Stick was obliged to chew a bread round. While they waited for the coffee, Reece leaned against the buckboard wagon and tended to Lin Jarret's Colt Walker Model 1847.

With expert practice she popped the cylinder free from the gun's frame, then used her bandanna to rub away the soot, running the cloth back and forth through the six chambers with a short stick. Once she finished, she cleaned the gun's barrel and polished the angled loading lever, frame, and butt.

Then, to load the gun, she turned her attention to the open box of balls and caps beside her.

First Reece charged the cylinder of the Colt, pouring a measure of powder—30 grains or so—into the front of each chamber from the powder flask still hanging on a cord around her neck. Next, she spun through the cylinder a second time, dropping a lead ball into each opening, pulling the lever under the barrel down to press the ball tight against the powder. Finally, she added the fire, snapping a tight round percussion cap into the back of each chamber.

As an extra caution, against wetness and also to prevent a cross-contamination of sparks that might launch a deadly chain-fire reaction, she filled the front of each chamber on the cylinder with lard from Micah's wagon inventory.

"Coffee's done," said Micah, bending over the fire to retrieve the pot. As soon as he passed out two full cups, he poured a third for himself. Then he put the cup down and prepared to snuff out the fire. But not before Lin's voice came from the edge of the river.

"Hello, the camp," he said, and Reece ran to him.

"Hello, yourself." Before she could stop herself, she wrapped both arms around him and buried her face in his neck. "Thanks be," she said.

"Hey, hey," he said, bringing her back out to arm's length. "I hope you haven't been worried about ol' Lin Jarret."

"We were just preparing to leave," she said. "Hornsby's men will be coming." She brushed at the tears on her cheeks, hoping the fire didn't give away her emotions. "Would you like some coffee? I've got your Colt reloaded."

Lin slung his arm around Reece's shoulder. "One thing at a time," he said, and she felt him shift more weight onto her than expected. "Right now, I just wanna stay upright."

They made it to the edge of the fire, and Lin got situated with a cup of hot coffee.

"You need to strip outta the wet shirt and britches," said Reece.

"Ma'am?" said Lin.

"You won't be worth a patch o' ringworm if you don't. One thing at a time, you said. Well, the first thing is to get you into some dry clothes."

"You may not have noticed, but I'm not exactly carrying a warbag full of suits."

"Stick," said Reece. "Go pull the trousers off the fellow Micah shot. I 'spect they'll fit. Shoes, socks, jacket. Anything else you can find."

Stick nodded his compliance and jogged over to the stretched out cadaver.

"Oh, no," said Lin. "Bad enough to be wearing a dead man's stockings."

"Would you rather catch pneumonia?"

"I'd rather just dry out here beside the fire with my coffee."

"We don't have time."

"I'd reckon Miss Reece is right," said Micah. "If anybody's coming here to look about the explosion, I'd rather be long gone."

While Stick worked, Reece double-checked Micah's shotgun and Lin's Maynard rifle. Both were primed and ready to fire. Stick's five-shot revolver was likewise ready to go. "I'll carry the Maynard," said Reece. Since Lin was armed with the Colt, it made sense.

Now each of them was armed.

When Stick showed up with a pair of cotton pants and a pair of soft moccasins balanced at the end a stick, Reece reconsidered. The odor of the rank attire preceded him by three feet.

"If it's all the same to you, I'll get along with the

clothes I've got," said Lin. "I might be damp, but at least I won't smell bad."

"No more than you already do," said Reece.

"At least you'll be able to find me in the dark." He winked. "After all, ain't that what's important?"

"Time to mount up," she said.

Within minutes they trundled away from the clearing with three horses and two wagons, Lin and Micah driving the buckboard, Reece and Stick on the high wheeler behind with Phillip Juarez riding in the box. They met three of Hornsby's men less than ten minutes later on the open range, and the wagons raced side-by-side.

Lin saw the first two men as shadows in the moonlight and lobbed a fast succession of thunder into their midst, confident he'd hit nothing but their sore nerves. The distance was too great, and his eyesight was still blurry after his river adventure.

He was right, but his antagonists weren't shooting any better.

When one of the men returned fire, Lin guessed the shots flew high and wild.

With a showy round of flares, the second man pitched an entire cylinder of lead ahead of him. Lin flinched as two of the shots skimmed past, flaming hot wasps with deadly stings.

Stick didn't hesitate to answer, triggering three rounds in succession. Lin could tell he was aiming at the moonlight glow of powder smoke.

A hit! The gunman's back arched and he fell to earth, kicking.

Without hesitation, the other two men threw their hands high into the air and waited for the horses to pass by.

But Lin wasn't about to be shot in the back. As soon

as he was sure of his aim, he pressed the trigger of his Colt, sending both men to their maker.

If Reece was still keeping count, Hornsby should be down to seven men, eight with Phillip Juarez. They rolled on past the twitching dead, pushing toward the embattled hacienda.

As they had agreed when they set out, they drove the wagons to the line of broke-down jacals behind the bunkhouse and convened at the grass-covered trap door above the underground tunnels.

The now-vacant livery barn was dark and silent. Likewise, the bunkhouse showed no signs of life. The house showed light in the front kitchen windows, and a dull amber glow from the back. A column of smoke rose from the Sinclair's fireplace chimney, but the cook stove stack was cold and dead.

Lin pulled a satchel from the back of the wagon and looped it over his shoulder. He carried his Colt at his hip. Reece held the Maynard in one hand and pulled open the dirt-encrusted door with the other.

Micah climbed into the back of the wagon with Phillip Juarez and used a sharp knife from his belt to cut his bonds. Then he gave him a firm kick in the pants. "Up, you," he said.

Juarez lurched forward, then rose to his knees, dizzy, rubbing circulation back into his wrists. The right side of his face was battered and swollen. He peered up at Micah. "I shoulda killed you, Ni—"

Micah dropped another kick to Juarez's backside, sending him face first into the floor of the wagon.

"Eat splinters, Phil."

"Just get him down here," said Lin. "In one piece, if you please."

While Micah tossed Juarez to the ground, Reece appealed Lin's plan.

"If it's all the same to you three, I want to follow Juarez in," said Lin.

"It's not all the same," said Lin, holding tight to her rifle. "You're staying out here with Stick and Micah. If I'm not out in twenty minutes, mount up and ride for leather to Mexico. Find Lash at The Drunk Duck."

"This is my home," said Reece.

"I didn't come this far to sit on my thumbs," said Stick.

"Seems I owe you my help, too," said Micah.

Lin sighed. "I don't like it," he said. "For all we know, Dub Hornsby is sitting in your bedroom, right on top of the exit to this tunnel. As soon as the door comes open, he might be ready with a cavalry's worth of powder."

"They haven't burned or destroyed anything," said Reece, looking around. "I don't think they'd risk blowing the tunnels unless Cardoza gave the go-ahead."

"We don't know he didn't," said Lin. "You'll notice he conveniently turned his back on his men and rode out of here earlier this evening."

"You're saying we shouldn't go in there? You're talking like a coward, and cowardice is the last thing I'd expect of you, *Mister Jarret*."

"The Ranger ain't a coward, Miss Reece," said Stick. "He just ain't crazy."

Jaw set, green eyes full of fury, Reece was at the brink of crazy herself. Her dad was probably dead, killed by the gargantuan slug waiting for her at the other end of the tunnel. She had a charged rifle in hand and the determination to use it. Lin scraped up every ounce of patience he could.

He remembered Otter the cat, and when he spoke,

his words were laced with empathy. "If you can show me a safer way of navigating this tunnel," he said. "I'm listening."

Reece's smile was a revelation.

"Who says this is the only tunnel?" she said.

CHAPTER 29

DUB HORNSBY LOOKED AT TOM SINCLAIR'S GOLD pocket watch through scratchy dry eyes.

It was well past midnight, and Hornsby hadn't slept for almost 24 hours. He'd been up long before dawn pulling together the last minute details of Cardoza's initial raid on the ranch. Then, after a full day of acting barmaid and sentry for the hired men, he'd considered a brief respite, alone in Sinclair's study by the fire.

He clicked the watch case shut. On the back was engraved a stylized letter S intertwined with an ornamental J. The Rancho de Jada brand.

It occurred to him to glance up at Jada Sinclair's portrait, but he didn't. Something about the intensity of the eyes, the accusatory way the painting stared down at him, caused him to avoid looking at it. If it wasn't for Cardoza's admiration for the piece, he'd have thrown it into the fire.

Marko had gone after the water wagon to find Reece Sinclair and the remainder of the men had finally settled into a dull routine of card games. There was no reason on earth why Hornsby couldn't lay back and watch the inside of his eyelids. A few minutes rest was long overdue.

Pushing back in Sinclair's plush chair, he made an embarrassing effort to lift his feet to the broad flat oak desktop. He nearly rolled from the chair and scolded Sinclair's dead body, stretched out where it was near the fire next to Barb Sanchez's corpse. "What's so funny, old man? At least I'm still alive enough to try."

Defeated, Hornsby chose to fold his arms across his enormous girth and simply dream of better days ahead. In the morning, the men would come about the cows. By afternoon, Hornsby would be back at the Muleskinner, swigging rye and plowing through a stack of rib steaks and gravy.

Within a month, he'd be managing Rancho de Jada.

And when Cardoza fell, because Cortina would fall, because the United States would never allow the Tejano incursions into Texas to continue, Dub Hornsby would have the spread all to himself.

First thing he'd do is get rid of the damned painting.

And he'd fill the grazing land with sheep.

He chuckled to himself. What the hell was Sinclair thinking going this deep into cattle? Imagine, he thought — *Texas as cattle country*? What a joke.

Hornsby had only just drifted off to slumber when a single dull thump from outside forced open his eyes. Far away was the heavy sound, he would've slipped back to sleep if not for the loud caterwauling of his man, Jed Akins.

The rawboned cowboy loped into the room like he owned it, and Hornsby jerked up with one hand reaching across the desk for his Colt revolver. "Careful, Jed. I could'a blown your damn fool head off."

"Sorry, boss. Thought you'd wanna know. There's

been some kind of explosion out there across the llano. Me and a couple others saw it flare up. Looks to be on the other side of the trees near the river."

Marko!

"Them two who was fighting took the water wagon out there, didn't they?" said Jed.

"They did," said Hornsby, pushing himself out from behind the desk. "I sent Marko after them. Do you know if anybody else is out there close to the river?"

"Can't think of anybody. It's just me and Landers and Todd. We been playing cards with a couple of the Mex in the kitchen. I think Walters is asleep in one of the bedrooms."

While Jed spoke, Hornsby's mind raced through the possible origins of an explosion at the river. More, he wondered what it might portend for the future.

If the blow up wasn't due to Marko, it was surely the work of Ranger and the girl. Or what if it was somebody else?

An unexpected variable he hadn't foreseen? It made Hornsby question Cardoza's hurry to leave. What if *el jefe* had called in a new wave of men with another cannon.

Or maybe somebody coming to rescue Sinclair. But who?

"Send three or four men out to see what it's about," said Hornsby.

"I'll send Todd and the two Mexicans," said Jed.

"Very good," said Hornsby, turning his attention to a second man entering the room. Walters was a fleshy as Jed was scrawny, and both men could do with a bath and a shave. Walters' expression was a mixed bag of eager anticipation and concern. Hornsby could tell he couldn't wait to speak.

"What now?"

"You ought to come look at what I found in the gal's bedroom," said Walters. "I was trying to get some shut-eye, but when the big boom went off, I could hear it through the floor—like it was coming from under the floor. I got down and inspected it and, well—you just need to come look-see for yourself."

"For your sake, this better be something important. I've had about enough stinking damn nonsense to last a coon's age."

"No nonsense, Dub. C'mon, follow me."

Reluctant, tired, Hornsby traipsed out into the hall and then left to the girl's bedroom. Once he'd led them through the door, Walters made a point of closing it behind them. "Ain't nobody else's business, unless you want it to be, Dub."

The room was stark and plain, though undeniably feminine with a frilly, lace-edged comforter spread across the brass bed, and a dressing table replete with perfumes and lotions. A mirror on the wall had ribbons tied around the edges, and above the bed was a crude painting of a horse. The wallpaper was a light sky-blue and the ceiling showed a brown stain where the roof leaked. Waiting behind the closed door, Hornsby felt the need to fidget.

He pulled Sinclair's watch from his pocket and saw the face. The morning was creeping on slow as hoof rot. "Get on with it, Walters," he said.

The thin man put his shoulder against the bed frame and rolled it out of the way.

"A trap door," he said.

By God, the man was right.

"A hidden tunnel, Dub. I heard the explosion up through a hidden tunnel." Walters opened the door with a creak of the iron hinges and the smell of raw earth wafted into the room.

Hornsby stepped forward to stand at the lip of the inlaid square.

Staring down into the pit, a good many things became more clear. "This is how Reece Sinclair and the Ranger escaped," he declared.

"I reckon so," said Jed. "There's tell the Sinclairs are part of them abolitionist groups. This must be how they help slide those Africans out of the country."

With the revelation, Hornsby's mind was more alert now. He was thinking fast.

"You suppose they mean to get back in here?" said Walters. "I wouldn't put it past your Ranger to try and sneak back in here."

"Just speculation of course," said Jed, "but if they wanted to try and take us..."

"This would be their means of doing it," said Hornsby. He walked over to the room's dressing table and picked up the wooden, three-legged stool beside it.

"Close it up, boys," he said. Walters let the door fall shut with a bang.

Carrying the stool back to the edge of the trap door, Hornsby put the seat down gently. Then he perched unceremoniously on top of it and pulled out his Colt. In the other hand, he held the ticking watch.

"If and when the door cracks open, I mean to be here," he said.

The men exchanged knowing looks.

"And God pity the poor devil who pops his head through," said Jed, laughing.

"A head's gonna get popped right off," agreed Walters.

Hornsby pressed his lips together into a grim smile.

"I have no doubt it won't be the last one," he said.

"You mind if we wait with you?" said Jed.

Typical, thought Hornsby. But why not? "If it will give

you something to do," he said. "Feel free to move your card game in here."

"Thanks, Dub."

Jed loped through the door only to return a few minutes later with two other men in tow. "Them other three ran down toward the river to see what the commotion was about," said Jed.

Hornsby nodded.

As the men around him got comfortable, he thought about the tunnel beneath his feet. He should've suspected such a thing, especially with all the stories about Sinclair's ties to this secret Hellbenders bunch. Hornsby wondered how such a thing was funded. Where did the money come from to outfit such a mission?

Private donations? Livestock?

No wonder the Sinclairs had such a puny spread. All their money went to help a bunch of ne'er do-wells who were better off under the whip.

Well, at least for Hornsby, the night was looking up. The men had something to look forward to, and Hornsby would have the last laugh at the Sinclair's expense.

Content he finally had the upper hand—despite the uncomfortable seat—he fell into a light doze.

———

"DUB! DUB, WAKE UP," said Jed, shaking his shoulder. Crouched down, close to his ear, the gaunt old devil pulled him from a dreamless reverie. "It's time, Dub. They're coming through the tunnel just like you said. Me and Walters heard 'em talking down there."

Hornsby pulled himself up and kicked away the tiny stool. "What did they say? How many are there?" The Colt was sweaty in his hand, and the watch case clicked open. He couldn't believe the time. Dawn wasn't too far away.

Jed stood with the other four men, arms akimbo, big iron guns dangling from their fingers. For his part, Walters was crouched against the floor, his ear pressed to the floorboards.

"It's a ways off, but there's for sure somebody down there, for sure," he said.

"You boys all get against the far wall," said Hornsby, positioning the men along the back of the room. "I'll stand here." He took a square position opposite them on the other side of the trap door.

Hornsby held his index finger to his nose, indicating quiet.

"When the door comes open, I'll make sure they see my gun," said Hornsby. "I'll tell 'em to freeze in their tracks. Then you boys unload into the floorboards here, and there." He pointed out path of the tunnel under the room.

Walters, Jeb, and the others showed their under-standing with giddy readiness.

"We do this right, all our worries are over," said Hornsby.

They waited as Sinclair's watch ticked off the minutes.

When the time came for action, things would happen fast.

The door in the floor cracked open an inch, and a man's voice sounded.

Wary. Apprehensive.

Scared.

"Hola?" he said, fingers gripping the edge of the trap, "Senor Hornsby?"

Immediately five sets of handguns erupted into a

barrage of roaring death. The symphony of lead was overwhelming in its effect, filling the air with splintered chunks of wood, slamming the door back down, and riddling the floor with holes. The room filled with thick smoke and one of the men let off a whooping cheer.

"I'd say we got 'em good. Teach 'em to sneak up on us."

Jeb strode forward, his six-shooter still aimed at the ruined floor. "There's more than one down there," he said.

Hornsby jammed a finger into his ear and tried to clear the ringing. He could barely hear his own voice above the after-effects of the shooting. "Swing it open, Jeb," he said.

The lanky man bent over, grasped the ring, and on the count of three, pulled it up until it braked to a stop on its hinges in a perpendicular position. Dust and smoke swirled deep in the pit and the outside air wafting in was cool.

"Empty," said Jeb.

"Senor?" Again, the same tepid voice.

This time a hand appeared from farther back in the hole—frantically waving a white shirt stained with blood. "Don't shoot. Don't—"

Jeb shot. Two rounds emptied his cylinder and put a smile on his face. "No surrender, right Dub?"

Hornsby berated him with rasping breath.

"You idiot. That was Phillip Juarez. He is Cardoza's man."

"Was Cardoza's man," came a voice from outside the room.

A girl's voice.

Hornsby's blood froze with recognition.

Stock still, he forced himself to turn and face the open door into the hallway.

It was like jogging through mud. Like pushing through a lake of icy slush.

It was almost too much for him.

Armed, with their guns ready to fire, Reece Sinclair stood with Lin Jarret across the hall in the door of the opposite bedroom. Just beyond them, a second trap door in the floor was open.

The girl had an impossibly long rifle pointed straight at Hornsby. An old gun, he judged. Eastern-made, unless he missed his guess. Maybe a .50 or .52 caliber. A gun like that would leave a hell of a hole in a man. Could practically tear off a limb.

The Ranger had his Colt backing her up, and there was no pity in their eyes. No sense that he had a chance at redemption.

In the last ticking seconds of his life, his guts turned to water, as he always knew they would. If it came to falling on his knees to beg, he knew he would do that too.

"Don't shoot," said Hornsby. "We can make a deal."

"Bring me my father," said Reece. "Let me talk to him, and we'll see about deals."

Hornsby started to tremble. "He's...uh...he's resting."

"You lying sack of shit," said Reece. She braced the rifle against her shoulder, didn't bother to take aim.

At point blank range, there was no need.

Hornsby felt his knees give way. "Oh, God, what do you think you're doing, girl?"

"Making up for lost time," said Reece.

Time?

Hornsby had one last mad glimpse at Sinclair's watch

as his ears were filled with a crashing reverberation. The glass on the watch was cracked, he noticed.

And then it was spattered with blood.

Dub Hornsby hit the floor of Reece's bedroom like a bag of rocks, and his five companions found themselves lined up as if for a firing squad.

"I'd say you boys have a choice to make," said Lin.

To a man they tossed their spent revolvers to the floor in a clatter of iron.

CHAPTER 30

THE RAP ON THE DOOR CAME EARLY, JARRING OSCAR Bruhn from a deep morning slumber.

Too early, he thought. What the hell time was it?

He pushed an arm out from under the covers, knocked over a half-empty bottle of rum, finally brushed against his silver pocket watch. A pocket watch engraved by the Texas Rangers.

He peered at the moonlit face—4:20.

"Aw, Jeezus," he moaned. Right on time.

"Mmmble-wfff?" said the old broad huddled in the blankets beside him.

Oscar popped her bare ass with the back of his hand and, just to be ornery, flung back the covers. "Rise and shine, rise and goddam shine, Rita."

He wasn't disappointed by Rita's loud squeal and hasty obscenities. "You sonuvabitch," she slurred before gathering the heavy folds back in on herself.

Oscar climbed to his feet and stretched, the pops and crackles of his back and shoulder joints competing for volume against the now constant soundings at the door. "Hold y'r damn water, I'll be there in a minute."

Where had he left his trousers?

The pounding on the door was incessant. "You in there, Oscar? We're ready to ride out here."

"Yeah, yeah. Just let me get on my damn pants."

Once partially dressed, he shuffled on bare feet to the door, scratching the course hair on his chest. His tongue was fuzzy and tasted like kerosene, and the back of his throat was hot. Behind him, Rita ripped off a loud passing of gas, and he grinned. By thunder she'd been a frisky one.

They'd had a wild night.

And daylight was coming far too soon. He yawned and unlocked the little apartment door. The good news was he was in charge of the day's work, and being in charge, could send Curt and Billy on their way with the rest of the men.

After a nice morning constitutional he could trail on behind.

He opened the door just as Curt raised yet another balled-up fist.

"You ready to go, Oz?"

Jade City was at peace under the dark Texas sky, but the seven horseman lined up in the street between Rita's place and the Sanchez Mercantile fidgeted with anticipation.

There was Billy on the end with his too-tall hat, and Scruff beside him—unshaved for more than a year, his beard twitched in the morning breeze. There was Hans and Ruth and Harry—Norwegian bachelors come down from up north and so tight with livestock you thought they were part sheepdog. Nick and Cardy on the far side. Oscar didn't trust either one of them. With their tied-down holsters and smart attitude, they were more gunnie than vaquero—more killer than cowboy.

But they'd have to do. These seven, with Curt making eight, were all he could wrangle up on short notice.

"You all know where to go?" said Oscar.

"I think so." Curt's teeth were stained and speckled with tobacco leaf.

"Place called Defilement. I'll meet you there after I check in at the ranch."

"You're going out to the Sinclair place?"

"Yeah," said Oscar. "I need to square up with Dub Hornsby. Then I'll ride over, and we can set out for Rio Grande City."

"Hell, the way I see it, Oz, we get out there to Defilement and start rounding the critters up, we just as well set out on the trail ourselves."

Oscar didn't see why not. It sounded like a reasonable plan.

"You've got my blessing," he said. "But by-God, watch out for them Indians."

Curt scoffed. "I heard somebody say something about 'em." He tipped his head back toward Nick and Cardy. "We've got plenty of experience killing Indians. I ain't worried."

"Good," said Oscar. "That puts my mind to ease."

Curt launched a long stream of tobacco juice into the dust. "We'll be on our way then," he said. "Meet you on the road to auction."

Oscar shut the door behind him and rubbed his hands together. "That morning air is crisp," he said.

"Wwllssay?" said Rita from the bed.

"I said you ought to haul outta bed and fix me some breakfast."

"Fix it yourself."

"Fix it myself?" Oscar trod to the edge of the flimsy

wood frame and pushed against it with his hip. "I'll fix you," he said. "How about I fix you?"

Rita tossed her blanket aside and rolled over. "How about you just do that?" she said, with a drunken purr.

"Still hot and bothered, ain't you? Damned if there ain't no satisfying you."

"I'll never be satisfied, Oz. You know that much."

Oscar knew how she felt. He'd accomplished more than any ten men. He'd sent soldiers into battle, buried some, decorated some with awards, killed his fair share. He'd run cattle and butchered savages until his head swam with the stink of blood. He'd amassed more money than he ever dreamed possible.

And bedded more dames.

"I know what it's like to never be satiated," he said. "I know the constant burning desire."

"Then what are you waiting for?" said Rita.

"Ain't waitin' no more. Not after today," he said, shucking out of his trousers. "C'mon, old woman. We'll go once more for the trail."

"Giddyap," said Rita.

————

ABOVE THE TREES of the Little Carlito break on the edge of town, the sun was a scolding ball of rolling bile, cussing Oscar for his indulgences, mocking his mistakes. He was late to the trail, and it was all that horny cow Rita's fault.

If she wasn't so eager all the time, a man might keep better track of the time. Might not be apt to doze back off to sleep.

At least she'd made him breakfast.

As ever, they ate good at Rita's place. One of her girls had a line on a pig farm, and she cut the bacon extra thick, loading it with pepper. Together with eggs, toast, and fried taters, Oscar had awakened to a full table. Rita even had jelly preserves set out with the butter.

Oscar carried a canteen jug of coffee with him and sipped on it as he cleared town on a handsome buckskin he'd trained all by himself. From snaffle bit to hackamore to two rein, the gelding was new to the bridle but handled like a dream.

Cowboying was in Oscar's blood.

He was glad to put the dust of Jade City behind for a while. Glad to put the Rangers behind as well. Leave it to the young men like his randy young nephew. Oscar had bigger plans.

A share in the new Cardoza estate on this side of the river would just be the start.

Oscar didn't get where he was in life without having a good guess at the future. Word was that Cortina wasn't giving up on his incursions any time soon. The Rangers would be called again at any time to close ranks with Cortina and his men. Oscar meant to profit on the chaos.

While his brothers-in-arms fought the good fight, him and Cardoza would continue to pick up the spoils. There were plenty of spoils here, along the border.

Riding along through the splendor of mid-morning, he couldn't help but think about his old friend, Tom Sinclair. No two ways about it, the man had never known which side of his bread was buttered. And when it came time for hard decisions, he'd always been reluctant to proceed.

To Oscar's way of thinking that kind of weakness made Tom not only squeamish, but downright stupid.

Take this situation with his daughter. What was Tom thinking, letting his girl get away with hiding Africans away from their rightful owners, helping them escape down to Mexico. No two ways about it—plain stupid.

Oscar breathed deep of cypress tree perfume, and his horse's dark mane was like Reece Sinclair's lustrous tresses. The gal was beautiful, and his nephew was one lucky buck. When the opportunity came to take Sinclair's spread, Oscar figured to kill two birds with one stone. Not only would he make a profit, he'd clear the region of its chief abolitionist—and set the kid up with a wife in the process.

He bore Reece no ill will. No doubt she'd see the error of her ways once she got a bit older. Once Lin put her in place a few times. Show her what it meant to love, honor. And obey.

Oscar just hoped the boy was smart enough to clear out with his pretty prize when the shooting started.

"Guess I'll find out soon enough," he said out loud, and a buzzard flapped up from the road in front of him. He watched it soar in circles above him, riding the warm air currents into the sky, joining in with its brothers and sisters in a crisscross of high altitude motion.

There sure were a lot of those bastards flying around this morning.

CHAPTER 31

LIN WASN'T ANY GOOD WITH WOMEN.

He had no idea what to do, standing next to Reece, his arm draped over her shoulders as she mourned the loss of her dad. No idea what to say.

Tom Sinclair was stretched out on the floor of his office, in between a half-dozen piles of books, his dead arms flat by his side, a hole in his shirt surrounded by brown, dry blood. Barb Sanchez was next to him, his head rolled sideways and his eyes still open staring at the wall.

At least Tom's eyes were closed, thought Lin. At least he wasn't caught for eternity in a hideous grimace of some kind. Beside him, Reece couldn't have sobbed harder were it otherwise. Her breast heaved with the effort, and Lin pulled her in close.

They assumed Sinclair and Sanchez would be killed, but to bear witness to it was a different thing. That an established ranchero wasn't safe in his own house was the kind of atrocity Lin joined the Rangers to prevent.

Or avenge.

"It's gonna be all right," he said, feeling like a fool, but not knowing what else to say.

Reece rubbed at the tears on her face, doing her best to catch her breath.

Lin couldn't help but think of the amateur *presa* Hornsby's men had built in the Little Carlito. Now that the worst of it was over for Reece, her emotional dam had broken. Now that she didn't have to be strong, she could afford to let go and the torrent had been released, if only for a few minutes.

"The ranch is yours again, *señorita*," he said. "Soon the well will be full of water again, the corrals filled with cattle."

"It won't be the same," she said.

"No, it won't," he said.

But to himself he decided, *it will be better*.

"I need to go deal with the remainder of Hornsby's men," said Lin.

"You go," she said. "I'll be fine here. I'd like to stay a while longer."

"Take all the time you need."

He kissed her forehead and walked to the door where he picked up his leather satchel. Inside was the gold Stick had retrieved from Manuel.

Lin eyed Sinclair's desk, and went to it. All the drawers were half-open, the contents in disarray. There was no chance Cardoza hadn't discovered the second bag of gold.

After a quick search, he confirmed his suspicions. Unless Sinclair had hidden it somewhere during the raid, the gold was gone.

His blood at a rapid boil, Lin strode out of the office and down the hall.

He found Hornsby's men around the kitchen table

sitting in the same wood folding chairs Lin and the others had used at their picnic supper. But the men's wrists were tied behind their backs and Stick and Micah watched over them with charged guns.

"I wish one of you skunks would give me one good reason we shouldn't cart all five of you outside and string you up by the neck."

The oldest man at the table was scrawny and rough-skinned. Lin had heard one of the men call him Jeb. When he answered, it was with a full measure of repentance—how much was genuine was arguable. "I guess we must seem like awfully bad men."

"Here's where poor old Jeb's gonna say he and his buddies had no idea what was happening here until it was too late to stop it," said Stick. "We've been through it once or twice already."

"Now, now...that's not entirely it," said Jeb. "Hornsby told us we were along as backup to a legal business transaction. Him and Cardoza had the papers. It's you all that showed resistance to the law. You tell 'em, Walters."

"It's just like he says," said Walters.

"You tell me how a legal business transaction left those two men dead in the office," said Lin.

"I wasn't there," said Walters. "I assume Sinclair threatened Mister Hornsby or Mister Cardoza."

"And Sanchez?"

"Sanchez was on Cardoza's side," said Jeb.

"That's a lie right there," said Stick.

"What are you talking about?" said Lin. "Barb Sanchez was Tom's brother-n-law. Family."

Jeb shrugged. "Just telling you the truth. Sanchez had been to the Muleskinner every other day or two for most of the past month. Drinking with Hornsby. Drinking with Cardoza. He was in on the whole thing. Wouldn't be the first time family went against family. The way this here thing with the states is going, it won't be the last."

Stick kicked the legs out from under Jeb's chair, cracking the flimsy wood, sending the old man down with a crash. "You damned old scum-sucker."

Jeb howled with anger and pain. "It's the truth, dammit."

"Okay, okay," said Lin. He held up the flat of his palm. "Micah, please help him up."

Stick said, "Lin, you can't believe this fish bait?"

Lin wasn't sure what to believe, but he'd heard a lot of lies in his time, and he'd heard a lot of truth. Jeb's words had the ring of honesty about them. At this point, there wasn't a lot to be gained by making Sanchez complicit in the plot to overtake the ranch. And Jeb didn't look to be the brightest lamp in the house. Why would he make up such a story if it weren't the truth?

"Somebody confiscated the powder and supplies we brought back from the mercantile on Wednesday," said Lin. "They did it before the dawn attack."

"Are you gonna be the one to tell Miss Reece?" said Stick. "She loved that old man as much as she loved her dad."

"I don't think anybody needs to tell Miss Reece," said Lin. "Let the dead keep their secrets."

"Does that mean you're going to let us go?" said Walters.

"Shut-up," said Stick.

"If Sanchez was working with Cardoza, why is he dead?" said Lin.

Walters hesitated, then raised his hand like he was waiting for a teacher to call on him.

Lin obliged.

"I seen it happen, Ranger. Cardoza shot Sinclair and Sanchez both. Cold-blooded murder."

"And yet, I can't help but notice you still continued to work for him," said Lin.

Walters hung his head. "He started shooting people and we was all skeered. We figured it was better to be on his side than get a belly full of lead."

The way these snakes turned on each other was pathetic.

Lin turned his attention to Micah. "The man you saw on the boardwalk talking to Morse about the cattle. Can you describe him?"

"Big, burly gent. Flushed, red face. Fleshy. He was taller than you."

"As tall as you?"

Micah's toothy smile was genuine. "Ain't many as tall as me," he said.

"But you're sure you heard him say he'd be at the ranch this morning to see about the cattle?"

"That's how I understood things."

Lin spoke to the men at the table. "What do you all know about this cattle deal? What were Cardoza and Hornsby planning?"

Again, Jeb took the lead. "This is another case of legalities. Hornsby said the man bought Sinclair's cows fair and square. He was to come to the ranch this morning for any final instructions, then ride out to the old sheep station to get a count and take them on into Rio Grande City."

"The old sheep station?" said Lin.

"I do believe he called it 'Defilement.'"

"That's where the cattle are now," said Stick. "With our herders." He looked at Lin. "How did Hornsby find out that piece of information? I mean, there's lots of places they might be grazing."

"Somebody told him," said Lin. "Probably Barb Sanchez."

Stick pressed his lips together and looked away. "I sure have seen some sorry situations in my time, but this might just be the sorriest. I can't stomach any of it."

"We've got to make sure those cattle don't reach Rio Grande City," said Lin. "As long as Reece still has her cows, Rancho de Jada can rebuild. Once the cattle are sold, there's nothing but land, and no money."

Micah spoke up. "Beg your pardon, Jarret, but aren't you forgetting about Cardoza? He isn't beat yet. And these men say he has a legal claim to the property."

"Just because a man says it's legal don't make it so," said Stick. "Anybody can forge a piece of paper."

"Cardoza said he was taking the papers in to Hollister Morse at the Muleskinner," said Jeb. "That's where he's staying. They're waiting for Judge Benteen to show up and file the papers proper."

"When does Benteen show up?" said Lin.

"Noon tomorrow," said Jeb. "He's supposed to meet Cardoza and Morse at the cantina."

"I hope it's damned soon for your sake, Jeb. I'm holding you over for trial, and you're gonna stay tied up until he gets here." Lin turned to Micah. "Bind 'em and gag them. We'll put 'em against the wall over there where they won't get lost."

"Is that really necessary?" said Walters.

"You're lucky I don't chuck you into one of them tunnels and cave in both ends," said Lin.

"Lucky we don't just shoot you," said Stick.

Once Hornsby's men were disposed of Lin carried fresh

water in from the well. It was still far from full, but at least there was water trickling into the bottom. Afterwards, he checked on Reece and found her asleep in her dad's chair. He got a blanket to cover her and left her to rest. Then he sat with Micah and Stick in the parlor, waiting for daylight.

"You told us about the man on the boardwalk," said Lin. "You said he was tall, sorta red-faced."

"Yeah," said Micah.

Lin thought about his next question for a long time. He knew he didn't want to know the answer, but he had to ask.

"I guess I never asked you if you caught his name."

"Yeah, Morse said his name as they were making their good-byes."

"I guess I need to know."

"I've been not sure about telling you," said Micah. "Not sure it would be good for my health."

"You still don't trust me?"

"I don't trust anybody."

"Yeah...well. Like I said. I guess I need to know this hombre's name."

Micah told him.

By the time dawn came, Reece had awakened and the four Hellbenders sat at the kitchen table nursing the wounds of their adventure with hot, black coffee.

Eventually, Stick carried in a portion of meal from the summer kitchen and made bread.

It was mid-morning when a knock came from outside.

Lin pulled out his Colt and opened the door.

It was Ramon and the two other Lipan herders.

The Apaches had come home.

CHAPTER 32

OSCAR WASN'T OVERLY SURE WHERE HE CROSSED ONTO Sinclair property, but by the time he reached the fork of the Carlito, he knew he was on the ranch.

His ranch, he reminded himself. Part of it was *his* ranch.

It gave him a thrill like he hadn't felt in a long time.

To be free of the Rangers. To be financially secure. After Cardoza was gone, his only real trouble was Hornsby.

With the fat bastard's doughy yellow spine, he'd be easy enough to dispose of. Besides, as a Ranger he had a unique skill set. He knew all about killing and disposing of problems.

The sun was farther along in the sky than he liked it. Not only did he make a late start of the day—thanks to Rita—he'd lollygagged along the trail like a school boy, admiring the autumn wild flowers and grassy llano, thinking and dreaming about his future.

A herd of sleek longhorn cattle grazed in the distance, and he couldn't help but pull his horse up short to stop and sip coffee.

He admired the view for some time. That was soon *his* view, he imagined. Dollars on the hoof.

But before his next drink from the canteen, something struck him as odd.

Cattle grazing on Sinclair property? It wasn't right.

Surely these weren't the longhorns he was supposed to drive to auction?

Hadn't he sent seven men out in the opposite direction to round those cows up that very morning? Defilement was still five miles away.

Gigging his buckskin away from the trail, he galloped straight for the herd, his heart beginning to race in his chest. "What goes on here?" he said to himself.

Presently he crossed a shallow arroyo onto the grassy field with the cows. The young buckskin wasn't too keen on getting too close to the heavy beeves. To compensate, Oscar rode a circumspect route through, squinting to make out the brand.

There was no doubt—these were Sinclair's cows, wearing the Sinclair brand.

"Damn blast the luck," he said. The Indians must have brought them in overnight.

Which meant half a day—or more—lost in time and wages to those seven yahoos he'd shooed out of town this morning. If the men didn't show up here, and soon, they might not make the auction.

Oscar turned his horse back toward the hacienda and slapped the buckskin's croup. "Yah, yah, yah," he said, venting his spleen in frustration. When he got hold of Dub Hornsby...

He rode at an all-out gallop. As fast as he was moving, he didn't notice the crucified man hanging from the gnarled mesquite tree until he'd nearly sailed past. Stomach hugging his backbone, he looped back around the tree and rode into its chilling shade. The once-human form was a flayed mass of skin and gristle. Minus its outer garments, blood still trickled along the lower limbs to form a puddle at the twisted roots.

It was Curt, Oscar's ramrod for the morning's cattle drive.

Jerking his eyes away, a low, dull wail started crawling up the back of his throat. When he pushed the buckskin back along the range, an all-out scream emerged.

Oscar drove on toward Rancho de Jada, pushing the horrific image out of his mind, blocking the implications of what he'd seen. In the sky ahead, more buzzards circled.

As he closed on the spot directly below the birds, he saw something pink and lumpy on the trail. He choked a little then, pushed back the sour taste in his mouth and advanced one step at a time, daring himself to avoid the scene, forcing himself to confirm what he already knew.

The wide-open bodies of Billy, Hans, Ruth, and Harry —all four who had only a few hours before been strong, capable cattlemen. All four left now to feed the buzzards.

He couldn't stifle the shriek pouring from his lungs as he slapped the buckskin with his leather quirt, again and again and again. Again the horse shot down the trail. Again, Oscar's thoughts were tangled, his imagination jumbled. All he could do was picture his men.

Oh, god, those poor men.

He had to reach Rancho de Jada, find Hornsby and Cardoza, report the unwarranted assaults—then a new terror clawed through his brain.

He'd butchered enough meat in his time to know— his men hadn't been dead long.

The killers might well be nearby, within striking distance.

Any instant they could rip him from the saddle. Any thought might be his last.

Might as well think of Rita. If he hadn't had that one last go-round with her, he would have been with his men. He would've had to face...whoever had done this.

Still he rode, clinging to every last shred of hope he could muster. He'd worked hard for his share of the ranch. He'd risked time away from his home, risked his standing with the Rangers, spent good money on meat for the recent supper.

Hadn't he given his nephew the greatest gift of all by sparing his life and the life of the girl?

At Rancho de Jada, Oscar found Nick and Cardy, the deadliest gunmen he ever laid eyes on, hanged from short measures of hemp rope in the open alleyway of the livery barn, swaying...swaying...swaying...

At the caliche block well where he'd recently greeted his only nephew with a jug, Oscar Bruhn dropped off his horse and tramped toward the front of the house. Where was Cardoza's string of black horses? Where were the men standing guard?

The howitzer cannon sat unattended in front of the front yard's rough retaining wall, but nobody walked out to greet him.

"Cardoza," he called. "Hornsby!"

When the front door opened, three figures emerged. Two men and a woman. Each of them carried a visible firearm.

What he saw wasn't right. This couldn't be.

"Lin? Reece?" Oscar didn't recognize the tall African, but he was young too.

What happened to the plan to take the ranch?

Oscar cleared his throat, but his words were strained, anemic. "What are you doing here, Lin? Miss Reece?"

Lin stepped forward and a trio of men draped in blankets appeared behind the original three.

Apaches.

Oscar's blood froze in his veins and a dull growl rose up from his guts. "Keep those animals away from me," he said. He hurled an accusatory finger toward his nephew. "Don't you people know the danger you're in?"

Lin's voice was tough and confident. Everything Oscar wasn't.

"Danger?" said Lin. "Yeah, we know all about danger, uncle. The thing is, we're just getting started."

———

THEY GATHERED in the yard beside the well, four Hellbenders with three horses. Stick and Micah had unhitched Cardoza's two black stallions from the water wagon and had them yoked to the howitzer's wheeled box cart, while Micah's grulla was back in front of the buckboard. Along with Hornsby's five men, Lin tossed his uncle, into the back.

"You ungrateful little piss ant," said Oscar. "After everything I did for you. After all the good words I've put in on your behalf, you'd think I'd receive a little consideration. Did you even hear me out, boy?"

"Shut-up, Oz," said Lin. "You lost your right to be heard when you betrayed your friends to Cardoza."

Oscar tried once more to explain. "That's just what you don't understand, Lin. It ain't about Cardoza or Cortina or any of this Mex nonsense. It's about the future of this here United States. It's about what's coming and our place in the Ivory Compass."

"You're one of them? The Order of the Ivory Compass?"

Oscar's voice took on a tone of pride. "I'm head of the local chapter. Humbles me to admit it. Saddens me to think we might've welcomed you in."

Lin asked Micah to fetch a bandanna. "Gag him," said Lin. "Then I don't have to listen to any more of his garbage." He smiled at Oscar. "Enjoy the ride. I promise it won't be comfortable."

The old devil barely struggled against his bonds. Ever since he arrived, he had looked ashen and sick. As Micah tied a kerchief around his mouth, he seemed shallow and weak, like he'd aged a decade in the past day.

Climbing down from the wagon box, Micah's voice was solemn. "Something sure set your Uncle off. Bad enough he's one of those Ivory Compass men, but he seems to have lost his senses t'boot. I'm sorry, Ranger. I know what it's like to lose family." The big man glanced at Reece as she adjusted a saddle on one of the stallions. "I guess we all do."

"Got me an idea what it was upset him," said Stick, joining them from the livery barn where he'd gone in search of an extra blanket. "There are two men hanging from the rafters down there. Looks like the work of our Indian friends. Holy cats, you never seen such a mess of blood and guts. Well, I mean, maybe you have, but—"

Lin recalled the bodies he and Stick had discovered outside the Muleskinner.

No wonder Oscar was in such a state. Especially if the men were friends.

"How about it, Oz? Are those two of your men?" said Lin.

On the back of the wagon, Oscar's eyes were twin white marbles in his skull. If he heard the question, he didn't respond.

"Did you cut the men down?" said Lin.

"I did. We'll go ahead and bury 'em tonight with the others." Stick fell back against the buckboard and took off his hat. Running a shirt sleeve over his brow, he said, "Did I mention this is the most sorry damn situation I ever saw? When I think about the Jensen brothers, and poor Mister Tom..."

"Where's the Apaches now?" said Lin, swiveling his head around. "After Oscar arrived, they vanished."

"They tend to do that," said Stick.

"And the cattle?"

Stick waved his arm. "They set them to grazing up north. Apparently they were in transit from Defilement when they met your uncle's crew."

"Why'd they leave Defilement?"

"Ramone got word from the auction house in Rio Grande City that Rancho de Jada was bringing in some cows today. Except he knew that wasn't true. He figured it meant somebody was riding in to steal the herd."

"Somebody at the auction house tipped him off?"

"Squaw man named Hutton. He runs the auction. The old man's married to Ramone's sister."

"Good to have connections," said Lin.

"Cardoza hasn't been as careful as he should. Around here, everybody is related to everybody else. He would have been well served to keep his mouth shut. I don't understand why people don't know when to keep quiet."

"Stick, that sure enough is a mystery. For now, we need to get these men to town," said Lin. "Judge Benteen is supposed to show at noon. I'd like to be there before he gets to the cantina." He cupped a palm around his mouth and called to Reece. "You ready to go?"

She put a foot in the stirrup and mounted one of the stallions. "Whenever you are," she said. "Lead the way."

Lin climbed aboard the buckboard's crowded bench

seat next to Micah and Stick, irritated that Reece had insisted on driving the cannon. Irritated, but proud at the same time.

She was setting off to make good on her dad's promise to kill Cardoza.

Lin reflected back on that first meeting in the study. It had been only a few days ago, but it seemed like ages had passed since them.

In Reece's case, the promise didn't sound so empty after all.

CHAPTER 33

IT WAS ALREADY A WESTERN MYTH, THE STORY OF THE gunslingers who walk into a saloon populated by their enemies. Lin had talked to Tom Sinclair about Western myth, had bought into a few of them himself. The idyllic life on a Rio Grande cattle ranch. The place of a woman in the hacienda kitchen. The right and honorable nature of the Texas Rangers.

Amazing how quick a man's beliefs can turn to powder, he thought.

But in spite of his uncle's betrayal, he opted to hold onto the ideal of the Rangers. One bad individual didn't mean the entire organization was corrupt.

By stepping into the Muleskinner cantina with Stick and Micah, Lin was putting another myth to the test.

"Let's just see how these young gunslingers fare," he said before leaving Reece at the spur of the Little Carlito. He kissed her cheek for good luck and patted the cannon. Primed with powder, wadding and a 12-pound ball, the howitzer was ready to fire.

"Don't go shooting that thing off until I give you the signal."

"I won't. Be careful."

"When you do see the signal, count five—slowly—and then put fire to the patch."

With his friends on either side, Lin led the way up the sandy incline to the cantina.

"I don't reckon we should outright blow up the place," said Stick.

"No, I don't reckon," said Micah.

"Not with people inside."

"Depends what people we find inside," said Lin.

"I meant we ought to get all the people out."

"Like the man said, depends what people," agreed Micah. "Some of them might benefit from staying behind."

"Reece ever tell you about Otter the cat?" said Lin.

"No, she never did," said Stick.

"Ask her about it sometime."

In front of the Muleskinner, a single horse waited at the hitching rack.

Lin, followed by Micah and Stick, walked through the door out of the sunlight and into the shade.

Lin's iron .44 was plainly visible on his hip. Stick carried the Maynard carbine high.

The Muleskinner's drinking area was more narrow than Lin expected, the back of the building being reserved for additional rooms. Adjusting to the light, he saw an enormous mahogany bar, scarred with nicks and missing chunks, painted barn red under the counter, with an iron rail and a series of tall wood chairs. Along the front wall were a few two-chair tables, and at the far space, in front of an open window, a round table for four.

Two men sat there, enveloped in a cloud of cigar smoke.

When Lin walked up to the counter with Stick and

Micah behind, Hollister Morse spoke. "We don't serve his kind. Tell him to wait outside."

Morse hadn't bothered to recognize Lin, and Cardoza kept his nose glued to a set of papers they shared.

Morse wore spectacles too big for his thin nose and his pallor was more sickly than Lin remembered. Dressed in a dapper gray suit with a thin pinstripe, he was nervous. Jumpy.

For his part, Cardoza's cufflinks gleamed in amber sunlight reflected from the bottle of rye holding down the table. On first glance, he immediately knew Lin and held up both hands.

"You have us at a disadvantage, Ranger," he said. "I would have thought you were too busy today to come to town."

"Never to busy to pay my last respects to a man."

"I told you to get that one out of here," hissed Morse through snarling clenched teeth.

"I think he's talking about me," said Micah.

"I know he's talking about you," said Lin, "and I guess I just can't hear him."

"Y'all ever read *The Three Musketeers* by this French fellow, Alexander Doo-moss?" said Stick. "Them boys stuck together," he said. He spoke directly to Morse. "Me and my friends do the same."

"I wonder," said Lin. "If you two would like to step outside and settle all this nonsense about the Sinclair ranch once and for all?"

Cardoza's smug expression set Lin's teeth on edge.

"Oh, please," he said. "Fisticuffs? Again?" He waved Lin away with his little finger and dropped his attention back to the papers in front of him.

"I'm sorry," said Morse. "I'm afraid I have to ask all of you leave. Now. And in case you have other ideas, let me inform you that we are expecting a Federal judge to arrive at any moment."

"We're happy to oblige you," said Lin. "We were just making sure you were home. It's not like we didn't give you the chance to come along."

Lin caught sight of Cardoza's twitch, a brief move of no more than half an inch toward the six-shooter on his hip, but then the *Cortinista* eyed his companion and obviously thought better of shooting it out. Instead of pulling iron, he again waggled his fingers toward the door. "*Vamanos*," he said. "Leave us be."

Lin walked back outside and raised his hand high in the air for Reece to see.

"Five seconds," he said, and the three men ran perpendicular to the building, away across the open ground like kids on the fourth of July—waiting for a firecracker. In this case, the firecracker threw nine-pound balls of lead.

———

REECE WATCHED LIN, Stick, and Micah traipse up the hill toward the cantina, then she appraised the long, fat barrel of the cannon, rolled a wooden lucifer between her fingers. Mourning her dad's loss, she felt a surge of righteous vindication in the big gun.

Dreaming of vengeance, she was sorry the men had opted to go inside.

Cardoza would be there with Morse waiting for the judge to steal her family's legacy.

No matter what, no matter how much she argued with him, she knew Lin would give them a chance. He'd ask them to come outside with him, and if they did, he'd push to carry them north in a gamble to find justice.

He'd lose that bet and get himself killed in the process.

Pigheaded and stubborn, she thought.

But then again, she didn't think Cardoza would come out. She figured—

Her thoughts were cut short by a sound from behind. When she pivoted around, a filthy, rough hand grasped her arm and yanked her forward.

"I'm surprised to see you again, gal."

Reece blinked at the overwhelming stench of river rot and burnt hair. She sucked in her breath and pulled back, slapped at the vicelike grip and tried to kick. "Marko," she gasped.

"Yeah, it's Marko," he said with a snarl. "I guess you weren't expecting me any more than I was expecting you." He licked his broken, black lips with a lizard's tongue. "What'cha doing with the hardware?"

Marko paid attention to where the cannon was aimed, pulled up Reece's fist to see the lucifer clenched there between her fingers. "Can I play, too?" His throat was a congested mass, and as he spoke he punctuated each word with globs of phlegm. "The last few day I've come to appreciate fire."

Reece put all her strength into a mighty heave, freeing her right arm, forcing Marko to widen his eye with surprise. She kicked him as hard as she could between the legs.

"Ooof," he coughed, expelling chunks of slime and sinking back. Struggling to catch his breath, he kept hold of her left hand, then slapped her hard across the jaw.

Reece reeled back, slamming into the steel side of the cannon, just missing the wide, spoked wheel of the cart. Stunned, she willed her eyes to focus. His stench was overpowering, his visage gruesome to bear. His long red hair was gone, reduced to a stubble of black pin-feathers on a gaping field of scabs. The width of his forehead was split and raw, the tips of his cheeks and nose burnt black.

"I almost didn't make it, you know," he said. "Your lover boy unleashed a hell of fire on me. But then came a bath of water, and I've got to tell you—I was baptized in that water. I was raised from the dead by the Lord himself."

Marko slapped Reece again and slipped behind to wrap an arm around her waist like an iron band. His other hand reached up and squeezed her neck while he nibbled at her ear and whispered. "I see now why He brought me back, don't you? Don't you see what I still need to do? What I always wanted to do to you, pretty girl?"

Frantic to break his hold, Reece got one foot on a spoke of the carriage wheel and levered the two of them away from the cannon by a couple feet, maybe a yard. Marko stumbled, but kept his fingers digging tight into her throat. Sparks went off inside Reece's head, and a gray fog started to set in.

Again, she kicked away, and again Marko held on.

"Oh, you aren't going to get away from me that easy," he said. The hand at her waist gripped her shirt and yanked it up, tearing it along the seam, exposing her midriff to the fresh Texas air. The shock of it forced a scream from her lips, and then her air was cut off.

————

"SOMETHING'S WRONG," said Lin, leaping up from the crouched position he assumed immediately after hurling away from the cantina. In the grass on the far side of the road into Jade City, Stick and Micah likewise pulled their hands away from their ears.

"Why hasn't she fired the damn thing?" said Micah.

"Somebody's with her," said Stick. "Somebody's got her."

Lin peered across the open distance, trying to make sense of what he saw. Reece was fighting with a man, kicking him, being swung around into the cannon. The bastard had her around the waist, his other hand on her neck.

"It's Marko," said Lin.

"It can't be Marko," said Stick. "He went up with the dam last night."

"Don't argue, dammit. Shoot him."

Because it was Marko.

There was no disguising the misshapen body, the way he lusted after Reece. How he survived the powder blast, Lin would never know, but it didn't matter. What mattered now is that he be put down once and for all.

Stick handed Lin the Maynard. "Take the shot," he said.

Lin pushed the long gun away. "No, Stick. You take the shot, dammit."

"Are you sure?"

"Yes, I'm sure. Take the goddamn shot."

Stick slammed the rifle against his shoulder, sighted down the barrel, pulled back the hammer and pulled the trigger.

————

THE AIR BLEW up with a concussion slamming against Reece's eardrums. At the same time, Marko's grip on her neck went limp.

Marko's mouth jerked away from her ear, and he tumbled backwards. Thrust forward, Reece regained her footing and put both hands to her beleaguered throat. Coughing, she spun around on her heel, reeled forward and caught herself on the cannon.

Marko lay twitching in the dirt with a chunk of his skull missing.

No time, she thought. No time to lose.

Miraculously, she still clutched the lucifer in a death-grip. She struck the match on the rough hull of the canon, lit the cotton patch and slammed it against the fuse.

The concussion dwarfed any gun she'd ever fired and its effect was equally immense.

One second the Muleskinner cantina was a whole structure, the next it was broken in half with timber and plaster from roof and frame erupting into the sky. Without a moment's hesitation, Stick and Micah were following up with an onslaught of lead, charging the cracked hull like a pair of mad hornets.

Even if Cardoza survived the howitzer, there wouldn't be any paper trail tying him to Rancho de Jada.

The second lucifer she held between her fingers would make sure of that.

She marched toward the carnage to meet her friends.

By the time Judge Harry Benteen rode into Jade City, there was nothing left of the Muleskinner but a pile of cinders.

"What happened here?" said the bespectacled old man.

"Kitchen fire," said Lin, greeting him in the soot-stained street. "I'm afraid it's a complete loss."

CHAPTER 34

"THE PROBLEM WITH GOOD-BYES IS THEY DON'T ERASE the memories," said Reece as she walked casually with Lin along the trail from Rancho de Jada to the sheep station at Defilement. Each of them led a horse. Hers was a supple black mare. His was the trusty bay from north Texas, loaded down with his bedroll, rifle boot, and other provisions.

"You and I have certainly made some good memories," said Lin. "Let's see if I can list them: crawling in the dirt underground, huddling together in a stinking hot grain closet, watching the Muleskinner burn to the ground."

"After two weeks, the stink of that place is still in my nose," said Reece.

They rode for a while in silence. The day was bright, with a promise of rain far off on the horizon. To Lin, Reece was as beautiful as ever with her hair tied back, dressed in a light linsey-woolsey shirt, corduroy britches, and felt, flat-brimmed hat.

The previous fourteen days had come and gone like a blur. The cattle were secure, the horses tended to.

The dead were buried.

A few of the less prejudiced neighbors had helped. Lin feared in the coming months they would become more few and far between.

"We made some good memories too, didn't we?" said Reece.

Lin stopped her in mid-stride and put his arms around her. It wasn't their first kiss, but it was the first one that meant something deep and meaningful. For the first time in his life, he didn't want to be the first one to let go.

Once back on the move, walking down the trail, Reece said, "Now that Judge Benteen has taken your Uncle Oscar back north, will they want me as a witness at his trial?"

"I suppose so. Hornsby's men, too. Turns out most of them are already wanted for one dastardly crime or other."

"That might require me staying in San Antonio for a long time," she said.

"Several days," Lin confirmed. "Maybe several weeks."

"I can't imagine what I would do with myself all that time," her voice was laced with humor.

"You'd be surprised. I'm not much of a city boy, myself, but I suspect I might be of some service showing you around."

She squeezed his hand and said, "I suppose I'd owe you something for the service you'd kindly be providing?"

"I suppose you would," he said with a sheepish grin. "But don't take that the wrong way. I'm nothing if not a gentleman. I'll come up with something to even things up between us."

Reece slapped him with her floppy hat, then jumped onto the back of her horse. "Follow me," she said.

Her horse outpaced his with ease, but Lin held back, content to watch Reece enjoy the fast gallop. She was going to need a lot of days like this—days filled with horses and sun and riding across the open range of her spread, because that's what all this land was now.

Hers.

And, whether she knew it or not, she needed time to heal.

Micah had agreed to stay on and help at the ranch. And Stick, well...he would always stick.

Lin's gut told him the ranch would prosper if they continued raising cows. Texas as cattle-country might seem a little far-fetched now, but he suspected change was in the air.

In fact, a lot of things were changing.

At Defilement, they reigned in next to a lone rocky outcropping, an anomaly on the otherwise flat region of long grass on both sides of the trail. Close to the rock was an old wooden shack, maybe fifteen feet tall, and as long as it was wide.

"This is the old sheep station?" he said. "Where the vaqueros stay?"

"This is the far property line," said Reece. She looked back across the range at the distance they'd covered. "Climb to the top of the rock and you can see all the way to the river. It's everything to me."

"It's your future," said Lin, gently. Then, "I wanted to ask you about the ranch." He took her hands in his. "Are you sure you'll be okay here, with Stick?"

"Micah's here too."

Lin chose his next words with care. "I can't deny that worries me," he said. "Micah being here." Before she could protest, he added, "Not for you. I'm concerned about him. A man shouldn't spend his days looking over his shoulder. As long as he's in Texas, he's a runaway. Trouble's gonna follow him."

Reece patted Lin's arm. "I forgot to tell you," she said. "Something Emma told me last night."

The young black woman had appeared on the hacienda's front door step the day before. Lin had been happy to make her acquaintance but had been too busy packing up his gear to see her again.

"What did Emma say?"

"Micah came to us from the Landers Ranch in north Texas. A few days ago, it was hit by a tornado. The place was wiped out, the whole family was killed."

"That's awful," said Lin. "Sorry to hear it."

"It was devastating, and unexpected at this time of year, but it's fortunate for Micah. The family is unaccounted for but presumed dead."

"They think Micah's dead, too?"

"Yes." Her expression was radiant. "It's a new life for him," she said.

"A new future with you and the ranch."

"It could be yours too," said Reece.

Lin's guts twisted in a knot like Cardoza's toughest gunnies couldn't have tied.

He barely managed to grunt, "Whoa, now, Contessa."

Reece laughed. "Whatever it is you're thinking, I'm pretty sure it's not what I'm talking about," she said.

"What are you talking about?"

"Help me with the door."

Together they approached the shack, and Reece led Lin to the back of the building. Two sorry doors, tied together where they met with a twist of rope, sagged on rusted iron hinges.

Reece pulled a gleaming iron knife from her boot and sliced the rope in half. The doors slumped to the ground.

Lin picked up his side and swung it outwards. Reece did the same.

Inside the shack was a dust-covered Concord stage coach, built of oak and braced with iron bands and leather. Covered in grime and bird droppings, the four wheeled vehicle somehow managed a serene majesty in the morning sun.

"I don't understand," said Lin.

"Dad bought it from an Overland Stage man last spring."

"What for? Was he planning to go into the stage coach business?"

"Because he thought it might help me."

"Help the Hellbenders, you mean?"

Reece nodded and fixed her attention on the sturdy vehicle. "You told me you always wanted one of your own. Now it seems you've got one. And I won't owe you for your showing me around San Antonio."

"I'm not sure what to say," said Lin.

"Emberville is a station on the Overland Mail route, straight north of here. They can help you with any repairs the coach needs."

"What is it you've got in mind, gal? Some kind of Hellbenders express?"

"Something like that," she said.

Reece crossed over to him and kissed him flat on the mouth.

Lin put his arms around her.

"What do you say?" she said.

There was no way to say no.

*A LOOK AT BOOK TWO: SEVEN
DEVILS ROAD*
BY RICHARD PROSCH

A RAGING GUNLET OF GUNFIRE AND DEATH.

Chuckholes and raging rivers, fog, rain, and impossibly steep grades—it's the spring of 1860.

The Butterfield Overland Trail is more than hazardous for a lone coach hurling down the Missouri run between Syracuse and Fort Smith, Arkansas. But for Texas Ranger Lin Jarret and his pack of Hellbenders charged with freighting $10,000 in stolen loot, it's a raging gauntlet of gunfire and death.

As the deadly Order of the Ivory Compass aims to engulf the Show-Me State, Texas Ranger Lin Jarret, Reece Sinclair, and Micah LeMay face an impossible assignment in their second explosive adventure in the exciting new Western series —*Hellbenders.*

AVAILABLE SEPTEMBER 2021

Thank you for taking the time to read *Hellbenders*. If you enjoyed it, please consider telling your friends or posting a short review. Word of mouth is an author's best friend and much appreciated.

Thank you.
Richard Prosch

Richard's western crime fiction captures the fleeting history and lonely frontier stories of his youth where characters aren't always what they seem, and the wind burned landscapes are filled with swift, deadly danger.

His work has appeared in *True West*, *Roundup*, and *Saddlebag Dispatches* magazines and online at Boys' Life. He won the Spur Award from Western Writers of America for short fiction, and his Jo Harper stories have received nominations for the Peacemaker award from Western Fictioneers.

Richard lives in Missouri with his wife and son, Gina, and Wyatt, assorted cats, and a Great Pyrenees named Moose.

Manufactured by Amazon.ca
Bolton, ON